TO PROTECT A PRINCESS

(REGENCY ROYALS BOOK 1)

JESS MICHAELS

To Harry and Meghan, for making me want to break a monarchy and write a better happily ever after.

And to Michael, a prince and a king amongst men.

There are a lot of conversations about the concept of Content Warnings in books and for other media. Having suffered from panic attacks that were triggered by trauma, I would NEVER wish that on my worst enemy. I want you to enjoy what you're reading, never be pulled away because you were surprised by triggering material. So, I will do my best to include Content Warnings in an author note in each book from now on. Also, look to my website for them, so that you don't accidentally buy a book that might give you pause.

Content Warning: Physical Assault on heroine (on page).

CHAPTER 1

Spring 1817

The Season of 1817 would become known for a great many things in the end, but at the beginning, all of Society was buzzing about one thing: the visit from the king and his family.

But they weren't referring to their own king, gouty and mad in his tower. Or their future king, who flitted from brothel to brothel with his demands for champagne with breakfast while his people suffered. No, the talk was about an entirely different monarch: the King of Athawick.

Such a tiny island for such a big stir, and yet Princess Ilaria, youngest sibling and only sister of the king, knew there would be stir. There was always stir when it came to her family. Their island's situation along the trade routes of the North Sea had made them important for centuries…and precarious if she could believe her eldest brother when he spoke, eyes hollow and distant, that newly placed crown so heavy on his head.

She leaned against the railing of the ship and closed her eyes as the salt air caressed her face. Every moment took them closer to England. Closer to a few months of madness. Her brother, of course, would not remain for that entire time, but their mother was insistent that Ilaria and her second oldest brother, Remington, take a Season in London. And their mother was not one to be denied.

"Your Highness?"

Ilaria opened her eyes and squinted against the bright reflection of sunlight on the water before she turned. Her brother's steward, Stephen Blairford, was standing there, his lips pressed in a tight, irritated line, just as they always were. She had never liked the man, not before when he served their father, not now when he served Grantham.

"What is it?" she asked.

"The king and the queen desire your presence," he said. "Immediately."

The way he added the last made it sound like an order. And she supposed it was, though it chafed. Here she was presumed to take precedence, but courtiers carried power. And this one knew it.

"Very well." He motioned as if he would lead her, and she jerked away from him. "I know where the family quarters are, Blairford. Thank you."

She walked away and, to his credit, Blairford didn't follow. At least he knew his place that far. She made her way through the doors that led off the ship deck and through a narrow hallway to a large, ornately carved door. It was open at present, and she could hear the voices of both her brothers and her mother drifting into the hallway.

"...how she will react..." came her mother's voice, and Ilaria stiffened. That didn't sound positive.

She thrust her shoulders back and entered the opulently decorated drawing room that was part of the royal family's quarters on the ship taken from Athawick's small but powerful armada. Occasionally this vessel served the family so it was finer than the rest.

"How who will react?" she asked as she pulled the door shut behind them for privacy.

Her brother, the new King of Athawick, stood ramrod straight in the middle of the room, every line of his clothing perfect, every hair in place. She could scarcely even recognize him as the brother who had run with her through fields in Athawick a decade before, two decades. He looked stern and cross and…tired. She could see he was tired.

Her mother, Queen Giabella, sat on a settee in the middle of the room, a cup of tea perched in her fingertips. She was stunningly beautiful, no matter her years. Her thick, dark hair was only slightly touched by gray and her sharp brown eyes flitted over Ilaria from head to toe…judging, no doubt.

Her mother's secretary, Dashiell Talbot, sat at the escritoire on one side of the room, a quill poised over a thick sheet of vellum. Ilaria's heart sank. Unlike Grantham's man, she adored Dashiell. He'd been working for her mother for nearly a decade and was always wonderful. But when he was about to take notes, it meant something official was happening.

Last, but certainly not least because he wouldn't allow it, was Remington. Her second oldest brother leaned lazily against the mantel, a drink in his hand and a bored expression on his face. Remi did his best to play layabout prince, though Ilaria knew there was far more to him than just that. He arched a brow at her, held her stare.

God's teeth, something *was* going on and she dreaded it down to her toes.

"You know, before you answer my question," she said, crossing to the sideboard. "I think I need a drink."

Her mother pursed her lips. "I expect that sort of thing from Remi, but you really must be more proper, especially as we enter English Society, my dear."

Ilaria bit back a sharp retort, but she still poured her drink and then crossed to stand beside Remi at the fireplace. He gave her a side glance that said multitudes.

"You called me here, Your Majesties," she said. "And clearly it isn't about family business in general, but about me. So what is it?

How could I have possibly offended during the last day and a half on board a ship in the middle of the North Sea?"

Grantham took a step toward her. "You've offended no one, Ilaria. Mother and I simply believe it is...time to discuss... the...the..."

"The future," their mother finished with a quick look toward Dashiell at the desk. He lifted his gaze as if sensing the queen's stare. He gave a tiny nod before he went back to madly scribbling.

"At present the future entails us disembarking on the shores of foggy, dirty London," Ilaria said. "And spending what will surely be a few boring months of balls and official events. I've agreed to attend them all in order to help you, Grantham. What else could you possibly wish of me?"

Her mother rose from the settee and moved toward her, dark eyes locking with Ilaria's. Now her heart rate rose, fear fluttered.

"It is time for you to be married, Ilaria," the queen said softly, almost gently. "At twenty-five, some would say high past time, and perhaps we would have pushed this issue sooner if not for your father's illness and death. But here we are, and we have been granted an opportunity by the fact that your brother has been officially coronated at last and the world has some interest in our family's tour."

"England is not the world," Ilaria snapped.

Remi chuckled. "They believe they are. They're certainly trying to conquer enough of it."

"*That* is the material problem," Grantham said, his gaze growing sharp as it focused on Remi. "Yes, they are land mad and resource mad. And Athawick may not have much of one, but we have plenty of the other thanks to the trade route. Generations of our family have fought and occasionally died to remain out of the Empire's reach, and I will not have that all fall apart during my watch. Ilaria, you are of an age to marry. And if you are linked to an important family of Britain, there is some thought that it will continue to protect Athawick."

She blinked. "You are going to barter me for freedom."

Grantham flinched, but then he hardened his expression. "Not my own, I assure you. But for our country…yes, I suppose you could call it that."

He turned away so he couldn't see her reaction, Ilaria thought. The one she couldn't keep from her face. It was as if someone had rolled one of the big waves on the sea right over her and she was now drowning in this new reality.

"Was this…was this always the plan?" she asked. "During all this preparation for this journey, were you two always lying to me about its purpose?"

The queen stepped toward her and caught her hand. Her mother's fingers were warm against her cold ones, and she squeezed gently. "We were not…sure how you would react, Ilaria. You have always been so independent."

Ilaria cocked her head. "Not so much anymore, I suppose. You will assure that, as will he." She jerked her hand from her mother's and used it to point at her brother's broad back. Then she turned on the other brother at her side. "Did you know about this, Remi?"

He lifted his hands. "No one tells me anything, darling, you know that. I'm just the spare."

"Remi, that isn't helpful," the queen said with a sharp gaze for her younger son. "Ilaria—"

Ilaria shook her head. "You waited until now to tell me while I was trapped on a ship and had no escape. You waited until we were half a day's journey to the shores of what you desire to be my prison. How could you, Mama? How could *you* do that?"

Grantham pivoted. "Your mother did not make this decision. Your king did. And you *will* respect both of us." He said the words harshly, but Ilaria could see the doubt in his gaze. The regret. But it didn't matter. As he had said, he didn't make this decision as her brother, but as her sovereign. They were certainly not the same man.

She swallowed hard and executed a small curtsey toward her

mother. "Your Majesty." She pivoted and did the same toward her brother. "Your Majesty. Is that all? May I be excused?"

Grantham's jaw tightened. "You will not fight this?"

"How could I?" she said softly, even as her mind spun off in a dozen different directions trying to find a way to do just that. "May I be excused?" she repeated.

She could see him grinding his teeth, but he inclined his head. "Yes."

She turned on her heel and exited the room, her hands shaking as she fled down the hallway to her own chamber. She rushed inside and slammed the door behind her, leaning on it with both hands as she tried to regain some semblance of control over her senses.

"Your Highness?"

She pivoted and found her companion, Sasha Killick, standing behind her, hands clasped and worry on her face. After the death of her parents when she was just a little girl, the royal family had taken her in and raised her alongside their own children. Not quite an equal. No, her father had required that. But Sasha was almost like Ilaria's own sister, as well as her companion…and when situations required it…her body double. They looked alike enough from a distance to serve that purpose.

Today, though, she only saw her friend and rushed forward to grasp Sasha's hands. "They are going to marry me off to some titled twit."

"What?" Sasha gasped and drew her to the settee before the low fire.

Ilaria told her what had happened, perhaps with a little more flourish than was required, but she was being bartered with like a horse, for heaven's sake. If there had ever been a time to be dramatic, this was it.

When it was all over, Sasha sat there, staring off into the fire, an inscrutable expression on her face. At last, she sighed. "I suppose we might have guessed this would happen. After all, royal marriages are very rarely for love or by choice of the particular parties. Look at your mother and father. They were a union to shore up alliances between Athawick and the kingdom of Everlay."

"And two more miserable people you never could have met," Ilaria sighed. "And *this* is what they wish for me. In these modern times."

"I think you're being a little silly, if you thought you would ever be truly in control of your future. You know that is not what your family is about."

Ilaria bent her head. Sasha wasn't wrong, of course. There were duties and expectations on her shoulders. There always had been. And yet somehow she had been able to ignore this possibility because her marriage had not been a topic of discussion since her father was alive. Grantham was such a different man from that cold, cruel bastard, she had hoped…

Well, it didn't matter now.

There was a light knock on her door and she huffed out a breath. "Probably my mother come to scold me."

Sasha squeezed her hand and then went to the door. But when she opened it, it was not the queen but Remi who leaned in her doorway.

"Sasha," he said with a wink toward Sasha as he entered the room.

"Your Highness," she returned as she closed the door behind him.

"Ugh, please don't do that," he said. "We're practically brother and sister, and I hate it."

"*That's* why I do it," Sasha teased. "And also because Blairford would blister my ears if he heard me being overly familiar."

"That piece of shit," Remi muttered as he flopped down on the settee next to Ilaria and slouched down.

"He looked so smug when he came to collect me," Ilaria said with a roll of her eyes. "You *know* he was part of this grand plan."

"Probably. He held the strings for Father and he's not going to let go of them easily for our brother." Remi shook his head. "Proximity to power is addictive, as we see every day." He nudged her with his shoulder. "How are you holding up?"

"Terribly," she said. "How about you?"

He laughed. "Me? I'm right as rain. They're not marrying *me* off to a simpering British virgin with no wit."

"You think not?" Ilaria said. "You're the second in line for the throne now, Remi. You're still in the crosshairs until Grantham finds a bride and produces a few heirs of his own to usurp you."

He flinched. "Christ, I hadn't thought of that."

"Well, you should," Ilaria grumbled. "If only so I don't have to be in this hateful situation by myself."

He grabbed for her hand, and for a moment her rapscallion of a brother looked serious. "I am…sorry, Ilaria."

"I know," she murmured, and rested her head on his shoulder. "I wish I could be like you and thwart them at every turn."

He chuckled. "If you started doing that, they'd have me shot for being a bad influence. Are you trying to get me shot?"

"If it would distract from this plan of theirs, perhaps?" She twisted her lips and batted her eyelashes at him. "Just in the leg maybe? Or the arm?"

He snorted out a laugh and pushed back to his feet. "Look, I'll try to talk to Grantham for you, but he doesn't listen to me anymore, not since he took the title. But I'll make the effort."

She smiled up at him. For all his foolishness, he was a good brother and she adored him for it. "Thank you."

He gave the most ridiculous bow of all time and then saluted Sasha. "Ladies," he said as he swept from the chamber.

But once he was gone, Ilaria couldn't help but think of what he'd said. In jest, perhaps, but still something to consider.

"What if I did that?" she asked out loud.

"Shot him in the leg?" Sasha asked mildly. "He might deserve it."

"No, not shoot him. Thwart *them*." She sat up straighter. "What if I thwarted their plans just like Remi always does?"

Sasha's brow wrinkled. "By drinking too much and seducing young women and generally having a good time?"

"I've never seduced a young woman," Ilaria mused. "I don't know that I'd hate it. But I think playing a little fast and loose with a young man or two might be the better way to frustrate their plans. Our island might not be so prudish about that sort of thing, but I know *theirs* is."

"Ilaria, think this through." Sasha's concern was plain on her face. "There would be consequences for any actions you take against the Crown. Your mother and the king are not to be trifled with."

Ilaria pursed her lips. Her friend wasn't wrong. She loved her family, but her mother and brother were forces of nature, and driven to protect the Crown. "But are there not consequences for falling in line, as well? Namely a loveless, empty marriage to some man who will marry me only for money and power?"

Sasha's expression softened. "You aren't wrong. I just want to see you come out of this as undamaged as possible. Perhaps don't make any hasty decisions until you meet the men your family will parade before you. See if you could *like* one of them. If you could, then everyone would win."

Ilaria sighed. "You are correct, as always. It's almost unforgiveable of you."

"And yet you always forgive me." Sasha laughed and Ilaria couldn't help but join in.

But as the subject changed to much more pleasant matters, her mind continued to spin. She would do as Sasha suggested, of course. She was no fool. Nor was she a pawn. She wouldn't allow herself to be.

CHAPTER 2

Captain Jonah Crawford clutched the drink in his hand with white-knuckled fingers as he looked out over the ballroom. God, how he hated these pointless exhibitions. Ballrooms filled with rich, stupid knobs hell-bent on getting drunk and making each other feel more important. All the while ignoring anything real or of value in the world.

He'd always felt an outsider in this sphere. A proud outsider. Except in the last few years his actions in the Royal Navy had allowed him invitation here more often. He'd been recognized as valuable, somehow, by the powers that be. And so he came and he stood and he watched this world spin by.

"Captain Crawford!"

He jerked from his wandering thoughts and forced a smile for the man coming across the ballroom toward him. The Earl of Bramwell was one of the men of this world he could actually stand. They had met through his brother-in-law, Nicholas Gillingham, a fellow serviceman he'd come to know after the man had suffered grievous injury in the line of duty.

"My lord," he said with a slight incline of his head. "I didn't realize you were here tonight."

"It's a crush," Bramwell said with a sigh. "Lady Gregson always invites too many people. Have you seen Nicholas and Aurora?"

Jonah shook his head. "No, are they here as well?"

Bramwell nodded. "Yes. Somewhat against his will, I think. But he will do anything to make my sister happy, as he always has."

"They are an excellent match," Jonah agreed, though he couldn't imagine finding a woman he would be so attached to. Such an odd thought.

"They are, indeed," Bramwell said, and he sounded happy, though there was something to the look on his face that made Jonah look a little closer.

"Troubled?"

Bramwell ducked his head. "Oh no, not really. I was just thinking about the upcoming Season. It will be full of crushes even worse than this one what with the royal family of Athawick joining the fray. It is all anyone has talking about for the last month."

Jonah set his jaw at the mention of Athawick and the impending royal visit. He would not react. He could not react.

"Ah yes," he said, keeping his tone neutral.

"You are acquainted with the family, aren't you?" Bramwell asked.

Jonah's mind flashed to two years before, to warm brown eyes that seemed to draw a man all the way in. That seemed to see too much.

He cleared his throat. "I was part of a group who went with the Regent to Athawick on an official visit two years ago. It was before the last king's death and yes, I got to know the family a little during that stay. Their new king, Grantham, is a decent fellow."

"I look forward to meeting him and his family," Bramwell said. "There is some rumor that they may be seeking a match for the daughter, Princess Ilaria, during their stay here."

Jonah's eyes narrowed. "Who said that?"

"My mother," Bramwell said. "And she is never wrong, at least when it comes to potential brides for men of a certain rank…for me, if we're being honest. Do you not think she is correct?"

Jonah gripped his hands in fists at his sides and then released them. God's teeth, he had no right to feel such a flood of emotion at this revelation about the princess's future. It had nothing to do with him, after all.

"I suppose it makes sense," he said. "Athawick has such a close relationship to Britain."

Bramwell nodded. "That was my mother's opinion on the matter. To bind their family to a titled family here would solidify all sorts of political relationships."

"Of course," Jonah said. "A title."

Bramwell's brow wrinkled, and for a moment Jonah had the horrifying realization he was going to be questioned further about his reaction. But before that nightmare could begin, a man stepped from the crowd.

"Gillingham!" Jonah said, happy for the interruption. "The earl said you were here."

Nicholas Gillingham leaned on a cane as he made his way to the two men. He extended his unoccupied hand and shook first with his brother-in-law and then with Jonah. He smiled at them both. "Excellent to see you."

"And you," Jonah said, and meant it. Though he might not have much patience with many of those in attendance tonight, he truly liked and respected Gillingham. They had bonded over military service, as well as being forced to leave the profession they'd each intended to take part in for life. For very different reasons, of course.

"Captain Crawford and I were just discussing the impending arrival of the Athawick Royal Family," the earl said.

"Ah, yes. Just before we departed for this evening's events, Aurora mentioned we had an invitation to Bleaking House tomorrow night for a welcome soiree."

"Staying at Bleaking House, are they?" Bramwell asked. "One of the lesser royal residences, but still, an official one. I suppose I will find the same waiting for me when I return home tonight. And I assume we'll see you there, as well, Captain? Because of that prior relationship we discussed."

Jonah shifted. He had no idea if he would be included on the welcoming guest list. It had been two years since he last saw any of the Athawick Royal Family. Perhaps the bonds of friendship he had formed with the now-king were long forgotten.

Or perhaps he would be dragged into their sphere, after all.

"If I am invited, I do not see a way I could refuse such an honor," he said.

The other two men began talking about some other subject then, but Jonah felt no relief about it. Now his mind was spinning, turning, recalling things he had used a great deal of discipline to forget.

Like the scent of Princess Ilaria's hair or the way she looked when she laughed. He would need to master some of that control again if he were to become a part of the family's time in London. Because he had no place in the life of the princess. He'd realized that once before and he could not forget it now.

Two Years Before
The Island of Athawick

Jonah was not accustomed to being a passenger on a ship so he was restless as the pleasure boat was piloted into the dock at Athawick. He stood away from the rest of the party, away from the Prince Regent and his lackeys, and stared out at the island that was their destination. He'd heard of the place, of course. Athawick was described in floral, fascinated terms any time someone spoke about it. It was a fairytale land to hear people tell it, but he had never believed it.

Until now. His breath caught at the sights before him. A clean, well-tended dock stretched out with men racing around to help pilot the ship to safety as the crowds of Athawickians waved from the shore and open windows and from behind barricades that kept them from the welcoming party.

The village beyond the dock was lined with colorful shops and homes, painted reds and blues and pinks and yellows, much like he'd seen many a time in Scotland over the years. A winding main road led up and up the rolling green hills toward a massive palace with towers and spires and a walled-in segment of the town at its feet, for protection from invaders in centuries past.

It was, unquestionably, the most beautiful castle he had ever seen, though he would certainly not say that in his current company. He could already see that the Prince Regent was staring up at the palace with pursed lips and unmasked annoyance. He wanted to have the finest toys and Athawick was showing him up with this display.

The docking was finished and the party began to exit the boat. The Regent went first, of course, waving to the cheering crowd as he approached the Athawick royal party. Jonah stood with the rest of the honor guard, chosen from each branch of the king's military for their acts of bravery. The Regent met the King of Athawick first, a tall and handsome older man who appeared a bit pale in the bright sunshine, and his queen, who was as stunning a woman as Jonah had ever seen.

Until she stepped to the side and her grown children moved forward to make their greetings. Two men, Jonah assumed the Princes Grantham and Remington, but behind them was a woman who could only be Princess Ilaria. His heat thudded almost painfully in his chest and he could not stop staring.

She was stunning, and he was well and truly stunned. With dark hair that was spun up in a complicated fashion, emphasizing her high cheekbones, brown eyes and full lips, she was uncommonly beautiful. A fact he could see was not missed by some of the other men in their party as all attention shifted to the princess.

She shifted her gaze toward the honor guard, flitting it around the various men without pausing until she reached…him.

Their eyes met, and for a moment she held there, without hesitation or blushing or simpering. She just looked at him, and in that moment he forgot to breathe.

Then she glanced away and it was like he had been released from a hold. He drew in a long gasp of air and tried to refocus as the King of Athawick announced, "Come, we will make our way to the palace."

Carriages arrived, trumpets blared and the parties situated themselves for the short trip through the happy crowd back to the castle on the hill. But Jonah could still feel the warmth of Princess Ilaria's stare coursing through his veins. A desire he hadn't expected when he reluctantly accepted this post from his old friend and mentor, Admiral Westing. A desire he would certainly have to control for the next month during their visit.

After all, he'd never see the woman again after that.

CHAPTER 3

1817
Bleaking House, London

"Do you think they know I am doing this under duress?" Ilaria asked as her maid slid yet another bejeweled clip into the complicated style she had created for Ilaria's hair. One that would later be matched in Sasha's locks so that she could race in as a stand-in if anything went wrong.

"I think *everyone* knows you are doing this under duress." Sasha lounged against the arm of the settee and laughed. "You have been bemoaning it since our arrival in London this morning. June, do you know Her Highness is doing this under duress?"

June giggled and her cheeks flushed in the mirror's reflection. "I think I'd best be left out of this, Miss Sasha."

Sasha rolled her eyes. "She knows where her bread is buttered, I suppose."

Ilaria felt herself smiling, no matter how she tried to retain an air of outrage. Sasha had always been able to do that and she loved her friend for it. Still, the relief of laughter didn't reduce the pain of reality.

"It is only that we haven't been in London a damned day," Ilaria huffed. "I apologize for the language, June, but there it is. And already I am being expected to exhibit for what will surely be a parade of disappointing potential grooms."

"And the Prince Regent," Sasha pointed out. "And virtually every other titled and important person in London. This isn't entirely about you, you know."

That brought Ilaria up short. She had been so annoyed at her family since their announcement of their plans for her the previous day, she'd become very focused on her role in their visit.

"You are…right, of course," she admitted. "I know tonight is about Grantham being recognized in his new role as king as much as it is about me. More, even. Did you see him after we arrived?"

She frowned as she thought of her brother, pacing the parlor as Blairford read him message after message from the courtiers for the Prince Regent and Queen Charlotte regarding the expectations and schedule of their visit.

Sasha nodded. "The weight of all this is enormous."

Ilaria sighed. "Fine, then I will not protest out of respect for Grantham. And I will dance and shake hands and behave myself."

"An excellent notion. You do look the part of proper princess in that dress."

Ilaria smiled as June stepped away. She got up and moved to the full-length mirror to examine herself. The gown was blue, with alternating paler blue stripes and highlights of gold. Atop her head, June had placed the sea crown, Ilaria's favorite from the royal collection because of its pale blue stones. It matched the gown to perfection.

"Come stand by me, let's compare," Ilaria said as she motioned to Sasha. Her companion joined her and they looked at their reflection in the mirror together. Though Sasha's hair was down—June would do it to match Ilaria's after she had left for the ball—they did look enough alike even now.

"You are prettier in it," Ilaria said with a smile. And she meant it.

Sasha was stunning and she always seemed more effortless than Ilaria, herself, felt.

Sasha snorted. "Unlikely. Anyway, no one will see me."

"Unless there is suddenly grave danger," Ilaria said, and then rolled her eyes. "Nothing is going to happen to me."

Sasha glanced toward the clock on the mantel. "Except that you are late and your mother might murder you."

Ilaria followed her gaze and yelped. "Oh, damn. Yes, I'll be off. I will see you later tonight with a full report on whatever wretched suitors they throw into my path. Good night! And thank you, June!"

She hurried from the room with the farewells of the two women ringing in her ears. She rushed down the hallway, taking the twists and turns with a bit of uncertainty, for she hadn't quite learned all the intricacies of the household yet. But she found the main stair at last and took it down toward the ballroom. Already she heard the strains of music lilting up the hallway toward her. She winced as she saw her family lined up to greet their guests.

She slipped into her place at the end of the line and smiled apologetically toward her mother. The queen was greeting someone, but the way she sent a side glance toward Ilaria could have frozen the depths of hell themselves. She was surely going to get a stern talking to later and she wasn't looking forward to it.

She pushed her shoulders back and fell into the role she had played for so long, she couldn't recall a time when it wasn't hers. She greeted attendees to the party, murmuring a welcome, making mindless small talk, watching them enter the ballroom.

This went on for what felt like a lifetime, until she could scarcely feel her fingers from shaking so many hands, until all their faces blurred together into one. She stifled a yawn and glanced toward the head of the line. Grantham was first to meet people as king, and her breath caught as she saw the gentleman who had approached him. One she knew.

It was Captain Jonah Crawford. The man had accompanied the

Prince Regent on a trip to Athawick what felt like centuries ago, considering all that had transpired since then.

Dear God, but he was handsome, in full naval dress uniform, his dark red hair cut short and neat, his gray-blue eyes focused on her brother as they briefly spoke. She'd tried to forget how compelling she'd found the man during their brief acquaintance. A few weeks, nothing more, and only a handful of private conversations and one dance had passed between them during that time. Still, she could recall every vibration of his voice, every turn of his head.

Now it came rushing back in a flood of racing blood and shaking hands.

He stepped away from Grantham and toward her mother as Ilaria greeted another partygoer whose face she didn't even really see. Captain Crawford was talking to Remi now, standing right near her. She could feel the heat of his presence even before he took another step and stopped just before her.

For what felt like a lifetime they stared at each other. She couldn't breathe, or at least she didn't recall doing so. She just stared up into those beautiful sea-gray eyes and thought of the last time she'd seen him. What he'd said to her then.

"Your Highness," he said at last, his voice low and rough. He took her hand and bent over it, the brush of his gloved fingers against hers awakening feelings she didn't want to have. Couldn't have.

So she drew her hand back. "Good evening, sir," she said.

"You remember Captain Crawford, don't you, Ilaria?" Remi asked at her side.

She blinked, pretending not to recall. "Hmmmm…"

"He was with the party of the Regent a couple of years ago," Remi continued to explain, utterly oblivious as usual.

"Oh yes," she said with what she hoped was a believably faint smile. "I do recall something like that. Good evening, Captain Crawford. It is good to see you again."

Crawford arched a brow. It was the slightest movement, but for a moment she felt caught. As if he could see through her act. "The feeling is mutual, Your Highness," he said. "I will leave you to the remainder of the receiving line. Good evening."

He stepped away and she drew in her breath at last. The man had presence, there was no denying that fact. He filled a space, he dominated all corners of it. And now that he was gone, she had to pretend that wasn't true and continue meeting the other guests, who now seemed even more boring than usual. Somehow she managed, and at last enough time had passed that Grantham stepped away from the receiving line and motioned the family into the ballroom.

People were staring as they came in. Ilaria saw the whispers behind fans, arched brows and slow nods. She scanned the crowd, pretending to herself that she was only taking in the scene, but she found Captain Crawford quickly enough. He was standing next to a tall gentleman with dark hair. He was not looking at her, so she refused to continue staring at him like a ninny.

"The Prince Regent will likely arrive shortly, along with his mother and brothers," Grantham said to their family group. "And we will be expected to greet them, so do not stray far and listen for the announcement." He arched a brow toward the queen. "And Mother, perhaps you could..."

Queen Giabella inclined her head. "I shall. Now go and greet your guests, Grantham. Remi, do try to behave yourself. And Ilaria, will you come with me, please?"

Grantham did not meet her eyes before he ducked into the crowd, all proper greetings and serious connections. Remi, however, did. His expression was rather pitying, but he did nothing to intervene before he stepped away, not that there was anything to do. How she wished she had the freedom he had managed to carve out for himself.

Giabella gave her an appraising look. "Do try not to look like I'm leading you the gallows, love."

"I certainly hope it shall not be so dire, Mama," she said. "But I am surprised you are not waiting to throw me in the path of the

Prince Regent's brothers. There are three, are there not? Decrepit specimen of the best and brightest this country has to offer?"

Her mother pursed her lips. "You would do well not to be overheard being so bold about the family that leads this country. And you will be happy to know that all parties involved have decided it is not in the best interest of anyone that you marry within the royal family itself."

"Why?" Ilaria asked.

"The official reason is that it would give both sides too much power. You could too greatly influence British politics in favor of Athawick and vice versa." Her mother shifted. "At least that is the reason the Regent has accepted."

"It is not the real one?"

"If you think I wish to marry you off to anyone who is thirty years your senior and with the wit of a wet sack, then you judge me too harshly." Her mother looked off into the crowd, refusing to meet her stare. "I'm going to do my best to find you a husband you can at least stand the look of."

Ilaria blinked. "You think if he is young that it will protect me?"

Her mother sighed. "I think there is a better chance."

Ilaria considered a retort, for her mother and father had been of an age and that had turned out dreadfully. But in the end she swallowed it back. Her conversations with Sasha had reminded her that she did love her family, misguided as they were. And she didn't want to hurt Grantham's chances of presenting well to Court and to kingdom. "Lead the way."

Her mother looked relieved at the capitulation and slowly guided Ilaria through the crowd. But with every step, Ilaria's heart leapt. They were heading toward Captain Crawford and his companion, and she could scarcely breathe as her mother came to a stop before the two men.

"Your Majesty," Crawford said, and he almost looked startled by their arrival.

He executed a bow, though his gray eyes slid toward Ilaria. She felt the heat enter her cheeks and hoped she wasn't turning as purple as a plum.

"Captain Crawford, let me repeat to you what a pleasure it is to see you again," her mother said, warmly and genuinely. The entire family had liked the man during his visit. And yet the queen didn't keep her attention on him long. Her gaze shifted to the other man. "Ilaria, you met the Earl of Bramwell in the receiving line."

Ilaria forced her gaze from Captain Crawford to the earl. He was handsome enough, no one could say it wasn't true. He had dark hair, a harshly angled jaw, full lips and warm brown eyes that seemed…kind. And yet she didn't even recall meeting the man a few moments before.

"Good evening again, my lord," Ilaria said softly.

He inclined his head. "Your Highness. How are you enjoying London?"

"Not much so far," Ilaria said. "We only arrived earlier in the day. This is a whirlwind, I'm afraid."

"Ah," the earl said. "Well, then I hope you will have a chance to settle in and see our city to its full potential in the next few weeks and months."

"Perhaps you could be a guide, my lord," Giabella said without even attempting subtlety.

The earl cast his glance first toward the queen, then to Ilaria again. He looked as she felt in that brief moment, like a rat caught in a cage.

"I would be pleased to give you some version of a tour if you would like that." He cleared his throat. "And perhaps you would honor me with a dance?"

Ilaria glanced again at Captain Crawford. He looked bored standing there, a witness to this first attempt to find her a husband suitable not for her, but for the future of her kingdom. She couldn't help but think of another dance, one he had been far more engaged in. She pushed those thoughts away and her shoulders back.

"I would very much enjoy a dance, my lord." She tried not to glare at her mother as she stood by, beaming from ear to ear. But she refused to look at Crawford as Lord Bramwell led her to the dance floor and they began.

If Captain Crawford didn't care, she didn't care. She certainly wasn't going to go chasing after some man.

"The entire country is aflutter about your visit, Your Highness."

She blinked and tried to refocus on the man dancing with her. "It seems so. They are all watching us dance, after all. The interest will not let up…unless someone else does something shocking and turns their attention."

He laughed and she examined his face closely. He really was very handsome and he had a nice laugh. He was a good dancer. For a first attempt at throwing her at a titled man, it wasn't the worst choice. And yet…

She stifled a sigh.

There was no spark here. No instantaneous connection that made her want to lean a little closer. To know more about him. Somehow she'd always pictured her future with a man who made her feel that spark.

Her gaze slid to Captain Crawford, who stood where she had left him, talking to her mother at the side of the ballroom. There were sparks galore with that one, at least on her side. Not that it mattered. If her mother and brother had their way, she would be matched for political connection, not desire or bond. Not spark.

Whether or not she was going to accept that future was another story entirely.

～

Jonah watched Ilaria glide across the floor in the Earl of Bramwell's arms and he tried to ignore the stirring flare of pain in his chest at the sight.

"They look well together, eh?" Queen Giabella asked at his side.

He flinched and forced his attention back to her. "Certainly.

Though I would wager your daughter looks well with any man lucky enough to dance with her."

The queen smiled. "That is true enough. She has grown into a beautiful woman, both inside and out. And whatever man takes her hand will be fortunate, indeed."

He cleared his throat as he stole another glance at Ilaria and Bramwell. She moved with such grace, such certainty. His stomach clenched at the sight. At the thoughts watching her created.

"I—" he began, and then stopped with a shake of his head. "Never mind."

The queen pivoted to face him straight on and speared him with her sharp, brown gaze. "Well, now you have piqued my interest, Captain Crawford. Whatever were you going to say?"

He opened and shut his mouth, staring at the woman before him. In her face, he could see where Ilaria had gotten her strength and her confidence.

"Speak now, young man," she said, her tone both playful and demanding.

He shifted. She was as undeniable as any admiral he'd served under in his years in the navy. "I…was…I was going to ask you an impertinent question about a rumor I heard."

"A rumor about Ilaria?" the queen asked, good humor replaced by concern. "Or…God forbid, Remi?"

"There are some who say that you are looking to match the princess with a husband on this trip," he said.

Queen Giabella's expression relaxed. "Ah. Well, those rumors may indeed be true. We do not verify or deny such things."

He nodded slowly. "And I suppose you must be considering Bramwell as an option."

Queen Giabella stared off for a moment, not at her daughter, but almost past her. Like she was seeing something not on the dance floor. "It would be a mutually beneficial match."

"Hmmm," Jonah murmured.

Queen Giabella arched her eyebrow all the higher. "*Hmmm.*

What does *hmmm* mean? Do you have an objection to the potential union?"

He drew back. "I...I would have no right to object, of course. And I have no knowledge of Lord Bramwell except that he is the brother-in-law of a friend and that he seems to be a very decent man. I was only thinking that I do not know your daughter overly well, but she does not seem like the kind of woman who can be... managed easily."

Queen Giabella sighed, and now she did look at Ilaria. "No, *that* is true enough. She is headstrong. And yet she knows her duty to her king and her country. She will do it. I have great faith in that." She smiled at him. "I do enjoy seeing you, Captain. My eldest son thinks highly of you. If you will excuse me, I must attend to my duties."

"Of course. I would not keep you, Your Majesty." He bowed deeply as she floated away through the crowd toward her next interaction.

Leaving him to return his full attention to the dancefloor. To Ilaria. To the thoughts he could not let grow or fester or intrude upon duty. His. Or hers.

I laria drew a deep breath as she trailed behind her mother and brother toward the entryway to the ballroom. They had been told by Grantham's courtier, Blairford, that the prince regent had arrived at last, late of course...far beyond fashionably.

There was a buzz in the room, a ripple through the throng. Though the masses might not love their future monarch, he still caused a stir. Ilaria had no doubt he enjoyed it, especially as the doors to the ballroom opened and he swept in behind bleating trumpets.

Her jaw nearly dropped when she realized the regent was wearing his formal court robes with all their feathers and golden stitching and silly slippers. They also left little to the imagination and she had to use all the control her mother had taught her to keep from staring at the exaggerated codpiece of his costume.

She saw Grantham's jaw twitch at the ridiculousness of it all. Unlike their father before him, he had a difficult time pretending when he thought someone a fool, and yet he swept the disgust from his face as he approached his fellow monarch. The ballroom held its collective breath as the bows and greetings were exchanged.

"Your Majesty," Grantham said. "You recall my family, I believe."

The introductions were made, along the lines of rank, which made Ilaria the last to extend her hand to the prince regent. He lifted it to his lips and lingered there just a little too long. "You are even more beautiful than you were two years ago, my dear. I could not have thought it possible."

She forced her court smile to her lips and ducked her head. "You are too kind, Your Majesty. I trust your Season has begun well enough."

The prince regent rolled his eyes. "Dreadfully, I'm afraid. This entire year has been a travesty." He pivoted away from her toward her brother. "You will understand, I think, now that you have taken the crown. The people can be cruel, indeed."

Grantham's lips thinned. "The people make demands, of course. But as their sovereign I feel compelled to hear them out."

The regent sniffed. "Your country is so small, it is different. I rule an empire. The best I can do is crush anyone who questions me. You'll learn soon enough, young man."

Ilaria saw Grantham holding back a retort. Luckily he was not forced to reply, for the prince regent's attentions were redirected toward Queen Giabella. "Your Majesty, would you honor me with a dance?"

If the queen was as put off by this silly man as the rest of them, she made no expression of it. Instead she took his hand with her most dazzling smile and let herself be led to the dancefloor. The music rose and as the crowd stared on, the pair began the intricate turns.

Grantham shook his head and walked away without another word, leaving Remi and Ilaria to watch their mother and the strutting regent who was a shockingly talented dancer.

"He is elegant, I give him that," Ilaria said. "And it is always lovely to see Mama dance. She is so good at it."

Remi sighed. "Indeed. Though I suppose the regent must be a good...*dancer*, mustn't he? Rumors are he...*dances* with a great many women."

Ilaria pivoted toward him. "You are an absolute cad, Remi. You can't refer to dancing as a euphemism when the man is spinning our mother across the floor. It's indecent."

"I'm sure if Mother would give him a second glance, he would happily...*dance* with her again." Remi snorted when Ilaria glared at him. "And judging from the way he drooled all over your hand, he'd *dance* with you, too."

"Ugh." Ilaria couldn't control her disgusted expression. "Well, luckily he is not in the running to be my future dance partner. Mama is making some attempt to keep me from the clutches of the English monarchy. And even if she wasn't, the regent already has a wife."

"Two, if rumors be true."

Her eyes went wide. "What?"

"His hated future queen and the one he married illegally decades ago."

"Great God, I'd all but forgotten that," Ilaria muttered. "And yet Grantham worries about using the wrong fork. It seems he could get away with almost anything."

"Not if he doesn't want our people to hate him," Remi said, and now he sounded more serious.

Ilaria sighed and watched as the regent executed a ludicrous bow as his dance with her mother ended. "Oh dear, he's coming back and he is staring right at me. It appears I am to be his next victim."

Remi chuckled. "At least it helps you escape the arms of the dozens of men who have been watching you all night."

She glanced over her shoulder. Behind them, the crowd was watching, and indeed, there were a great many male eyes focused on Ilaria rather than the queen and the prince regent. Most of their expressions could only be described as mercenary but as the crowd stirred, she saw Jonah Crawford also watching her.

Unlike the other men, his gray eyes were not filled with visions of importance or fortune...no, he had a very different expression. She had seen it once before, been drawn to it all those years ago. But just as her body gave a great shiver or reaction, he turned and walked away. She couldn't track him because the regent and her mother returned and she was forced back into the role of dutiful princess rather than woman with a beating heart. One that wanted what it wanted, even if she could never have it.

Ilaria was exhausted and her feet hurt. The party was winding down at last, even as the first hints of dawn brightened the horizon outside. She had danced with what felt like every eligible man in entire country, plus most of the married ones. And after her dance with the regent, the attention of the room had focused more fully on her. Something she could not have imagined possible. Even when she wasn't dancing, hoards of eligible gentlemen had crowded around, practically drooling on her. Her mother had pushed and prodded and her eldest brother had encouraged and all the while Jonah Crawford had stood off to the side, a witness to every moment of her humiliation.

And it *was* a humiliation. Anyone who had attended the ball tonight had to be certain of Ilaria's status. They knew that her family was willing to barter her for gain. Her stomach turned at the thought.

"And how was your night?"

She tensed as Grantham stepped up beside her and smiled as if he weren't the very one holding the keys to her future.

"Fine," she said through clenched teeth. "Though I'm not certain why you ask."

His brow wrinkled, and for a moment she no longer saw the passive expression of her king, but the hurt of her brother. At least he was still in there, though she wasn't sure for how long. The Crown tended to change a man and perhaps not in the best ways.

"Because I care about your well-being," he said softly.

"Hmmm. Well, you were watching me all night, keeping track of your investment. So I'm sure you already know all the twists and turns of my evening. Your little spies and bodyguards must have reported anything you didn't see, as well."

"Ilaria," he said on a sigh. "Please."

"Please what?" she asked, pivoting to face him head on. "Please tow the line? Please stop wanting more from your future than the exact nightmare we watched our mother live out all our lives? Please be dutiful and never have a thought for my own happiness?"

His shoulders rolled forward and his mouth twisted. "There is more at play here than perhaps you realize," he said softly.

She wrinkled her brow. "What do you mean?"

He opened his mouth, and for a brief moment she thought he might actually let her in. But then his expression went stony once more. Sibling gone, king returned. "Trust that I do what I do for the good of us all, Ilaria."

She shook her head. "I don't know what to trust anymore, *Your Majesty.*"

He flinched at the use of his title, but he said nothing. He just turned on his heel and walked away. Back across the now-sparsely populated ballroom to where their mother stood with one of the many potential suitors who had been thrown in Ilaria's path earlier. She couldn't even remember the man's name, but she did recall his absolutely terrible breath.

She shuddered and looked toward the doors which led to the

broad wraparound terrace behind the ballroom. If she was not to be found, she could not be forced to do something she didn't want to do. That was what Remi did to avoid duty, after all. Why should she not exercise the same option?

She slipped through the terrace doors, shut them firmly behind her and then drew a long breath of the cool, early morning air. She moved to the edge and rested her hands on the rough stone wall to look down at the garden below. Once she had slept for a while, she would have to explore the gardens. She had always loved the peace of a green space like the one below.

"Your Highness."

She froze at the sound of a man's voice behind her. Not just any man's voice either. One she recognized even though she didn't wish to do so. She slowly turned and found Captain Crawford coming from the shadowy corner of the terrace.

"Captain," she said, fighting to measure her tone when she feared she sounded excited to see him again. "I did not realize you were out here. I'm surprised you have not already departed."

He shrugged as he joined her at the terrace wall, close enough that she could feel his body heat. Smell the spicy hint of his skin. He still smelled the same as he had all those years ago and she only barely resisted the urge to lean in a little closer.

"There is a bit of a crush on the drive," he explained. "I thought it made more sense to wait a short while before I asked for my horse. I'd rather do it here than out with the half-drunk partygoers."

"More than half for many of them," she said.

"Most."

"Well, you never seemed the kind of man who indulged *too* much in anything," she said. "So I suppose that shouldn't surprise me."

He turned slightly and caught her stare. "Ahhh, so are you no longer pretending you didn't remember me from my visit to Athawick two years ago?"

Heat flooded her cheeks. "Oh…I…" She shook her head. "You've caught me, Captain. I did pretend to not recall you earlier tonight."

He held her stare for a beat. "Playing games, princess?"

She swallowed hard. There was something about the drawl to his voice as he asked that question that seemed to drive through her bloodstream. Settled in the most inopportune places. This man set her on her heels and she did not allow many people to do that.

Any people.

She forced a smile. "No, just doing as you once asked me to do," she retorted, and was pleased when he shifted. It seemed he recalled the last time they'd seen each other, too. Those words he'd said that had stung her. She pushed them away and asked, "What about you, Captain?"

"You're asking if I'm playing games?" he said.

She nodded.

"No, Your Highness. I can't afford games, I'm afraid." He backed away from her, his hand flexing at his side as he did so. "I should not delay and I'm sure you have other things to do. It was a pleasure seeing you again. Good…good morning."

He didn't wait for her to respond, but pivoted on his heel and strode from the terrace, leaving her alone. She sucked in a breath, hating that her hands shook.

"Is that who I think it was?"

Ilaria looked down the terrace to find Sasha coming toward her. Now that most of the partygoers had gone, she could come out from the wings where Ilaria was sure she had been spying off and on all night. Her friend was still dressed in the same gown she, herself, was wearing, not a hair out of place of their shared style. She looked like a mirror image, except cooler and not as off kilter as Ilaria now felt.

"Who do you think it was?" she asked, dully she knew.

"Captain Jonah Crawford," Sasha said. "Or was I seeing things?"

Ilaria struggled to find her breath. "You weren't. It was, indeed, the esteemed Captain Crawford. He was an attendee at the ball and we were just saying our…our farewells."

Sasha arched a brow at her. "Ilaria, you forget that I am your confidante and friend. I know you...well, you *liked* the man during his visit to Athawick, what was it...three years ago?"

"Two," Ilaria corrected. "It's been two years, and yes, I thought him very handsome when he visited me...my family back then."

"When he stepped off the ship back then I thought you'd stopped breathing," Sasha said.

"Perhaps I did," Ilaria mused. "There we were, in the midst of foolish pomp and circumstance and down the gang plank of the royal yacht comes this...this *man*. All certainty and angles and sharp gaze." She realized she was letting herself drift away to that moment and jerked herself back to reality. "But you can see by the way he walked away without so much as a backward glance that he thinks nothing of me. And I can think nothing of him, thanks to my family's plans."

Sasha tilted her head. "Ilaria—"

"I'm simply tired," Ilaria said. "With the travel and then this huge event. I'm tired. Come, we'll have little chance for rest before the next event this evening. Let's go before I fall over or my brother and mother find ten more men off the street for me to meet."

She could see Sasha wished to say more about the subject, but instead her companion wrapped an arm around her waist and the two walked down the length of the terrace, toward a door that led to a parlor, not the ballroom.

She hadn't lied, of course. She *was* tired. But she feared her sleep would be restless thanks to the man who had just left her on the terrace.

CHAPTER 4

Jonah weaved his way through the club, looking for Grantham. The king was impossible to miss, seated in the back, a circle of men staring at him from the main hall, while his bodyguards stood by, anything but inconspicuous. He sipped his drink and read the paper as if he didn't even notice all the attention being lavished on him. Attention that would certainly extend to Jonah the moment he joined the man.

He drew a deep breath before he did just that.

"Your Majesty," he said, bowing before he extended a hand. The closest bodyguard twitched as if he would move if need be.

Grantham rose to his feet and took the offered hand. "Crawford, very good to see you again, old friend. Please, join me."

Jonah did so and the steward rushed forward with another glass and the bottle of whisky that was apparently what his companion was drinking. It was a bit early for Jonah, but he didn't refuse as the libation was poured.

As the steward stepped away, Grantham raised his glass. "To old friendships, eh?"

"Indeed, sir," Jonah said, and the crystal clinked as they touched glasses. Jonah took a small sip of the drink and set it aside. "I admit I was surprised to receive your message to meet here today."

Grantham smiled. "Why is that?"

"This is an official visit. I assumed you would have a packed schedule of activities and obligations."

The king's mouth tightened. "Yes. There is hardly a moment free. I had to argue with my courtier for what felt like an eternity to force him to find time in my day today to sit with you. Sometimes it feels as if *they* are running the country and my life, rather than me."

"I suppose that is a hazard of the job," Jonah said. "I recall the influence of the courtiers when I was traveling with the regent. They can be quite a bit to manage."

Grantham rolled his eyes before he took a long drink. Then he set his glass down. "I suppose each of us have a great deal more to manage than we did when last we met."

"Indeed," Jonah said. "There have been big changes for us both."

"Mine are obvious, and trust that I am sick to death talking about them," Grantham said with a chuckle. "Indulge me for a moment by pretending I am not a king and you and I are just old friends catching up."

Jonah inclined his head. "If that's your wish. Yes, when last we saw each other, I was still in the Royal Navy. I thought I would be there the rest of my life. But then a..." He hesitated. "A family member passed and suddenly I was left an inheritance and an estate to manage. It was evident doing both was not an option."

"So you chose the estate," Grantham said.

Jonah sighed. "There were duties and dependents that came along with it."

"Ah, heavy is the head that wears the crown. *That* I understand." Grantham shook his head. "And do you find the gift you were left a blessing or a curse?"

That was a question whose answer Jonah had avoided for some time. "Both, if I am honest. I didn't want to leave my position. I sometimes long for what I once had. And yet...I am good at managing the estate. I have made it a better place in the last year and a half. That has meaning, at least to the lives of those who are impacted by what I do."

Grantham took another sip of his drink and nodded. "There is a good feeling to knowing you are helping others. It's almost worth all the rest."

"I know you said you were sick to death of speaking of your own change of fortunes, but may I ask how things are going here in London? This is your first official visit as monarch."

Grantham strummed his fingers against the edge of his glass restlessly. "Yes, and it is with our most precarious ally. So there is a great deal riding on what happens here."

"I can see how that would be true," Jonah said.

Grantham held his gaze a moment and let out his breath slowly. "I'm going to say something to you now that I hope you understand must be kept in confidence."

Jonah wrinkled his brow. "Of…course. What is it?"

"This entire endeavor is less than a week old and I already feel like I'm herding cats. I'm shuttled from event to event, shaking hands, having the most ridiculous conversations about the weather and the roads. Any encounter with the regent makes me wonder if I'm going to say the wrong thing and be invaded the moment I return home." Grantham paused and ran a hand through his hair. "And home is an entirely other conversation. One I ought not to get into with an acquaintance."

"There is trouble?" Jonah asked. "My recollection is that you and your family are well liked by your subjects."

"For the most part it seems that is true, but there are factions and—" Grantham stopped himself suddenly and shook his head. "As I said, I ought not to talk to you about this."

Jonah nodded slowly. "I understand the reticence. But I hope you know that I hear this only as a friend. I have no ulterior motive, no desire to use the knowledge against you in any way."

"I…appreciate that. Normally I would discuss this with my

family, but things have changed since I took the title of king. And coming here has created even more of a wall between us."

"How so?"

"From the moment he arrived, Remi went off to whore his way through London," he explained.

Jonah chuckled. "I will only say that doesn't seem out of character."

"Not in the slightest," Grantham agreed, and a flutter of a smile turned up this lips. "Only there is the potential for greater consequences. My mother is…worried. I see her trying to hide it, but it's there in her every stare, her every movement. Thank God her secretary, Dashiell Talbot, is accompanying us on this journey. Sometimes it feels like he is the confidante she needs."

"And then there is Princess Ilaria," Jonah said softly, bringing them around to the topic that interested him most. The topic he had not been able to forget since he'd last seen her after the welcome ball three mornings before.

"Yes, there is Ilaria." Grantham stared off into nothingness for a moment. "She thinks me such a villain at present—she can scarcely look at me. And she's determined to punish me. Make my life difficult."

"Why?" Jonah asked, though he knew why. He'd seen the why as she danced with all those eligible titled men.

"She doesn't like my plans for her," the king said softly. "And perhaps I don't entirely blame her for that. I only wish she understood that to refuse this future is to create problems. And perhaps even dangers."

"Dangers?" Jonah asked. "What does that mean? Does it have to do with the unrest you mentioned a moment ago?"

Grantham rested his tightly clenched hands against his thighs. "The beginnings of unrest. My courtiers try to tell me this is normal during a transition. They try to convince me to crush it swiftly and cruelly enough that no one ever attempts it during my reign again. But that does not seem right."

Jonah hesitated. He was in no position to advise a king. The lemon-faced courtier standing staring at them from a few feet away had that job. And yet this wasn't advising a king, was it? It was helping a friend.

"I think," he said carefully, "that you must do what you think is right for yourself and your country."

"Yes. As soon as I figure out what that is and manage to finagle my family back into line."

"Do you really think the princess will step out of line?" Jonah asked. "That she won't do as you wish?"

"Not only am I not certain that she will do as is required, she might thwart me entirely. At home she has a nasty habit of slipping her guards. I'm sure she is already plotting the same here and could do all manner of things to make this hard on me and herself."

"I could…" Jonah swallowed hard. He should not continue that sentence. He should cut it off and stand up and end this conversation. But he didn't. "I could look out for her."

Grantham tilted his head. "Now that is an idea." He set his drink aside and steepled his fingers, strumming them together. "I could present you with her schedule and help arrange for you to be invited to any events where she would be present. If she saw you, she would never guess it was because you were following her, guarding her. She only vaguely recalled you from your time on Athawick."

Jonah bit his lip. There was no need to inform Grantham about Ilaria's subterfuge. Or their encounter after the welcome ball on the terrace that he had been pondering for days.

"Would it put you out?"

Jonah blinked and pulled himself back to the present. "Er…no. I have a few matters to attend in Town, but most of my time is taken up by frivolous activities. I really don't mind having a vocation."

"Excellent," Grantham said. "There is a garden party in two hours, actually, that my sister will be attending." He lifted a hand

and snapped his fingers, and the courtier who had been standing by stepped up.

"Yes, Your Majesty?"

"Blairford, can you arrange for Captain Crawford to get a last-minute invitation to Lady Questington's garden party?"

The courtier cast Jonah a quick and rather dismissive look. "I can certainly do everything in my power, sir. Is there anything else?"

"No, just that." Grantham waved his hand as if to dismiss the man. As he walked away, Jonah couldn't help but take note of Blairford's sour expression.

"Friendly fellow," he said.

Grantham laughed. "He is that. He was my father's right-hand man and I inherited him. He is very knowledgeable about the goings on in my country, so I keep him."

"Hmm," Jonah murmured.

"Thank you for offering to keep an eye on my sister. It will be helpful to know that a friend is doing so." He rose, and Jonah saw that this was his dismissal, and done very politely and royally.

He took the hint and stood, as well, extending a hand, which the king shook. "I'm happy to do so."

"I'll follow up with you soon," Grantham said. "Good afternoon."

Jonah stepped back, executed a bow and then departed, back through the buzzing club. Normally he might have taken note about who was there, what they were doing, but at that moment, his mind was occupied with other things.

Such as the fact that he had just agreed to trail Ilaria across London. Follow the woman who had inspired several entirely inappropriate dreams over the past few days. Years.

"Bloody idiot," he muttered.

"Mr. Crawford?" He turned to find Grantham's courtier, Blairford, at his heels, looking unpleasant as ever.

"Captain," Jonah corrected, though he thought the man already knew that. He was calling him by the wrong honorific as an insult, not a mistake.

"I have sent a message requesting that you be included on the guest list for the tea this afternoon. A reply will be sent to your home directly."

"Thank you, Blairford," Jonah said. "I'm sure the king appreciates your hard work."

Blairford arched a brow as he looked Jonah up and down. "There are many who look out for the best interests of Athawick, sir. Whether you are one of them remains to be seen. Good day."

Jonah watched as the man flounced away and sighed heavily as he exited the club and motioned for his horse to be brought around. It seemed he had upset the applecart, the chain of command, and the courtiers weren't pleased with it. One more mess to potentially deal with.

But it was too late to go back now. So it seemed he would have to go prepare for tea.

The royal carriage rumbled over the uneven cobblestones that lined the London streets. Ilaria hardly noticed the motion as she stared out the window and tried to block out the never-ending stream of conversation coming from where her mother sat. It was all jabber about the upcoming garden party and the expectations to be found there.

At last Ilaria leveled her gaze at her. "And which suitor will be there waiting for me, Mama?"

Queen Giabella blinked. "Suitor? What makes you think there is a suitor at today's gathering?"

Ilaria pursed her lips. "You have never been one to chatter idly, but since we stepped into the vehicle half an hour ago, you haven't stopped talking. Which makes me think you are nervous. And it can't be because of the gathering, you hold court with ease."

"Ilaria," her mother began, and she sounded weary.

Ilaria didn't stop. "And Grantham is not attending because he has some tedious meeting elsewhere. Remi is nowhere to be found so he can't cause a scene. Which means you are worried about me. And since I don't think I've ever humiliated you when it came to a party, that makes me think you're worried about something else." She folded her arms. "Such as how I will interact with one of the suitors you insist on throwing in my path."

Her mother tossed her head. "I've never thrown anything in anyone's path in my life. The thought, Ilaria."

"Which one, Mama?" Ilaria arched a brow and knew it was exactly as her mother did it. She had learned the action from the queen, after all. "Or is it some new one? Will I be forced to meet every eligible man in England?"

"Very well, you are not wrong. There will be a potential suitor in attendance this afternoon." Her mother folded her arms. "The Earl of Bramwell."

Ilaria wrinkled her brow and tried to conjure an image to go with the man. Finally she recalled him as the one she had first danced with at the ball a few nights before. The friend of Captain Crawford's.

"You certainly cannot have anything against the man?" the queen asked, almost triumphantly when Ilaria had been silent too long.

"I don't know him well enough to claim an objection against him, Mama. Nor is it likely I will come to know him in any meaningful way in the short time we will be in London. And yet you and Grantham are determined to leg shackle me to him or some other man who looks almost exactly like him." She sighed. "What if he is dreadful under that façade? What if he is cruel?"

"I'll have you know, he has had a good source vouch for him."

"Who?" Ilaria asked, wrinkling her brow.

"Captain Crawford."

"Cr-Crawford?" Ilaria repeated, and there was a sting that worked through her at the thought.

"And I doubt you have anything to say about *that*. You liked the man well enough when he visited Athawick with the Regent years ago."

Ilaria turned to look out the window. Though Sasha knew about her past interest in Crawford, she'd never told her mother about the attraction she felt. Once she might have, for despite the fact they were knocking heads now, they had been close in the past.

But back when Crawford had come to their island, her mother had been busy dealing with issues with the king. His illness had just begun, and sometimes her mother had been forced to cover. So Ilaria had kept the truth from her, and now she didn't want her mother to see her true reaction to this news. Didn't want to reveal too much of herself.

"I'm surprised Captain Crawford would have an opinion whatsoever about my future," she said at last.

Her mother did not respond because the carriage turned into the drive and she was now distracted as footmen raced to help them down and their hostess, Lady Questington, hustled down the stairs to deeply curtsey. Her servants lined the stairs, waving large feathered fans to cool the entryway.

Ilaria rolled her eyes at the grandeur. Sometimes it felt like it kept anything from being real at all. She sighed and followed her mother down to the drive.

"Lady Questington," the queen said, extending a hand.

The woman blinked at it before she took it, then awkwardly kissed it before she flushed and managed a wobbly curtsey. "Oh, I am a-titter to meet you, Your Majesties."

Ilaria forced a smile to sooth their hostess's nerves. She had committed at least four breaches in royal etiquette in the span of thirty seconds, but none of it ever mattered. Queen Giabella was never anything but kind and her children had learned to behave the same way.

As they entered the house together, Giabella cooed and complimented everything from the paintings hanging in the halls to the color of the wallpaper. And slowly, Lady Questington seemed to relax. By the time they exited to the garden she was chatting amiably.

The other guests were already gathered there, staring as Ilaria and the queen joined them. Murmuring and Ilaria was certain also judging their every move.

She scanned the crowd for Lord Bramwell, just so she would be prepared for greeting him again. But before she could find him, her gaze fell on Captain Crawford instead, and her heart, traitor that it was, leapt. He was not in uniform today, but dressed impeccably in a dark jacket, perfectly tied cravat and gold-threaded waistcoat. His thick, ruddy hair was swept away from his forehead in waves that were almost too perfect.

She set her jaw. Handsome or not, she was irritated with the man and she intended to do something about it. She moved to do so when her mother caught her elbow and pivoted her instead to face Lord Bramwell, who had apparently joined their party while she was staring at Captain Crawford.

"Ilaria, you recall Lord Bramwell, do you not?" her mother asked, and her fingers dug just a fraction harder into Ilaria's elbow. A warning, a reminder.

She forced a smile to her face. "Of course I recall you, my lord. How nice to see you again."

Lord Bramwell executed a bow and he smiled, though it did not entirely reach his eyes as he said, "Your Highness, the pleasure is all mine. I wondered if I might introduce you ladies to my mother. The dowager countess is very anxious to make your acquaintance."

The queen said something, but Ilaria hardly heard it as she glanced back over her shoulder toward Captain Crawford. He was watching her now, there was no denying it. His gray gaze was focused on her face, and when she glared at him he smiled just a fraction.

She turned away as she was all but dragged across the grass to an older lady with a bright smile and a dark pink gown. As they drew closer, Ilaria could see the similarities between Lord Bramwell and his mother, including the kindness of their eyes.

The introductions were made and Ilaria felt herself being analyzed. Not judged, perhaps, but sized up certainly. A strange thing since she felt no interest in the objectively handsome man standing with his mother. And when he looked at her, it was not with a great deal of interest in return. He was polite, kind, even amusing, but there was no spark there. No heat.

"Your Majesty," Lady Bramwell said after a short time. "I wonder if you have ever played cribbage?"

Ilaria cast a side glance at her mother and was not surprised when her expression lit up. "Oh my, yes. I often play with my private secretary, Dash—Mr. Talbot."

"That is excellent news," Lady Bramwell said. "Would it be too impertinent to ask you to join me in a little tournament a group of ladies plays twice monthly? It is nothing formal, but it is high fun."

Ilaria watched a plethora of emotion pass over her mother's face, and for a moment she forgot her own annoyance with the queen's plan. Sometimes it was hard to recall all her mother had sacrificed for her children, for her country. She was not allowed many friends, she rarely indulged in frivolity like the game that was being offered now.

Ilaria squeezed her mother's hand. "I think you should, Mama. It sounds like grand fun."

There was another beat of hesitation, and then Queen Giabella slowly nodded. "I would very much appreciate the invitation. And I'm certain we can make the time and place work. Mr. Talbot is very good at managing my schedule."

"Wonderful. Why don't you come with me, then?" Lady Bramwell said. "And I will introduce you to a few of the other ladies who come to our group."

She sent a meaningful glance toward Lord Bramwell, and Ilaria's heart sank. As much as she was pleased that her mother might make an actual friend during this trip, it was clear that did not change the goal of either lady. They both seemed determined to make the match of their children.

The queen sent Ilaria much the same look and then the ladies moved off together, chatting as they went. Ilaria sighed. "It was kind of your mother to offer. Sometimes the queen finds it hard to indulge in pleasures due to the reverence people hold to her title."

Lord Bramwell smiled. "Well, she will find both reverence and companionship in my mother. The countess has never met someone she didn't consider a friend. She can do nothing but welcome all comers."

"That sounds like a very nice quality," Ilaria said, and meant it. She examined her companion a bit more closely. As choices went, he was not the worst. He was handsome enough, he had a nice smile and thus far he had not said anything foolish or irritating.

"It is," he agreed. "She is the best of women."

Ilaria nodded and they stood together in silence a moment. Long enough that it became uncomfortable.

He gave another of those false smiles. "I-I think she is a bit taken in with all the court intrigue. My mother."

Ilaria shifted. "I suppose there is some of that. Though in comparison to the machinations in this country, I think we are staid."

He chuckled. "I don't know. I've never met a lady who had a double."

Her smile slowly fell. Sasha had played the role of her double for years, though very rarely. It allowed Ilaria to skip processions if she was needed elsewhere and provided safety in some dire situations. But the purpose of it was secrecy, which was why at certain parties Sasha only lurked where she wouldn't be seen. Ilaria's husband would know of it, of course, but this man was not yet her husband.

"I-I'm not sure what you mean," she said slowly.

He tilted his head. "I met her at the ball. Miss Sasha Killick, yes?"

"You met her?" Ilaria asked. "How?"

He shrugged. "I went onto the terrace to get a bit of air and saw you standing at the wall, staring up at the stars. I thought I would come speak to you, but as I approached and the woman turned, I realized she was not you, but someone dressed and styled as you. It didn't take long to figure out the rest."

She shifted. There was no danger from this man, she felt that in her very bones, but she was still uncomfortable with him knowing even a small part of her secrets. "Did you speak?"

"We did," he said, somewhat slower. "For a moment."

She pursed her lips. "Sasha never said anything."

Now there was a flicker of something in his stare. A brief flash of…pain. "Ah, well, perhaps I did not make much of an impression."

Ilaria glanced him up and down. She wished this man could make an impression on *her*, that she could *will* what her family desired to be something she wanted just as badly. But she couldn't. There was just no spark here with this man. There was nothing.

"Ah, it seems my mother is coming back to us," Ilaria said. "I suppose she will wish to introduce me all around."

"Indeed," Bramwell said with a small bow. "It was a pleasure seeing you again."

She met his eyes and held there a moment. "And I'm sure it will be a pleasure we will soon repeat."

He gave her a tight smile that said everything. That he understood. That he was just as uninterested in the situation being created by their families. And that he had no way to fight it, just as she had no way to fight it.

He stepped away, and within a moment, her mother had returned to her side. She smiled at Ilaria, expectant. "I was watching you."

"Of course you were," Ilaria sighed.

"You two look well together. And you seemed to be having a good time."

Ilaria faced her mother. "He is fine, Mama. Perfectly pleasant. But I feel nothing when he speaks to me and it's evident neither does he."

Her mother's mouth went tight and she edged a little closer. "This isn't about feelings, my dear. That is a childish notion. And one I shall not discuss in the middle of a garden party."

"Mama," Ilaria began.

"No," her mother insisted, cheeks pinkening. "Now I must speak to more of the attendees. I suggest you do the same."

Her mother stepped away and Ilaria gripped her hands at her sides, frustration pulsing through her. Of course this wasn't the time for the conversation she wished to have, but damn it. How could she be truly offered no say in her life?

She drew in a long breath and settled herself as best she could. As her mother had said, this was not the place for a breakdown. She would simply have to gather herself and perhaps try again in a more private setting. At some point her mother or Grantham would have to listen to her.

She turned, but before she could find herself a person to approach, she saw Captain Crawford standing a short distance away. Still watching her.

The frustration she had been trying to fight returned in an instant. After all, he had been encouraging her mother to press her toward Bramwell, hadn't he? And if she could not have words with her mother about it, she was absolutely going to have them with him.

CHAPTER 5

Jonah knew that Ilaria was coming toward him. He'd seen her as she made her initial approach and dropped his gaze so his stare wouldn't be too obvious. People were watching her, after all. Everyone was watching her, not just him. But he felt her as she moved closer, closer. Felt her down to his bones and in his rapidly heating blood.

"Just what the hell do you think you're doing?" she hissed as she reached him.

He lifted his eyes and let his gaze flit over her face. One had to appreciate that her expression could remain cool and detached even when her words were heated and the spark in her eyes said she was raring for a fight.

She was absolutely stunning in that moment. He had to use every ounce of control in his arsenal not to be well and truly stunned.

"I beg your pardon?" he drawled, glad he could sound far more detached than he felt.

She clenched her jaw and her tone was tense as she said, "My mother tells me you made your exalted opinions public when it comes to Lord Bramwell and our potential union."

Jonah's jaw dropped at that and he stared at her. "What are you talking about?"

She folded her arms, which only served to highlight the lovely curve of her breasts. Still, he had to maintain focus. No ogling.

"You encouraged the match," she declared with a quick glance around her to make sure no one was eavesdropping.

They weren't. People were watching, of course, but no one was close enough to hear them. Still he stepped a little farther away from the main group and motioned her to follow.

"I did no such thing," he argued softly.

"You didn't talk to my mother about the Earl of Bramwell?" she snapped.

He pursed his lips. "Queen Giabella *did* ask me what I knew about Lord Bramwell because he is the brother-in-law of a friend of mine. And yes, I did recommend him to her because he seems a decent man. But that was as far as it went. I never suggested you should be matched with him. I never gave a stamp of approval for such thing."

She shifted and he could see some of the starch coming out of her. "That...makes sense, I suppose."

"I certainly hope so. I don't think I have any place in encouraging any matches for you." He had said the words but immediately wished he could take them back. Especially when she tilted her head and examined him more closely.

"Why not?" she asked.

A dozen answers raced through his mind. All of them inappropriate. None of them something he could say to her as she stood what felt like too close, staring up at him with those beautiful dark brown eyes.

"It isn't my place," he said at last, his voice choked.

She sighed and the sound seemed to shudder from her very soul. "Well, I am sorry. I was upset and it seems I've taken it out on you."

He shrugged. "This—" He waved his hand around to indicate the gathering. "—can be overwhelming."

She nodded. "What you say is most definitely true. No matter how long you are raised in it. Honestly I don't know why you'd put yourself in the middle of *this*. Where do you fit?"

He cast her a side glance. "You think me unsuitable for Society, Your Highness?"

Her eyes widened a fraction and her breath hitched. "Of course not. I just think you are a military man and one with little patience for frivolity."

He smothered a smile. She wasn't wrong there. At least about the second part. Though the first...

"I was *once* a military man," he corrected.

"Once?" she repeated.

"I thought you knew. I am retired."

She blinked. "No, I didn't know. No one told me. But you loved the Royal Navy, that was evident any time we talked about it back in Athawick. What could compel you to take your retirement at such a young age? You are vital and potent—certainly you could have continued."

He sucked in a breath at the descriptors she used. Certainly he felt a bit potent at present, with the lilac scent of her hair wafting on the light breeze to his nostrils and her gaze focused so intently on him.

He swallowed. "I could have in body, yes. But you see I received..." He hesitated, just as he always hesitated at this subject. "I received an inheritance just after we last met. And it came with responsibilities I would not have been able to aptly discharge if I were still serving. So I was forced to take on this choice."

Her eyes widened a fraction and he saw how much she understood that statement. How much it connected them that circumstance forced them into situations they did not want. Her gaze flitted down his body and he tensed. Added to that emotional connection was the physical one. Because he knew she...well, *wanted* might be a strong word. A woman like Ilaria had likely been raised not to recognize those types of things.

But they were still there, burning hot under the surface. And they mirrored his own wicked feelings that he had to control under all circumstances.

"And so you are here seeking a Society bride then?" she asked, her voice a little rougher and lower.

A Society bride. He had a few in his life encouraging him to do so, both voices he respected and ones he did not. But he never thought about that future. It didn't feel like his. None of this did.

But he couldn't say that to Ilaria. Nor could he tell her that his real purpose in being here was to watch her, report on her to her brother. Keep her from doing something reckless.

So he inclined his head. "As you are seeking a husband."

"No," she said. "No. My brother and mother are seeking a Society husband for position and rank and *duty*."

"You say that word as if it is a curse."

"If it is all anyone cares about, to the detriment of all else, then I think it is," she said softly. "I saw what a union only about duty entails, Captain. That they would want that for me...that *she* would want that for me..."

For the first time since he'd met this woman, glittering in her palace on her island, he saw a crack in her. And behind it all the pain and darkness and fear that she so carefully hid behind a façade. He saw it all, in a brief moment that she erased almost before it began. And he wanted desperately to help her. *Truly* help her, not just keep her from making her situation worse.

"I am sorry, Ilaria," he said softly.

Her eyes widened and he realized he had been far too familiar. Now her cheeks flamed and she worried her hands before her. "I-I see Remi has somehow made his way here and I need to speak to him. Please excuse me."

She did not wait for his response as would be expected, but cast him one last quick glance and then skirted away toward her brother. He watched her as she made her way through the crowd, and shook his head.

Now that he knew the depth of her emotions when it came to this situation, he recognized how truly dangerous this was. And he feared she might go too far and go to a place where even he could not save her. So he would have to be more vigilant, more focused, even though he knew he dragged himself to hell by doing so.

Ilaria felt like she was listing as she made her way to Remi across the grass. Her brother looked half-drunk still and she suddenly felt like it. Off-kilter, uncertain. She blamed Captain Crawford entirely. He had thrown her off with his questions, with his ability to extract explanations she normally kept to herself. With the way his gaze focused so entirely on her in a way no other man had ever done.

Remi sighed as she reached him and forced a bleary smile. "There she is."

"And there you are," she said, trying to bring herself back to the present. "You didn't come home last night, did you?"

He chuckled. "Are you playing the role of disappointed courtier? Trust me, Ilaria, I'll have enough chats with those later. I don't want a preview."

She frowned. For all his ridiculousness, Remi had his serious side. She knew being spare to the heir had been difficult. Their father had cared little for anyone but Grantham, and only so the king could browbeat him into becoming the kind of monarch he expected. Ilaria and Remi had been left out of the cold. Remi had behaved accordingly.

"Where were you then?" she asked softly.

He darted his gaze toward her and actually looked guilty. She caught her breath because Remi *never* looked guilty.

"Nowhere *you* should know about," he said with a nervous chuckle.

"Should I worry?"

He wrinkled his brow. "No. I just...it's not a place for ladies. Or...it is a place for ladies. But it's not a place for you."

"What does that mean?" she asked, unable to mask her outrage.

He held up his hands as if to surrender. "You shouldn't know about it. It's not yours."

She glared at him slowly. "You're as bad as the two of them."

He drew back and she knew the barb she'd thrown had landed, just as she intended it to. There was nothing Remi hated more than being compared to those in power. Their father, but later their brother. And the sycophants who ruled over it all.

He pursed his lips. "Fine, nosy noodle..."

She laughed at the silly quip that reminded her of childhood days when she and her two brothers had made a game of insults that shared the same first letter. God, those days seemed like another life now.

"...I'll tell you, but you might be sorry."

She tilted her head. "Well then?"

"It is called the Donville Masquerade. It's an underground club with gaming and music and...er...entertainments."

She rolled her eyes. "So some slightly rowdier version of the same clubs you gentlemen have made exclusive of ladies for decades. Bravo, Remi, you're as boring as the rest."

He shook his head. "It's not...it's not that kind of club. There are women in attendance for one and everyone wears masks and it gets a little...a little..."

He was plum-red now, and Ilaria's eyes widened. "What?"

"Sweaty," he whispered, looking around as if he feared someone would overhear.

"What does that mean?" she whispered back. "You're being very unclear."

"Because the subject is not one talked about in polite company," he said. He gave her a look laced with meaning. "It's a club for people to enjoy each other. You know what I'm saying, Ilaria. *Enjoy* each other. With anonymity. Without consequences."

"Enjoy each other without—*oh!*" She stared at him, gape-mouthed as what he meant sank in. "You mean it's a club for, er…for, er…"

"Yes. For *er.*"

"Remi!" she gasped. "That cannot be true. The English are known prudes—how could they have such a club and have it acceptable?"

"Well, I'm not sure it *is* acceptable," he said. "The masks make it less dangerous, that is all. And the man who runs the place, Marcus Rivers, seems to keep a tight ship so that no one is taken advantage of…and so that nothing that happens in those walls exits them."

She continued to stare at him in disbelief. What he described was tempting, indeed. She knew about pleasure. She had learned how to give it to herself. She had even found a hint of it with a lover a few years ago. Nothing serious, but a bit of fun to pass the time. Life in court was so very boring.

But it had been a long time since she indulged in anything like that. Her father's death, the upheaval after, it had muted all pleasure. And now that she was here, everything in her life was further turned on its head. Her family was encouraging her to throw her life away for duty.

And everywhere she turned she saw Captain Crawford and his ruddy hair and pale eyes, watching her. Tracking her. Drawling at her until her body trembled.

Perhaps that was just because she had been alone for so long. Perhaps if she changed that—or at least did something shocking, even if it wasn't so far as taking a lover—she would forget those thoughts and feelings and desires.

Perhaps she could regain a little control.

"This is an entirely uncomfortable subject," Remi said, interrupting her thoughts. "And I no longer wish to have this discussion."

"Fine, I don't want to talk about it with you either," Ilaria said. "But you might want to gird your loins, because our hostess is coming over and she is very interested in our monarchy. Or at least the male lines of it since Lady Questington has a daughter of a certain age."

"Christ," Remi muttered, and glanced over his shoulder to find Lady Questington indeed heading in their direction. "I better make myself scarce."

He shot her a look and then nearly sprinted away, leaving her laughing after him despite her annoyance with her current situation.

And yet her laughter faded as she thought, once again, of what her brother had revealed to her. She looked around and found Captain Crawford once again. He was impossible to miss, after all. He almost stood out like a beacon, hateful...*beautiful* man.

She wanted him. It was something she had recognized all those years ago in Athawick when they had talked and, yes, flirted, and almost...well, sometimes she wasn't certain what they'd *almost* done one warm summer's night. She'd tried to forget him, and yet the moment they were in the same space, it was clear she had not.

But it was impossible. Crawford was too respectable a man to give her what she wanted. She was already locked into a life she didn't desire.

So that was a hopeless case. And maybe the only way to forget about it was to seek pleasure elsewhere. This club seemed a good enough idea. She just needed to find out a little more about it. Luckily there were people on her brother's payroll who were willing to take blunt and ask no questions when she needed information.

And she intended to use those people. As soon as possible.

CHAPTER 6

Ilaria sat at her dressing table watching in the mirror as Sasha gently brushed her hair. Though she could have asked her maid to do so or done it herself, she and Sasha had long done so for each other.

"You have been very quiet about the garden party earlier today," Sasha said. "Do you want to talk about it?"

Ilaria pursed her lips. "My mother misses no opportunity to shove me into the faces of any eligible man of a certain rank and situation. This afternoon it was Lord Bramwell again."

Sasha hesitated in her strokes, and in the mirror Ilaria saw her gaze lift. "The Earl of Bramwell?"

"The very one." Ilaria shook her head. "He seems a nice enough man and he's not unpleasant to look at, but there is no spark there whatsoever."

"That's too bad," Sasha said, and returned to her brushstrokes.

"He said the funniest thing, though. He said that he saw you on the terrace the night of the welcome ball."

The brush clattered to the floor and Ilaria pivoted. "Are you well? You are pale."

"I'm fine," Sasha muttered as she bent to pick up the brush. "Just tired, I suppose."

"Well, sit down," Ilaria said, waving her toward the settee. She got up from her dressing table and joined her friend, searching her face. "Is it because I mentioned Lord Bramwell?"

"Of course not," Sasha said, her tone unexpectedly sharp. "I have no connection to the man. He happened to come outside the night of the welcome ball and found me there. I tried to put him off the idea that I might be your double, but he is too clever for his own good. We talked for but a moment—there was nothing else to it."

Ilaria wrinkled her brow. "If you say so."

"I do," Sasha said. "And you are changing the subject."

"Was I?" Ilaria asked. "I thought the subject was the garden party this afternoon."

Sasha tilted her head. "I've known you since we were girls, Ilaria. I can see you're holding something back. What is it?"

Before Ilaria could answer, there was a light knock on the chamber door. Sasha shot her a look that said the conversation was not over and got up to answer. She spoke softly to whoever it was in the hall and then returned to Ilaria with a few sheets of folded paper in her hands.

"From Darby," Sasha said with an arched brow as she handed the message over.

Ilaria's heart skipped as she leapt to her feet and snatched the papers. She paced off, reading through the notes, face heating with every word she wrote.

"Do you want to tell me what's going on?" Sasha asked, placing her hands on her hips like she was ready to scold.

"Nothing," Ilaria said absently as she clutched the papers to her chest.

"Are you truly going to lie to me?" Sasha asked. "I grew up the same way you did—I know Darby is the servant all of us turn to when we want discreet information for a price. And your expression gives you away even if I didn't know that. What are you up to, Ilaria?"

Ilaria swallowed hard and met Sasha's gaze. She would need her help for her next step, so she couldn't be coy. "Do you swear you will not tell another living soul what I am about to share with you?"

Sasha's brow wrinkled. "I suppose."

"Remi told me about this wicked club here in London, the Donville Masquerade. I wanted to know more, so I asked Darby for the information." She handed over the papers.

Sasha read for a moment and then she gasped as she jerked her head up. "Ilaria, this is a…a sex club. Where people can have masked…encounters."

"Yes," Ilaria said. "Which makes it a perfect place for me to visit, as I'll be masked, as well, and no one will ever recognize me."

Sasha stared, mouth agape. "You're going to go to this place."

Ilaria nodded.

"Why?" Sasha asked. "Masked or not, it is a great risk to take. Why do you feel you need to do such a thing?"

"Because…" Ilaria bent her head as exhaustion flooded every part of her body and soul. "Because I'm not so foolish to believe I will be able to escape my family's plans. I can fight all I want, but they will win and I'll end up leg shackled to Bramwell or some other man just like him."

Sasha flinched but didn't interrupt, for which Ilaria was pleased. As she said those words, she felt the sting of unshed tears in her eyes, the catch of her breath. She didn't want to break down because she feared if she did, she would never be able to fully pull herself together again.

"When Remi talked about this place I was…intrigued," she admitted. "Because it seems utterly out of the line of the duty I'm expected to fulfill. And I want to…I want to go there."

"For what?"

"Just to see," she said. "And maybe to have one last little moment that is just for me. Just about me."

Sasha bent her head. "But is that wise, Ilaria? In your position—"

"My *position* should not be any different from that of my brothers, who are allowed to do such things, provided they are discreet about it."

Sasha closed her eyes. "You're right. And yet this is not the way of the world, especially this one. What will you do if you're caught? Or threatened? Or…"

"I won't be caught," Ilaria said. "I'll be sure of it. And you read the information. The owner of the club is named Marcus Rivers, and he seems to be a highly cautious man and protective of his business and clients. There is not even one report of bad behavior in his walls. It is likely safer than walking through a park in London."

Sasha let out a long, heavy sigh. "You can't be talked out of this, can you?"

Ilaria smiled. "No."

"Then how can I help?"

Ilaria rushed to her and enveloped her in a hug. "First, we have to find something for me to wear that won't be recognized. And a mask. Oh, and a carriage."

Sasha laughed as she motioned Ilaria back to the dressing table so she could arrange her hair, and she practically danced back to her place. This was going to happen! Tonight! And she couldn't wait.

J onah sat on his horse in the narrow alleyway behind the house the royal family was occupying. Grantham had arranged it so that his armed guards were aware of Jonah's presence. When one of them came around, they nodded toward him in the darkness and he acknowledged them back just as silently. But his attention was always drawn back to the window two floors above. Ilaria's chamber.

The curtains had been drawn there an hour before, and he could have simply accepted that she'd gone to bed and returned home, but something in the back of his mind tickled.

He'd watched Ilaria, probably far too closely, at the garden party. He'd felt her tension increase with every moment. Oh, she looked serene enough. She talked to the always-swarming guests who were drawn to her power and beauty and influence. She smiled and laughed as she should. But there was something beneath that surface. An ever-increasing dissatisfaction about her circumstance that he'd seen a glimpse of when he spoke to her.

And he feared she would soon break under the weight of that and perhaps do something...foolish.

As if conjured by his expectations, the curtains to the bedroom opened again. Behind them he could see Ilaria as she moved about the room with her companion and body double, Sasha Killick. From this distance, they did look a great deal alike—he could see why the young woman had been brought into that duty.

But he could easily tell them apart. There was something about the way Ilaria moved. About the way she used her hands to talk. The way she tilted her head just so. Now, why he had memorized these tiny details, he did not wish to explore. But there they were, burned into his mind as he watched her.

By God, but she was beautiful. Up close, from a distance, none of it mattered. She was a flame and he was always drawn to her, impending burns be damned. Which was exactly why he should not have suggested he become her secret bodyguard.

In fact, what he ought to do was go around to the front of the house, knock on the door and tell Grantham he would not be able to perform this role. Suggest that he find some other arrangement and then stay away from Ilaria for the remainder of the family visit, even if that meant going back to his estate along the Welsh border and hiding there until this temptation had passed.

And perhaps he would have done that. Perhaps he would have packed up his inappropriate feelings and desires and done the right thing, only just as he moved to do so he noticed Ilaria step up to the window. She looked out, down toward the alley, as if she were looking for something. He backed his horse farther into the darkness, uncertain if she could see him. Only it wasn't him she was looking at. She said something over her shoulder, likely to her companion, and pointed farther up the narrow lane.

He frowned. A carriage unmarked by the royal crest was parked there now.

What was going on?

He glanced up at the window and watched in utter disbelief and creeping horror as Ilaria raised the sash and then delicately stepped out onto the narrow ledge. She eased along it and then stopped. She drew a few breaths before she grasped the flimsy trellis near the window.

It was mightily impressive, actually, to watch her make her way down the wall. She didn't hesitate, but made slow and steady progress as her companion watched from above, her nervousness as clear as Jonah's.

For a moment, as she neared the ground, she wasn't visible behind the high walls that surrounded the small estate.

He waited, holding his breath, hoping what he guessed was about to transpire was incorrect. But then a hidden gate along the wall opened and Ilaria stepped into the alleyway and bolted to the carriage. She was helped up by the driver, who retook his place, and they began to drive away toward the main street in the distance.

"Bloody hell," Jonah muttered, then urged his horse to follow.

The woman would be the death of him. He just hoped she wasn't about to do something that would be the death of her.

Ilaria set the mask on her face and secured it as best she could with her hands shaking. She was practically bouncing in the carriage as a thrill worked down her very bones.

Oh, she had snuck out before, back in Athawick. Often she

slipped from the oppression of the palace down to the lake on the property. Without watchful eyes, she could swim naked in the cool water to clear her mind. It was heavenly.

Never had she made an escape in a strange city to go do something as wicked as she was about to do. Her heart throbbed at just the idea, though her mind had not yet formulated a plan to go along with this impulsive decision.

Would she just look around? Would she participate? She didn't know. And the lack of a plan made her both nervous and excited. She'd had every moment of her life planned for so long.

The carriage began to slow, and she peeked out to see a nondescript building with an elaborately carved door before her. The vehicle rocked as the drive stepped down and opened the door for her. With a little extra blunt slipped into their pockets, there were a handful of servants who were willing to help the royal family's children. Darby was one of them. The driver, Nicholson, was another.

She took his hand and stepped out. She looked up at the building with a shiver of excitement.

"I'll wait, Your H—"

She lifted a hand to stay his words. "Perhaps we ought not use formalities in this situation, Nicholson."

"Of course. I shall wait for you," he said with a bow.

She nodded her understanding and then turned to the door. It was drawn open by a perfectly liveried servant who did not seem curious about or surprised by her appearance here. She acknowledged him silently as she passed through the door into an antechamber where another finely dressed gentleman stood by at a podium which contained a large book.

"Good evening," he said as she slipped inside. "May I have your membership name?"

She blinked. There had been something about this in the notes Darby had given her. Memberships were attached to a false name so that no one would ever suspect those who wished to remain anonymous.

"I-I have heard a nonmember may purchase a night here?" she said.

"Of course, madam." He wrote something on a slip of paper and handed it over.

When she unfolded it, it contained the sum she must pay. Luckily she had been prepared by the recognizance of her servant, so she carefully pressed the notes she had brought with her into the paper and handed it back.

"Excellent. What name would you like to use for the evening?"

That was the one thing she had not fully decided. To go incognito was such a thrilling thing and she wanted to find something that would fit.

When she didn't answer immediately, the gentleman smiled with indulgence, as if he saw this sort of thing all the time. And she supposed he likely did. "It can be a last name or a first name. Often people choose the name of a friend, slightly altered, of course."

She swallowed because as she stood at the precipice of this adventure and all the passion it could bring, she could think of only one name. Only one man.

"Miss Crawford," she whispered.

"Very good," he said, scribbling the name down. "Please leave your mask on at all times. To remove it is at your own risk of exposure. Do not ask any other guest to remove their mask. They may do so only of their own volition. If you are told no by another guest, you must cease whatever you are doing. If you say no at any time, your partner or partners must do the same. Mr. Rivers vets his membership very well, but if you are ever in need to aid, tap your cheek three times with your forefinger. Guards are on the lookout for that signal from ladies. You may also say the word 'chestnut' to anyone who works here and that is also a signal that you need assistance. Do you have any questions?"

She swallowed hard. "No."

"Then welcome to the Donville Masquerade." As he said it, he moved to the door and swung it open to reveal a huge room. She stepped forward in wonder and stared at the brightly lit hall filled with people laughing and dancing and gambling…and also kissing and touching and even more.

"Oh…" she whispered, moving forward like she was being drawn by a magnet.

She was no innocent, but this was far more than she'd ever been exposed to. Women and men ground together in passionate displays, naked bodies were visible. In the distance she saw a stage where a fully nude woman was doing an erotic dance as men and women alike applauded and left coins on the stage for her.

Ilaria's breath hitched, her body tingled and it felt like she was in a dreamy fog as she glided forward to see and feel even more. But before she had made it even a few steps, she felt the grip of fingers against her elbow.

She jerked to face the person who had been so bold, only to find herself staring up into gray eyes she knew well. Gray eyes that were dilated and hard with anger and concern…and something more. Something heated.

"C-Captain," she whispered, her voice barely carrying.

He shook his head slowly. "Princess, I think you'd best come with me."

CHAPTER 7

Two Years Before
The Island of Athawick

Jonah stood on the terrace outside the glittering ball, staring up at the stars. In the three weeks since his arrival on the island, he'd had little time to himself. The party always seemed to have something to do, somewhere to be and it was unfailingly tedious. It never amounted to anything but those with power showing off for each other. So far removed from his world.

And then there was the other problem with this visit. The one that had sent him dashing from the ballroom as much as the ridiculous speeches and grandiosity of the regent and the king.

Ilaria.

He shut his eyes as he thought of her, as if that would block out the stirrings of his heart rather than make them all the stronger. After all, the woman haunted both his dreams and his every waking moment.

Three weeks and he had spoken to her beyond a polite greeting all of six times. And yet each one was seared into his mind. He could picture every smile that had flitted over her face, every time their eyes had met, every word of every conversation. They never delved into anything too personal, nor too deep. Sometimes he felt like they danced around reality, but Ilaria never allowed them to jump over the edge. Still, he liked her, with the fire in her eyes and the slightly wicked tilt to her smile. Liked her too much. Which was why he'd left the ballroom, because he couldn't stop staring at her in her pale pink gown with a sparkling diamond tiara perched amongst the perfectly arranged brown curls.

At some point, someone was going to notice.

"Captain?"

He tensed, his hands fisting against the terrace wall edge. It seemed someone already had.

He turned toward the voice and barely kept himself from catching his breath. Ilaria stood a few feet away, hands clasped before her, a small smile on her face.

"Your Highness," he said softly. "Good evening."

She inclined her head. "Are you hiding, Captain?"

He swallowed hard. "I am not a very good dancer, I'm afraid. So I was hoping to avoid being dragged into humiliating myself."

She tilted her head. "That is disappointing. There are a great many ladies who were looking forward to taking a turn around the dancefloor with you tonight." She moved a little closer. "Including this lady."

His lips parted. Her face was still utterly serene as she said those words and perhaps she only meant them in a friendly way. Still, the idea that she would want to do something so intimate as dance with him was thrilling.

She smiled as the strains of the music drifted out onto the terrace around them. "Ah, this is my favorite," she said, and held out a hand. "Will you dance with me now?"

He blinked as he stared at the outstretched fingers. "Here? On the terrace?"

"If you truly fear your skills being judged, then the terrace seems the best place to test them. No one is looking. That is a rare enough thing in this place." She flexed her fingers toward him. "I am not accustomed to being refused, Captain Crawford."

He took her hand, barely holding back a shiver when her fingers tangled with his, even though they were both wearing gloves. "No one could ever refuse you, Your Highness."

He drew her closer, catching a whiff of the lilac fragrance of her hair as he pressed one hand into her hip and they began to turn. She smiled up at him after he had maneuvered her in time to the music for a moment. "You are not so bad a dancer as you advertised, sir."

He found himself chuckling. "Underselling is always best, I've found. Then I can only impress later."

She broke into a wide grin that was unlike any other he'd ever seen grace her expression. It made him realize just how false those other smiles had likely been these last few weeks. This one was very real and it lit her up like a dozen candles. It made him want so very desperately to know what those ruby lips tasted like.

She must have sensed that desire, for the smile faded and her gaze locked with his for far too long. They slowed their movements, out of time to the music now, only dancing to their own rhythm. She turned her face toward his a touch more, lifting her lips as if offering them.

He might have done something foolish like draw her closer, like duck his head and kiss her, but the door to the terrace opened and she tugged away, spinning toward the terrace edge, her cheeks bright with color. It was her father who came upon them, and the king did not look particularly pleased as he moved toward them.

"Ilaria, you cannot neglect your guests," he said sharply.

She tossed Jonah a quick look before she smiled at her father, another of those very false expressions. "I am not, for as you see, Captain Crawford is here. I came out to get some air and was very pleased to chat with him a moment."

The king inclined his head toward Jonah. "Well, I think the good captain has been blessed with enough of your time. Go back inside, now, and find out who your mother has put on your dance card."

Ilaria gave Jonah another brief look and then nodded. "Of course. Good night, Captain."

"Good night, Your Highness."

She slipped away, back toward the ballroom doors, and Jonah expected the king to follow her. But he didn't, at least not immediately. He simply stood where he was, staring at Jonah. And then, he slowly shook his head. He said nothing, but the message was entirely clear as the king pivoted on his heel and stalked after his daughter, leaving Jonah with no doubt as to his place.

And it was *not* kissing a princess on a terrace.

~

1 *817*

The Donville Masquerade, London

Jonah hadn't meant to let things go so far. When he realized Ilaria's carriage had stopped at the Donville Masquerade, he had thought to try to stop her before she entered the hall. But a cart had blocked his way so he could not stop her from entering, and when he reached the entrance, the doorman had kept him from following her, as was the custom, to protect each member's identity.

But when he got into the hall, there was no mistaking her reaction. Her full lips were parted, her dark eyes darting from one delight to the next. The way she squirmed ever so slightly, the way her hands shook. He knew she was intrigued by what she saw. Aroused.

And it drove him to the edge of madness. But he'd also seen something else: the way the eyes of the entire hall had shifted to her. He didn't think anyone recognized her thanks to the plain gown she was wearing and the mask covering the top half of her face, but that didn't mean she was safe.

The men and women in this room were hunters. They wanted to play, to catch, to devour. How in the world could Ilaria react to such a thing? How could her innocence about the world not be changed by seeing what she was seeing…or even seduced into doing some of what she saw?

If he had been charged to protect her, he was damned well going to do it.

Which was why he had rushed forward and demanded she come with him. It was evident she recognized him, even though he, too, had donned a mask that had been provided at the door. Perhaps it was his voice or his eyes, it didn't really matter. She was allowing him to guide her through the room, away from as much of the debauchery as he could manage. The back rooms at Donville were quiet. They were private, as long as one was careful.

They were the perfect place to escape with a lover. Not that that was his intent. They were also the perfect place to have a conversation with a recalcitrant princess.

He nodded to the guard at the back hallway and lifted his hand in the signal for what he wanted. A flash only members knew. The guard nodded back and made the sign for five with his fingers.

Jonah hustled Ilaria to Room Five and slammed the door behind them. At last he released her, shaking out his hand in the hopes he would stop feeling the heat of her, the softness against his skin. She stared at him as he stormed across the room and flicked shut the peephole that allowed guests to watch the activities of those in certain rooms.

When he pivoted back, Ilaria's mouth had dropped open. "Was that…?"

"Yes," he snapped out as he tugged off his mask and threw it aside. "Now explain yourself."

"Captain Crawford…I…what are you doing here?" she asked.

He lifted both brows. "Right now I think we'd best deal with you. Stop stalling and out with it."

Now her shock faded from her face and he saw her shift back into royal mode. She lifted her chin and looked at him with ice in her stare. "You can't talk to me that way. I am Princess Ilaria of Athawick."

"Say it louder so everyone can hear," he snapped. He was pleased that at least her cheeks heated, so she was taking this somewhat seriously. "And please, spare me the indignation. You snuck out of your home and took yourself to a notorious sex club."

She stared at him a moment. "How—how did you know I snuck out?"

He cleared his throat. He hadn't meant to say that. It seemed she was not the only one who needed to be more prudent in this situation. He shifted as he tried to come up with an excuse. "Your mother and brother cannot possibly know you are here, and given that it is very late, one must assume you snuck out," he said at last.

"Oh," she said softly. He saw the starch go out of her. Saw her shoulders roll forward a fraction.

He moved toward her a step, even though he shouldn't. He'd brought her back here for privacy, but they were in a bedroom. Next to a bed with satin sheets. The walls were covered with erotic art from all places in the world. This was an entirely inappropriate situation, especially considering the thoughts he sometimes had about this woman.

"What are you doing, Ilaria?" he asked, softer this time. More gently.

She paced away from him, worrying her hands before her for a moment before she let out a great sigh and sank down on the edge of bed. His throat tightened, because now the situation was even more precarious. It would be very easy to lower her back against the mattress and show her what coming here entailed.

He wasn't going to do that. But it would be very easy.

She slid a finger beneath her mask and took it off, mussing her hair slightly in the process as she set it aside. "I...I don't want to marry. Not this way."

He nodded slowly. He already knew that. But the pain of how she said it was new. Honest. Heartbreaking. "So you came here to, what, Ilaria? Trade your virginity?"

She glanced up at him. "Not my virginity."

He shook his head. "You see, that is what makes this so frustrating. You came here without thinking it through. It would be difficult to leave this place without trading your virginity, Ilaria. Sex is currency at Donville."

"I can't trade it because I no longer have it," she said softly. Not with embarrassment. She didn't look embarrassed in the slightest.

"I...oh."

"There is no sad story, which is what I think you assume from your facial expression. I know a woman's hymen is of great interest to men of this country."

He flinched at the directness of that statement. "It is not in Athawick?"

"If a person is careful not to produce illegitimate offspring, why should one not indulge a little? That is how we view things in Athawick, for either men or women."

"Very progressive," he said.

She arched a brow. "Do you wish to judge me for having disposed of the construct of my innocence before wedlock? Despite the fact that men are expected and encouraged to do so?"

"I have no place to," he said, though his mind was still reeling at the casual way she discussed this subject.

She stared up at him, dark eyes wide and holding his steadily. "And what if you did? What if you had a reason to care about that sort of thing? Not generally. When it came to me."

He swallowed. She was treading in extremely dangerous waters now. He could not allow her to drag him in just as deep. Not if he wanted to get out of this without betraying a friend. Without betraying his own sense of honor.

"I happen to like the idea that every person should have control over their own body and what they do or do not do with it," he said, wishing his voice didn't have the slightest tremble.

"Very open-minded of you, Captain Crawford," she said softly. "But while I may have not been judged for youthful dalliances in my country, my body is certainly not my own to control. Not really. Not for the long term."

"I know you feel trapped," he said, and stepped closer. She inched to the side, and he realized she was leaving him a place on the bed next to her. With a sigh, he took it, carefully perching so he didn't touch her. "But Ilaria, this is not the best route to escape."

"Isn't it?" she said on a long sigh. "I just wanted to…to forget. I wanted to forget that I can't fight what's going to happen. I could fight them forever and I'll still lose."

He felt her desperation like acid on his skin. "You truly think you could never learn to love anyone you were matched with? The Earl of Bramwell…he really is a good man and—"

She held up a hand with a humorless laugh. "Don't become my matchmaker, Captain. Not you."

He wrinkled his brow. "Why not me?"

"You know why." She worried her hands in her lap before she glanced up at him. "*I* know why. We can pretend it away all we like, but we both felt it when we saw each other again here in London. We felt it in Athawick, too, all those years ago." He drew in a breath, but she shook her head. "Don't deny it. I was on that terrace, too, that night. I'm not a fool."

He clamped his lips back together and didn't say those hollow words. "No, you're not a fool."

She turned a little and examined his face in the sparkling firelight. "What is your first name?"

He blinked down at her. "What?"

"I've only ever called you Captain Crawford," she explained. "I've only ever *thought* of you as Captain Crawford. But if we're going to talk about my virginity and admit that we want each other, desperate as this may be, I would like to know your first name."

He swallowed hard. "Jonah," he said.

"Like in the Bible?" she asked, blinking.

He choked on a laugh. "Though I'm not a particularly godly man, especially in this moment…yes. I do believe that is what my mother named me after. Seems fitting that I was drawn to the sea. Though I've never been swallowed by a whale."

"Why are you not godly especially in this moment?" she asked.

He cleared his throat. "Because I'm sitting on a bed in a sex club next to you, Ilaria. And we've already determined that you and I desire each other. It's difficult to think of anything pious under these circumstances."

She stared at him for what felt like a lifetime as the room got hotter and smaller, then she leaned a little closer. He felt her breath brush across his chin, warm and soft and sweet.

"Then why try to be pious, *Jonah*?" She said his name and it was like nails raking across his naked back. Wicked. "I don't want you to be."

She leaned up, cupping his cheek. He felt the weight of every one of those soft fingers, pressing into his skin, burning him like a brand. Time slowed until it meant nothing—the only thing with meaning was how she was leaning up into him. Closer and closer, inch by inch until there was no distance between them anymore. At last she pressed her lips to his.

He caught her upper arms as she did so, intent on pushing her away. Only he found he couldn't. It wasn't possible when her mouth was like heaven on his, impossible when she parted her lips slightly and whispered his name against his mouth, impossible when her tongue darted out and traced the crease of his lips.

He opened to her instead of turning away, tugging her even closer as he forgot his promises to himself and to her brother, forgot that this was wrong, forgot everything except the never-ending drumbeat of desire that roared through his veins.

She felt it too. That was clear in the way she sucked his tongue as he breached her mouth. She lifted into him, clenching his lapels with both hands as their mouths collided harder and faster and with less and less control. His entire body thrummed with need, and he recognized he had very little time left to pull away before he was going to be swept into the sea by her. Lost to her.

If that happened, there would be no going back.

Ilaria had been kissed before…or at least she thought she had. This moment was making her question that fact, along with everything else in her life. Kissing Jonah had been a curiosity that had haunted her for two years, but also a way to retain the control he wanted to strip away.

That was a colossal failure. There was no control in this moment of clashing lips and tongues and teeth. No control in how she lifted to him, her body aching for more, begging for more. There was no control in any of this, and for one of the first times in her life, she didn't care. If she could feel this man move inside of her, she would trade all the control in the world.

But he had different ideas. With a curse that was muffled against her lips, he yanked away from her, pushing to his feet and striding across the room to the fire. He stood there, back to her, shoulders lifting and falling with his panting breaths.

"I can't do this," he said without looking at her.

Her heart sank, far more than she wished it to. She folded her arms as if she could shield herself from the disappointment, from the rejection. "You mean you won't."

He turned at that and his gray gaze pierced through her, held her in place with an ease that frightened her. "Same difference," he choked out.

She got up and shook her head. "No, it isn't. And you know it."

He let out an exasperated exhalation and ran a hand through his thick, ruddy hair. She could see his frustration, how close he was to coming undone. It was a crack in that façade of perfect, military precision and she longed to see what he would become if she shattered it. What was under there? What kind of beast would be unleashed?

"What do you want from me, Ilaria?" he barked.

She met his stare and moved toward him, hoping she looked more confident then she felt. He didn't move, but tracked her as she crossed to him. He watched as she took his hand and lifted it, resting it against her breast. His fingers flexed just the slightest, but enough to send a shock of awareness through her.

"I want you to do exactly what *you* want to do."

They stood like that for what felt like a lifetime, and she thought he might bend to her. Break for her. But instead he pulled away, tugging his hand away from her body and flexing it at his side. "We both know that's impossible."

"Why?" she pressed.

He shook his head. "I'm not the match for you, Ilaria and I never have been. That's all that matters now."

She flinched at his reminder. "Repeating the party line for my family, I see. You should be on their payroll."

Now he was the one who flinched and his gaze darted away. But he didn't move toward her. He didn't touch her.

"What just happened mattered to me, Jonah," she said softly. "Just so you know."

He glanced at her. "Ilaria—"

She turned away this time. She had already been rejected once— she didn't feel like repeating it. She straightened her spine and tried to make herself as cold as possible as she lifted a hand to silence him. "You needn't tell me twice, Captain. You don't want me…or you do want me but you're too cowardly to pursue it. Either way, I'll find someone else who isn't so concerned about propriety."

She moved for the door with those words, but he lunged for her, catching her elbow in a surprisingly gentle, if firm, grip. "You cannot stay here," he said, his voice rough.

She arched a brow. "I have no intention of staying, Captain. My night has been ruined and I'm in no mood to play. But understand something, you can't thwart me forever. No one can."

With that, she pulled her arm from his hand and exited the room. She almost expected him to catch her again, to try to stop her, control her. But he didn't. Though she felt him watching her, following her at a safe distance, she supposed to insure that she did, indeed, leave this place.

Out in the main hall, the crowd was still writhing, and she caught her breath. After that kiss with Jonah, after all the pleasure it had implied, the activities of the attendees felt even more powerful. They made her already edgy body react even further.

The music felt so loud, and every time the crowd jostled her she almost couldn't breathe. She moved toward the door and had almost reached it when she felt something scrape along her side. She jerked her gaze down and then looked around for who or what had touched her, but the room was too close and busy to determine it.

She made it to the door and exited into the antechamber with a gasp. The same man who had helped her earlier looked up from his paperwork. "Ah, hello again, Miss Crawford."

She almost tripped. She'd used Jonah's name for her false identity—she'd almost forgotten. If he found out…

"I-I need my carriage," she whispered.

"Of course," the gentleman said, and moved to the front door where he said something to the guard outside.

She followed him, and within moments her vehicle was sliding to a stop before her. The guard helped her up and off they sped, back toward the high walls of the fortress where her brother and mother wanted her to stay. Far from the crowd and from the man who tempted her to more.

She smoothed her hands along her gown as if that movement could soothe her discombobulation, and that was when her fingers caught something in the fabric. She glanced down in the dimness of the carriage and saw that there was a large tear in the folds of fabric across her midsection. A clean cut, as if not torn but sliced. She pushed the silk away and found a slight scratch across her stomach beneath.

"What in the world…?" she mused, running her finger along the light abrasion. It had to have happened when she felt that very area touched as she exited the club, but what could have made such a mark was beyond her. All she knew was that Sasha was going to be cross, indeed. This was one of her favorite gowns.

Ilaria pursed her lips. All she'd managed to do tonight was rip a gown and annoy a friend. The whole evening was wasted, after all.

Well, except for that kiss. She couldn't regret that, even if her time with Jonah hadn't ended as she'd wanted it to. Even if he was frustratingly determined to keep her from getting what she wanted. What she needed.

Which meant he was just one more person she'd need to subvert to do just that.

One thing Jonah had always prided himself on was his focus. It had served him well during his time in the Navy, it had become something he relied upon after his inheritance when there was so much to learn and to repair. Yet today he sat at his desk in his study, staring at the paperwork in front of him. He had read the same sentence in the ledger at least five times and could not have told someone what it said if he were held at gunpoint. His errant mind kept wandering, traveling down winding paths that always took him to the same place. The same moment.

When Ilaria's lips had touched his at the Donville Masquerade just the night before.

No matter what he did, he could not seem to make his mind file away the feel of her mouth to be forgotten. He couldn't make his body stop hardening at the memory of her touch. He had pleasured himself last night and again this morning to make it stop, but to no avail. She intruded upon his every dream and his every waking moment.

"I beg your pardon, Captain Crawford," his butler said as he stepped into the doorway. "Admiral Westing is here. Would you like to receive him here or in the parlor?"

Jonah blinked. The admiral was not supposed to be here until one and it could not be that late. Except the man was always on time, which meant Jonah had been woolgathering and fantasizing for hours.

"Captain?"

"I apologize, Hudson," Jonah said, rising from the desk. "Clearly I am out of sorts. Why don't you bring the admiral here? It is as comfortable a meeting place as the parlor."

"Very good, sir. I'll have tea brought shortly."

Jonah inclined his head and smoothed his jacket, putting himself in perfect order almost out of habit. He could hear the admiral's quick, certain steps as he approached and smiled slightly at the memories they created. Happy ones, mostly.

The admiral led the way in, with Hudson at his heels. The butler drew a breath to announce him, but Jonah raised a hand with a chuckle. "Thank you, Hudson, I see him."

He saluted his former superior officer, and the admiral quickly returned it before his lined face tilted in a smile and he held out his hand for a shake. "Good to see you, my boy."

Jonah let his shoulders relax. "It is good to be seen, Admiral. I was glad to receive your missive, I wasn't certain you were in London."

"Mrs. Westing is the reason, of course," the admiral said as the two men took a seat before the fire. "She wanted to be in Town for at least part of the Season, and when she heard the royal family of Athawick was here, she could not be deterred from her desires."

Jonah fought to keep a reaction from his face. It seemed he would not escape this topic, even with his old friend. "I'm certain you are already connected to far more exalted company than I, but if you are in need of an invitation to one of the royal events, I might be able to assist."

"Ah yes, your connection to Athawick," the admiral said. "During Prinny's pomp and circumstance visit two summers ago. I'd almost forgotten I chose you for that ridiculous duty. Was I angry with you at the time?"

Jonah chuckled. "I believe you acted like it was an honor at the time, sir. And it was, I know that. But yes, I do know the family a little."

"They're causing quite the stir with all the rumors of marriages to come."

Jonah pushed to his feet. "Drink?" he asked as he moved to the sideboard. The door opened as he did and a maid slipped in with a tea set. She placed it on the sideboard and Jonah nodded her away. "We have, as you can see, both the staid and the not-so-much."

"As much as I'd like to try that whisky, the wife is insisting I make a few better choices. So tea for me. No milk, no sugar."

Jonah fixed it as such, taking his time so as to avoid the continued conversation that made him think even more of Ilaria's scent.

"Are you drying the leaves, yourself?" the admiral groused when Jonah had clearly taken too long.

Jonah snorted out a laugh as he handed the cup over. "Aren't you the one who preached patience, old man?"

"To you recalcitrant youth. I've earned my haste through age and experience." Jonah retook his place and the admiral looked at him closely. "You don't seem to like this subject."

"The subject of tea?"

The admiral arched a brow. "Of the Athawick business."

"I wouldn't say that. I have no feelings one way or another."

"Liar," the admiral said as he sipped his tea. "What is it then?"

Jonah sighed. This man had been his superior officer, yes, his sponsor to greater things, but he had also taken Jonah under his wing when it came to the personal. He'd been a father figure, the only real one Jonah had ever had. And now he was torn between getting good advice and the fear he might let the admiral down.

"The new king and I became friendly during my summer in

Athawick," he said slowly. "And he has asked me to take on a duty that I am…uncertain about."

The admiral tilted his head. "Explain."

Jonah did so quickly, leaving out the fact that he'd followed Ilaria to Donville and kissed her. "So I'm to trail the princess, keeping an eye out."

"Interesting," the admiral said.

"Don't lie," Jonah snorted. "You think all this court intrigue to be as foolish as spring lambs."

"It is," the admiral said with a shake of his head. "People with too much time and money and not half enough sense. But I'm also no fool as to how your situation has changed. This is an opportunity, you know. One to make a name for yourself in the minds of those with rank. It could align you with those who could help you. Raise you up."

Jonah bent his head. "God's teeth, that sounds dreadful."

"But it is the way of your new world."

"Is it? Because I am the bastard son of the dissolute youngest child of a minor viscount. That I inherited his little estate and all its problems is a weight on my shoulders and it stole all I worked for over the decades preceding. I have a hard time seeing it as an opportunity."

"Oh, don't sit around feeling sorry for yourself," the admiral harrumphed, and once again Jonah smothered a smile. The man was direct, he had missed that. "It's a shame that you had to give up your future in the Navy, but since you did, it would be just as shameful not to do something with the opportunity you are afforded. One that can be multiplied by aligning yourself with the family du jour."

"Ugh, you just love to be right, don't you?"

"It happens so often, I scarcely notice it."

"I think I need a stronger drink than tea," Jonah teased. He had gotten up to return to the sideboard to retrieve the whisky when there was a light knock on the study door and Hudson reappeared.

"I am sorry to intrude, Captain, but we've received a message from the staff of the King of Athawick. He is intending to join you in half an hour."

Jonah stared for a moment and then nodded. "Thank you. I'll be prepared. Do follow whatever protocol they have laid out."

Hudson looked slightly dazed, but he hurried off to do just that. When he was gone, the admiral blinked up at Jonah. "Doesn't muck around, does he?"

Jonah drew in a long breath and added a large splash of alcohol to his tea, then waggled the bottle to offer the same to his companion. The admiral laughed and held out his cup.

"The man is accustomed to getting his way," Jonah explained before he returned the bottle to the side table. He sat down and the two men clinked their cups.

"Why the urgency today?"

"I wrote him a note last night telling him I wanted to meet to update him on a...situation with Ilaria." He realized in a flash how familiar that was and shifted. "Princess Ilaria. His sister. The—the princess."

The admiral's eyes widened a fraction at his stammering. "I see."

Jonah ignored the tone and continued, "I assumed we would arrange some time in his schedule over the next few days, but apparently he did not feel it could wait."

"What is your connection to this young woman?"

"I don't know what you mean," Jonah said, but his tone sounded so hollow to his own ears, he was certain the admiral heard it too.

"Lying to a commanding officer?" he said softly.

Jonah rolled his eyes. "You're not my commanding officer anymore."

"Then allow me to be your friend." The admiral leaned forward and draped his elbows over his knees. "What is your connection to Princess Ilaria? And don't tell me there is none because I see you go gooey eyed at the mention of her name."

It was a markedly irritating thing to have a person who could see one so closely. This man had known Jonah when he was little more than a pup. He'd been hard with him when he needed, gentle when he needed that. And he was one of the few people in this world with a window to Jonah's soul.

"When I met Ilaria in Athawick, there may have been an…attraction there. Nothing came of it, of course. I was just a captain in the Royal Navy. It was a flirtation at most, harmless."

He blinked as he thought of that heated moment on the terrace all those years ago. It hadn't felt all that harmless.

Jonah cleared his throat. "Just for good fun. And I will admit that I still find her very attractive now that she's here. More than that, I think it would be unwise to say. I know the folly of it and I will exert all the control you taught me to keep myself in line."

To his surprise, the admiral's face softened slightly. "I see. Under normal circumstances, I would be very pleased if you were mooning over some woman. I've had a very happy marriage for nearly thirty years and I would wish nothing less for you. But in this case…I suppose we know there is no good end to it."

"No," Jonah said quietly. "And so I think it best not to discuss it. I took on the duty that the king requested of me. I intend to fulfill it to the best of my abilities. And you seem to think that there could be some benefit to me because of it, which remains to be seen. Other than that, there is nothing more to say on the subject."

The admiral nodded slowly. "As you say. Then let us speak of other things, shall we?"

Jonah nodded, and for a little while they talked about the admiral's duties, his impending retirement and a few mutual acquaintances. Jonah was able to relax for the first time since the arrival of the Athawick Royal Family, and so he was almost disappointed when Hudson reappeared to announce that the King of Athawick had arrived.

The king was led into the room with little pomp or circumstance beyond Hudson nearly prostrating himself as he bowed. Jonah shook his head as he moved to the man and bowed with far less grandeur.

"Your Majesty," he said as the two men shook hands. "May I present Admiral Westing, my superior officer when I served."

The admiral stepped forward and executed a polite bow. "Your Majesty."

"Good afternoon, Admiral, a pleasure to make your acquaintance. I'm sorry to intrude upon your prior business," Grantham said.

"Not at all," the admiral said. "I'm sure the captain will be well pleased to be free of my foolishness." He winked at Jonah, who laughed in response.

"I fear I bring enough of my own," Grantham said with a quick glance for Jonah. "As I'm sure you are well aware."

"You and your family are the talk of London," the admiral admitted. "One could scarcely not be aware of your every move thanks to the gossip sheets and whisper campaigns. My wife is enthralled."

Grantham chuckled. "It seems an even split between irritated and enthralled. Depending on how we disrupt the flow of traffic."

The admiral let out one of his booming laughs, and Jonah and Grantham joined in because it was impossible not to. "It is good to be so self-aware, Your Majesty. And now I shall leave you two to what I'm certain is a matter of great importance." He turned to Jonah. "It is always good to see you, my boy."

"And you, sir."

They saluted and then the admiral bowed to Grantham again, this time with what Jonah felt was more warmth and sincerity. He slipped from the room and closed the door behind himself, leaving them alone.

"Seems a good sort," Grantham said, and nodded as Jonah motioned toward the tea set.

"He is. The best of men. His wife is wonderful, as well." He said the last knowing it would evoke the very response Grantham gave.

"Ah yes, the one who is enthralled by us. I shall make sure they are invited to some of the events."

"Thank you, that would be very kind." They returned to the seats he and the admiral had abandoned a moment before. "I admit, Your Majesty, I am surprised to have your company."

Grantham pursed his lips. "The way Ilaria was acting this morning, I felt I had to see you given your note."

Jonah blinked, trying to keep his countenance from showing too much. "And how was your sister acting?"

"She was in a mood all morning," Grantham said with a sigh. "Angry with me, frustrated with our mother. When I asked her why, she lashed out, but I could see she was on the verge of tears. She didn't look like she slept at all. I fear she is becoming more and more willful with each passing day."

Jonah hesitated. He'd had every intention of telling Grantham that his sister had gone to the Donville Masquerade, though he'd never meant to say that they kissed. But now, hearing about Ilaria's tears…he questioned that intention. She'd said over and over that she felt trapped by this situation. Would trapping her more really be of help? Because that was what telling Grantham would do. The king would lock her down even further, extinguishing her light more and more until she was nothing but a husk beneath it all.

Jonah didn't want to do that to her.

"I think your sister needs more coverage," he said. "She does need a closer eye overall. That was what I wished to discuss with you."

Grantham's brows lowered. "And you could not have written that in the note you sent, rather than implying we needed to speak in person?"

"Of course," Jonah said, inclining his head. "I am sorry, Your Majesty."

"No, I am." Grantham sighed. "I am being no better than my sister, for all my judgment. I suppose the pressures of this visit are weighing on us all. I am making Ilaria unhappy, I know that I am. I don't like doing it, despite what she thinks."

Jonah could feel the anguish in this man coming off of him in waves. He couldn't help but want to assist. After all, he liked

Grantham. Perhaps their disparate situations would never allow them to truly be friends, but in another life he knew they would have been.

"And?" he encouraged gently.

Grantham eyed him carefully. "And...and I am considering leaving my family here and returning home to Athawick."

"The situation there is getting worse?" Jonah asked.

Grantham shrugged. "It is hard to assess from here. There are reports of increasing unrest in small pockets of the population."

Jonah shifted. He knew, and he was certain this man knew just as well, that small pockets could become explosive if not managed one way or another. "What does your family think?"

"I haven't told them."

Jonah drew back. "You haven't...why?"

For a moment it seemed Grantham might answer that question. Might unburden himself from the weight he carried. But then he hardened himself. "This is not your problem to fix, Captain Crawford. I should not have brought it to your doorstep. I will increase the coverage on my sister, as you have suggested. But I hope you'll continue to watch over her."

Jonah caught his breath. He knew he ought to refuse that. To tell Grantham he couldn't. Being near Ilaria was too much a temptation, and after the kiss he knew it would only get worse, not better.

"Please," Grantham said softly. "For a...for a friend."

Jonah flinched. He couldn't refuse that. "Yes."

The relief that washed over the king's face was palpable. "Very good. Tonight we're having a small gathering. Just the family and a few select others. Will you attend?"

Jonah knew Grantham was stressing the intimacy of the gathering in order to entice him, but instead it raised his anxiety. He would not be able to avoid Ilaria the same way he could at a gala event with hundreds of people.

"Captain?"

He nodded. "Yes. Of course I will attend."

"Very good. I'll have my man send you the particulars. And now I must rush off, yet another tedious session with the Prince Regent this afternoon. He really is unbearable company."

Jonah smiled. "An experience I have shared. Good luck and good day, Your Majesty."

"Good day," Grantham said, and then he was off, leaving Jonah to stare after him.

He thought about the admiral's admonishment that he could further himself with his connection to this family. The old man was probably right, and yet he feared that would come at a cost. To his mind. To his body.

And if he wasn't careful, to his heart.

Ilaria came down the staircase and up the long, winding halls toward the parlor. She was early, which was a miracle in itself. She was never early to anything. Princesses were to be fashionably late, her mother had always said, so their entrance could be seen and enjoyed by those who had come a long way to view them.

She snorted her derision. Perhaps *that* was why she had insisted on being early tonight. To thwart her mother. Or maybe it was that she couldn't sit still and needed to move, so she had rushed June in her preparations.

Whatever the reason, she only knew she felt out of sorts. Uncomfortable. She kept thinking of that kiss with Jonah, sitting on the bed at a bawdy house. She kept thinking of how he'd refused her. How much that hurt, even if she pretended it didn't.

"Foolish girl," she grunted to herself as she entered the parlor.

She had expected it to be empty yet, but as she stepped inside she was shocked to see the very subject of her angry musings standing at the fireplace, staring up at a landscape hung there.

"Jonah," she gasped, and he turned toward her, his eyes as wide as her own. She cleared her throat and quickly gathered herself. "Captain Crawford, good evening. I didn't expect to see you here."

"Nor I you, Your Highness," he said, his voice rough.

She arched a brow. "You did not expect me in my own house?"

"I didn't expect you to be down so early," he corrected.

"And yet *you* are here abominably early, Captain," she said, glancing at the clock on the mantel pointedly. "Were you raised in a barn?"

"No, madam," he said, his lips twitching like he wanted to laugh. Suddenly she wished he would. "In a middle-class home in central London." His cheek tightened and his gaze got a little darker. "Occasionally in a barrister's office."

She blinked, for he had just given her a glimpse into his past that she had never thought to explore. Now, though, she wanted to know more about him. What had made the man who stood before her, so handsome in his formal attire, every auburn hair in place, gray eyes boring into her?

She cleared her throat. This man had rejected her the night before. She really had to attempt a little decorum. Just a little.

She sniffed and pivoted to the sideboard. "Drink?"

"Yes," he said.

She felt him watching as she poured herself sherry and the same for him. When she handed the drink over, his fingers lightly brushed her own and she caught her breath despite herself. Lunging for control, she said, "So, my brother invited you to his little pony show."

He said nothing, but continued watching her closely.

She shrugged. "I wonder if Grantham would be so solicitous if he knew about that kiss."

Now his jaw twitched. At last she had elicited a response. "Ilaria."

The way he said her name, almost a low growl, made heat sluice through her. Settle in the most inappropriate places. She forced a smile. "*Jonah*," she said. "Don't worry yourself. I won't tell him. I would hurt myself more than you by doing so."

He snorted before he took a long drink. "I don't know about that."

"I do," she insisted. "Grantham is in no mood for me as of late, I assure you."

Jonah's brow wrinkled. "He must manage a great deal."

She sighed. "Yes. I know."

Jonah took a small step closer. Such a tiny distance, and yet she suddenly felt very close, very hot. She looked up at him and her breath disappeared. It was like the previous night when he'd kissed her. Suddenly he was all that mattered.

"You know *some* of it," he said softly.

She drew back, the spell between them somewhat lifted by that odd statement. "What does *that* mean?" she asked.

Before he could respond, there was the bustle of people entering the room. She turned and somehow manage to smile. Sasha was laughing with Remi, the queen was on Grantham's arm. Behind them came a small collection of guests, and suddenly Ilaria recalled she had been meant to meet them in the foyer. Judging by her mother's pointed glare, she would pay for that distracted mistake.

She stepped away from Jonah and glided toward the newcomers to welcome them and smooth the feathers she had ruffled. It was only when she reached the parlor door that she realized the last guests into the chamber were the Earl of Bramwell and his mother.

She sighed and cast one last glance at Jonah, who was standing in the middle of the room just watching her. It was obvious it was going to be a very long night. One she would have to smile through and hope she would not break and make things worse.

Jonah had watched Ilaria all night. It had been a challenge, for the gathering wasn't particularly large and it was too easy for someone to catch him staring at her. So he'd glanced from the corner of his eye, positioned himself to be able to see her over someone's shoulder as they talked, moved himself to and fro just to catch a glimpse.

She always had a smile on her face, but he was coming to realize how often that expression was false. It hadn't reached her eyes at any time during this long night. He'd observed her talking, laughing, and yet he'd heard the strain in her voice. Seen it in the way her hands fisted at her sides, opening and shutting over and over.

And when she was alone? When she thought no one was observing her? That was when he saw how very close to the edge she was. She shuddered every time she spoke to the Earl of Bramwell, even though no one could ever accuse the man of being anything but decent. And Jonah knew many considered him handsome. There was no denying that was true. But when Ilaria looked at the earl, it was clear she saw him as nothing more than a trap ready to spring shut and hold her forever. Her future was slipping through her fingers, and as the night wore on, Jonah began to realize just how dangerous that was.

Ilaria had already flung herself out of a window and raced alone to a sex club in order to escape her future. What else might she do if her desperation rose?

He didn't want to find out, so as the dwindling crowd milled around the parlor, he moved toward her and stepped up beside her. She glanced over at him with a questioning look on her face. "Good evening again," she said softly. "I thought you would avoid me all night. And yet here you are."

"Here I am," he drawled, wishing his heart weren't beating so damned fast. Could she hear it? "Ilaria, I'll help you."

She wrinkled her brow. "I'm sorry?"

He sighed and looked around to ensure no one was listening to them. "You want a taste of freedom, you said. You want a little escape before the inescapable, yes? A moment before the cage is fully locked and you cannot escape what you believe is inevitable?"

She pivoted to fully face him now and her eyes had gone wide, her mouth dropped open. "You'll help me?"

He shook his head at her lack of decorum in the half-full room.

"If you create a scene now, you'll make this harder on yourself, you know."

She snapped her mouth shut and gripped her hands before herself, but she was practically vibrating as she repeated herself, this time on a whisper, "You'll help me?"

"Yes, but there will be a few rules," he said.

She nodded. "Of course."

"We will disguise you any time you are out. Your family doesn't deserve censure and I think you would agree about that."

"They don't," she said, and glanced toward her mother. "I know they are trying their best, even if I don't like the methods. What else?"

"You must listen to me when we are out. I don't want to argue for ten minutes with you about what is safe and not safe and then have you hurt or worse." He arched a brow. "Do you understand?"

She extended her lower lip in the prettiest pout. One he wanted to nip with his teeth until she sighed against him like she had last night. He pushed those thoughts away as she nodded.

"Finally," he said, hearing how rough with desire his voice now sounded. He hoped she couldn't hear it. "You will not go out by yourself in some misguided attempt to go wild. You will allow me to protect you."

She stared up at him silently, but he didn't need words. He saw her desire flare in her eyes, felt it in the way her breath caught just a fraction, in the way a little pink entered her cheeks. Whatever her thoughts were, they were not chaste. Heat sliced through him at that realization, settling in places where he would soon not be able to hide it. He quickly thought of anything else to keep himself from humiliation in the King of Athawick's parlor.

"Whatever you say, Jonah," she said softly, and then she slowly licked her lips.

"Don't play with fire, Princess," he said. "You might not like getting burned as much as you think you will." He noted that Grantham was watching them, so he inched back a fraction. "We can't talk about this here. I'll meet you tonight at one in the alleyway behind your home. Do not, and I mean this, do *not* climb out your window. Slip into the garden from a door."

She tilted her head. "How did you know I came out a window before?"

He caught his breath. He was so wrapped up in this woman, he was forgetting himself. "Lucky guess. I'll see you in a few hours."

He turned away and went about the business of goodbyes to the rest of the royal family. But as he stepped out and motioned for his horse, his hands began to shake with anticipation. He had just made what he knew would likely turn out to be a huge mistake. But it was done now. So it was time to make his plans, both on what the next move was, and how to keep Ilaria from crawling even deeper beneath his skin.

The night was utterly still when Ilaria and Sasha stepped from the servants' entrance and into the garden. Ilaria looked around, though she was certain there would be no one outside. If they were going to get caught in this endeavor, it would have been in the hallways. And yet her heart throbbed.

Sasha caught her hand before she could move farther and Ilaria turned back. Her friend was worrying her lip as she looked out into the dark garden. "Ilaria, this cannot be a good idea. Sneaking out once was trouble enough, but doing it again, this time to meet with a man in the alley…even a man we know…"

Ilaria shook her head. She hadn't told Sasha about her encounter with Jonah at the Donville Masquerade earlier. How could she? And reveal what she'd seen? Reveal that passionate kiss and how he had denied her afterward?

No, she couldn't say that, even to her best friend. Her sister, for all intents and purposes.

"Captain Crawford won't let me come to any harm, Sasha. I can guarantee that. And no, it might not be the best of ideas, but I *need* this." She clasped Sasha's hand tighter. "I need it, Sasha. I feel like I'm going to come out of my skin every time I have to shake another hand, smile another smile, pretend I'm fine with being used as chattel for my brother's ambitions."

Sasha's expression softened. "I know it's difficult. I know this isn't what you want."

"No," Ilaria whispered. "But I'll do it, won't I? In the end I will have no choice, not unless I wish to destroy my brother's hopes. But until that moment comes, can I not have just a tiny escape? Just some small pleasure for myself before all of my pleasures are ripped from me."

"That is a little dramatic, love," Sasha said.

Ilaria bent her head. "Perhaps it is. But it feels so very real to me that I can hardly breathe."

Sasha leaned forward and bussed her cheek. "Then go with him. But promise me you'll be careful."

"I will," Ilaria said.

"I'll try to stay awake and look for your return," Sasha whispered as Ilaria raced into the twisting maze of the garden. The gate hidden in the high wall took a moment for her to find, but she managed and turned the rusty handle to hurtle herself into the alleyway.

She looked around in the darkness for any sign of Jonah, but before she could call for him, he stepped from the shadows. A cloud blew away from the moon in that moment and the light fell on him. She caught her breath. He looked like some fallen angel. Wicked and beautiful, a temptation embodied that would drag her to hell.

But oh, what a journey it would be.

"Ilaria," he said softly. "Come."

She blinked at the order and the double meaning of that little word. He tilted his head when she didn't move and motioned to the phaeton parked just up the alleyway. She jumped, pulled from her thoughts. "Oh, yes," she whispered.

She followed him to the vehicle and stared up at it. Somehow when she pictured Jonah making his way around London, she hadn't ever put him in a rig like this. It was sleek and modern with its big back wheels on swan-necked leaf springs and its body mounted daringly high. The body of the phaeton had been painted a bright, lemon-yellow with shiny black highlights that glistened in the moonlight.

She let out a whistle. "This is a thing of beauty."

He gave a half-smile. "Thank you. I do not often wish to race around London streets, but tonight seems the time to be dangerous." He held out a hand to help her up.

She grasped his fingers. "Yes."

After she had settled herself in, he took the driver's seat and they trotted off toward the street. For a while, they were silent. He seemed comfortable in that quiet, she was less so. She simply couldn't think of anything to say to a man who so confused her. He kissed her, he refused her. He watched her, he told her he would help.

The man was a riddle, that was certain.

"Where...where are we going?" she asked when it felt like a lifetime had passed.

He gave her a side glance as he turned down yet another street and then motioned his head forward. She followed the flick of his chin and caught her breath. The Donville Masquerade was just before them.

"There is a mask on the seat," he said softly.

She grabbed for it and tied it on with shaking hands, even as she asked, "Why?"

The vehicle slid to a smooth stop and he set the reins down. Pivoting in his seat, he faced her full on.

"You want to play, Ilaria? Then let's play."

CHAPTER 10

Jonah's mind was spinning as he followed Ilaria into the antechamber and they stopped at the station to check in. He knew what he was doing was wildly irresponsible. For her, for himself. And yet he couldn't stop. He could tell himself a hundred times that he was doing this to overload her senses, to let her have everything she wanted so she would know it was too much…

But that was a lie. He had taken her here because he wanted her here. Because he wanted her, full stop. He was driven to take this path and the consequences be damned.

"Welcome back, Mr. Harlen," the man at the desk said, checking his name off. "And Miss Crawford."

Jonah swiveled his head to look at Ilaria but found her staring straight ahead, cheeks bright with a blush beneath her mask. She had chosen *his* name to be her false identity? Out of all the names in the world? He couldn't believe she hadn't done so it for some reason. *He* had certainly chosen his own name with a thought to the meaning.

"Will Miss Crawford be joining you on your membership, sir, or purchasing her own?"

Jonah forced himself to focus. "Er, on mine. Thank you."

"Excellent. Do you need a reminder about the rules of the club?"

"No," Ilaria said, so softly that the word almost didn't carry.

The man inclined his head and then motioned to the door. "Enjoy yourselves."

Ilaria gave Jonah a quick glance and he saw her nerves. Strong as she tried to be, as she was, this was a challenge to her. Which was what he'd claimed to want when he allowed for this ridiculous plan. But seeing her pupils dilate, her tongue come out to wet her lips, her hands shake at her sides, he wanted to protect her, not break her down.

He placed a hand on the small of her back, feeling the flutter that worked through her when he touched her so intimately. He was exquisitely aware of how her spine straightened, how her body leaned back just a fraction to increase the pressure of his fingers.

And he wanted to fuck her so badly he could almost taste her surrender.

The doors opened and the cacophony of sounds from within swirled around them as they entered the bright chamber. As with the previous night, they had come late enough that the debauchery of the hall was well underway. Half-naked bodies writhed on the dancefloor, a game of strip whist was being played with a mixed group of men and women who were touching as much as playing. And against the back wall, a woman was being given enthusiastic oral pleasure by another lady while a small crowd watched.

He saw Ilaria's gaze flit and hold on that particular image and another shudder worked through her. He marked the interest and guided her to the edge of the room.

"You want to look," he said, leaning down to whisper close to her ear. "Look. You want to touch…"

"No," she said, glancing up at him, eyes wide. "I don't think I want to…to touch a stranger. Not yet at any rate."

"You think you might wish to do so at some point?" he asked. He waited for jealousy to arc through him, but the idea of watching Ilaria receive pleasure was a potent one. At least in the realm of fantasy. Reality might be harder to take, though he had no place to tell her what to do or not to do so long as she was protected during her games.

That was what he was here for, wasn't it?

"I don't know," she whispered. "I want to look."

He nodded and let her do so for a while, guiding her around the room, marking what made her breath hitch or her cheeks pinken with high color. Eventually he motioned her toward a side room where a woman writhed on stage, mimicking masturbation as she stripped item after item of clothing from her body. They stood in the back of the crowd, watching. Well, Ilaria watched the show.

Jonah watched her. It was impossible not to do so when her increasing desire was slashed across her face. Powerful. Potent. She weaved ever so gently on her feet until he caught her elbow and held her still.

She stared at his fingers clenched against her elbow and then slowly slid her gaze up to his face. They held stares for what felt like a lifetime as everything in the room faded but her. He cleared his throat.

"How do you feel?" he asked.

She swallowed hard. "Unsteady," she admitted before she lifted a hand to his chest.

Her fingers curled against his jacket. Three layers of fabric and she might as well have been licking his skin, the reaction was so strong. His cock, already at half attention from the moment her breath caught for the first time, came to be fully so.

"Like I want more," she murmured, leaning against him with no subtlety. No hesitation. He felt the warm length of her molding to his side, the way her leg lightly crooked around his, just as it would if he were driving between them.

He shook his head. He had to stop this madness some way, any way. "Then come with me," he said, and guided her from the room and back into the main hall.

~

Ilaria forgot how to breathe as she staggered after Jonah through the crowded, sweaty hall. All around her were moans and sighs, and it was like every sound sent a shiver through her, sent wet heat to settle between her legs, sent electric sensation into every nerve. She felt so tightly wound that she feared she might pop.

But he didn't hesitate, and she realized he was maneuvering her toward those back rooms again. The place where they had been alone before. Where he had kissed her and made her want so much more from him. From them.

"Jonah," she whispered, a harsh sound. A desperate and needy sound that left no question about the desires in her body.

He held her tighter, drawing her against him as he said, "The hall," to the guard.

The man arched a brow and nodded, then got up and led them not to a room, but to a secret door. He unlocked it and motioned them inside. "You're the only ones at present."

"Very good," Jonah said, his tone a little garbled, as if strained.

"What are we doing?" she whispered as he took her hand and led her into a narrow, dark space lit only by a few candles set high on the walls and shafts of light coming from someplace she couldn't determine.

"You want more," he said, and led her to one of those shafts. "This is more."

He turned her toward the source of the brightness, and she gasped. The light was coming from one of the private rooms—this was a peeping place to look into the chamber.

"This is what you were doing when..." she began, looking over her shoulder at him.

She couldn't see the fullness of his expression, but he nodded. "I closed the barrier the last time we were here so no one in this hall could see us."

She moved closer to the opening and lifted a hand to cover her mouth. A man and woman were in the room, and it was obvious they had been there for a while. Both were naked from the waist up, her gown drooping at her full hips. He was bent over her, sucking hard on her nipples as she arched beneath him, moaning softly with every lick.

"Jonah," Ilaria whispered, and staggered away until her back hit the opposite wall.

He leaned in closer and the light from the room hit his face, giving her a half-view of his taut expression. "We can leave."

"Do they know I'm watching?" she murmured.

He shrugged. "They know someone might be. Some people like that. A lot of people, as you can see from how they behave in the public room. But here it's more intimate. Is that what you want, Ilaria?"

He was testing her, that was clear. But his voice was rough, filled with desire even though he wasn't even sparing a glance for the couple in the room behind him.

She swallowed and looked over his shoulder through the little window again. The man had stripped the woman's dress off and knelt between her legs. His head bobbed as he pleasured her with his tongue and her moans turned to keening cries.

Ilaria found herself moving closer, eyes wide as she stared at the two. She'd had a lover before, back in Athawick. The son of a courtier who she'd always found somewhat handsome. He'd been bound to go to the continent for his education and so they'd both known nothing more would ever come of their attraction. It was for fun, nothing serious. No emotions had ever been involved, just a drive for the heady first blush of pleasure. Neither of them had been very experienced. He'd certainly never done *that*. Her body thrummed at the sight, her sex gripping against nothing as she stared.

She felt Jonah move behind her, his heat at her back, and she couldn't resist. She leaned into him, her back to his chest, her bottom pressed against his pelvis. She felt his cock there, hard and ready. Proof that he wasn't as unmoved as he sometimes pretended to be.

The woman in the room came with great, gulping cries and the man between her legs never let up as it happened. It was only when she went limp against the pillows that he shoved his trousers away and took her. Ilaria watched as his backside pumped, as her legs latched around him, still shaking from her first orgasm, clearly building to a second.

Jonah's hands touched her hips, and she gasped as she realized she had been grinding back against him in slow circles. She thought he would stop her, but instead he pulled her back harder, increasing the friction. She reached up, cupping the nape of his neck, arching against him and seeking the same pleasure she watched the couple in the room find.

"Please," she murmured, shoving a hand against her skirts and between her legs. "Please."

Jonah went still for a moment, his entire body quivering with desire. He turned her to face him, his gray stare glittering in the dimness. "You want this."

She nodded without hesitation. "Yes."

He closed his eyes and she saw the fight on his face. The uncertainty. The drive to keep up whatever he called honor.

"Please," she repeated softly, tracing a finger over his jawline.

He grunted rather than answer, and then he pushed her, pivoting her so her back was against the wall opposite the window again. He leaned into her, letting her feel the full length of him as his mouth lowered to hers, not with gentleness or finesse, but with animal passion. Heated desperation. Reluctant surrender. She lifted into him, trying to pull him closer, trying to make him a part of her because that was what she needed so desperately was this man driving inside of her the way the man in the room was doing to the moaning woman he took.

Jonah broke the kiss. "Just once," he said, she thought more to himself than to her. "Just once."

She didn't know that she agreed to that statement. But she didn't get the chance to argue because he surprised her by pressing his mouth to her throat, dragging it lower, over her collarbone, her still-clothed breasts, her stomach, her hip. He dropped to his knees before her and looked up at her as he began to slide her gown up her legs.

His palms were warm, even through her silky stockings, and she pressed her hands against the wall behind her as if she could somehow maintain sanity by gripping the rough surface of the wallpaper.

"Watch them," he ordered, glancing up at her even as he lifted her skirt over her knees.

She forced herself to do so, looking across the narrow hall back into the chamber. The man had shifted to his back on the bed and the woman now straddled him, hands pressed to his chest as she slowly ground down over him.

Jonah pulled her skirt up to hip level and then caught one of Ilaria's hands. "Hold this," he said.

She caught the fabric and shifted her attention to him. He chuckled as he fingered the edge of her stockings. "You aren't wearing drawers," he said, his face very close to her naked sex.

She shook her head. "I…never…do," she gasped out.

He glared up at her. "Of course you don't. And now I know it and it is all I'll think about every time I see you. That and…" He leaned in closer and let a puff of warm air blow across the apex of her thighs. "This."

He stroked his fingers there and she widened her stance immediately, granting him better access. He leaned his head forward and rested it against her hip. "You'll be the death of me, Ilaria, one way or another."

He pressed a hand to each of her inner thighs and gently pushed, making her stand even wider still. He let out a ragged sigh before he pressed his mouth to the flesh of her thigh, licking languidly, sucking gently.

Ilaria gripped at the wall with her free hand, trying to find purchase when it felt like everything in the world was spiraling to focus on the place between her legs. Especially when his tongue glided higher, teasing the spot where her leg met her pelvis. Then he pressed his mouth to her sex and everything stopped.

It was a fairly chaste kiss as kisses went. Closed mouth, no tongue, but she was on fire. He was kissing her between her legs. Like she'd seen outside, like she was watching right now, for the couple in the room had switched positions yet again and now the woman ground down against her partner's tongue even as she took his cock deep into her mouth.

Ilaria flexed her hips against Jonah's mouth, and he parted her folds with one hand and licked her as an answer. She nearly came apart right then, with that perfect pressure stroking across her clitoris. He cupped her backside beneath her skirts, pulling her more firmly against his mouth. She ground down against his tongue, watching the scene in the room across the hall, then squeezing her eyes shut because what he was doing was infinitely more arousing and intimate than anything she could watch.

He swirled his tongue around her, over and over, keeping just the right pressure there. She rode the sensation, gasping out moans and cries in the quiet hallway. Perhaps those in the rooms could hear her. She didn't really care. She just wanted this, wanted to come for this man.

And he clearly wanted the same thing. He didn't tease her, perhaps because they were in the public hall, perhaps because there was little time, perhaps because he just didn't have the desire to. He drove her forward, always toward the cliff edge she could feel in the distance. He did it without effort. It was like he knew the instrument of her body, like he'd played this melody before even if they'd never touched like this.

Whatever it was, it didn't matter. She writhed against him, the pleasure building, arcing through her, making every inch of her tingle and clench and lean toward the pleasure about to overtake her.

He sucked her clitoris, and the explosion was immediate and powerful. She rocked against him, her back bowing, her fingernails raking the wall behind her as noises unlike anything she'd ever heard escaped from deep within her chest. He continued to torture her, never easing his tongue until her knees buckled. He cupped her backside harder, supporting her she leaned against the wall and stared down at him.

"Come here," she whispered.

He hesitated a moment but then pushed to his feet. She wrapped her arms around his neck and lifted her mouth to his, tasting the sweet and salty flavor of herself on his tongue. She shuddered at that and the kiss deepened. She wedged a hand between them as he pressed her more firmly against the wall, and cupped the hardness of his cock. She had very much enjoyed his mouth, but this was what she wanted.

But he pulled away rather than taking the next obvious step in this encounter. "Ilaria," he whispered, an admonishment rather than an endearment.

She blinked. "You won't?"

He shook his head slowly. "I won't try to lie and tell you I don't want to. It's obvious I want to."

She stroked him again and he muttered a curse.

"Then why won't you?" she asked. "Here in the dark, no one will know. No one will see."

He rested his forehead on her shoulder for a fraction of a moment. "I want to protect you, not make everything worse. Or more confusing."

"You don't think licking my pussy until I spasmed in a hallway was making it more confusing?" she asked.

He stiffened at the language she had chosen, not out of offense, she didn't think, but desire. Her bluntness aroused him. She would file that fact away.

"Probably," he admitted. "And that's why I can't go further."

He stepped away then, raising his hands as if to show her he wasn't armed. He wouldn't hurt her. Only that wasn't true. He hurt her every time he refused her. Every time he drew her close only to push her away.

She smoothed her wrinkled skirt, letting it fall to her ankles to cover her again. With as much of an air as she could manage, she thrust her shoulders back and arched an eyebrow at him, though she didn't know if he could see it in the dimness of the hall.

"I'm not confused," she said. "Just so you know. If you are, that's on you."

She pivoted then and moved away from him, back toward the exit into the main hall. She heard his frustrated sigh, but he said nothing else as he followed her, a few steps behind back into the light. As if the whispered pleasures in the dark had never happened.

As if they had meant nothing to him. But she knew that was a lie. She'd felt how much they meant in the moments when she lost herself. And she wasn't about to forget that, even if he wanted to.

CHAPTER 11

The light hit Jonah in the face and he winced. It felt like waking from a dream as he and Ilaria entered the main hall together, and he was dazed by it. He could still taste her on his tongue, still feel the rhythm of the waves of her pleasure as she came. He'd never felt anything like it, not with any woman he'd been with before.

Despite all his promises to himself, he had almost gone further. When she touched him, cupping his cock, stroking him, it had taken every ounce of discipline in his body not to pin her and take her hard and fast against the wall. Make her scream with even more pleasure. Give her every inch of himself and forget all the reasons why he couldn't. Shouldn't.

He blinked those thoughts away as she maneuvered them to an empty table and sat. When she looked up at him, he saw her disappointment, mixed with whatever satisfaction from her release remained.

"I need a drink," she said, her tone cooler and more detached than it had been in the hall when it had just been them and the pulsing passion they shared. "Will you fetch me one?"

He shifted. It seemed she was ready to put a wall back up

between them. And perhaps that was for the best, even though his heart ached a little at the idea.

"I'm not certain I should leave you alone," he said, looking around at the sea of masked people.

She arched a brow up at him. "You see exactly what I do. These people have no interest in me—they are too wrapped up in their own pleasures. It will be but a moment and I will sit right here and not speak to anyone."

He pursed his lips. She was not going to be deterred, it seemed and the last thing he wanted was to have this conversation 'round and 'round until they drew attention to themselves. And she was right that those around them were far too invested in their own games to pay attention to anyone else.

"Very well," he grumbled. He edged off into the crowd, unable to keep himself from looking back over his shoulder to ensure she was safe. She had bent her head and was staring at her hands, clasped on the table before her.

He reached the bar and motioned to the man behind it. He was busy and held up a hand to indicate he'd seen Jonah and would join him shortly. Jonah sighed and leaned against the bar top. His entire body still felt on edge from his encounter with Ilaria in the hallway. And he wanted so much more.

"Good evening, Mr. *Harlen.*"

Jonah turned at the usage of his false name and found Marcus Rivers, the proprietor of the infamous club, coming through the crowd toward him. He was a giant of a man, physically intimidating, which Jonah supposed was the point considering his business. He had dark hair and green eyes that seemed to see everything around him.

The two had met years ago, when Jonah was still in the Royal Navy. A casual acquaintance outside the club had turned to an invitation to become a member. He hadn't come all that often, but when he did, he enjoyed himself.

Never more than tonight, however.

"Rivers," Jonah said, extending his hand. "Good evening."

"Been a while since we saw you here. Annabelle will be pleased to hear you've returned," Rivers said as the two men shook.

Jonah smiled. Annabelle had been married to Rivers for a few years and helped manage the club. He had never seen the man so settled as he was since their union. In that moment, he was a little jealous of his friend's certainty.

"I'll have to say my good evenings if I'm lucky enough to see her." Jonah tilted his head. "How in the world do you keep everyone's secret identity and real identity straight when your club does such a brisk business?"

Rivers tapped his temple. "It's all up here, my friend. I just have to access it."

"Remarkable."

"I'm not sure that's true." Rivers looked out over the crowd. "I must say I do not know who your companion is. That is rare enough a thing."

Jonah tensed. "I would prefer not to give her true identity if you don't mind. She isn't a member of the Masquerade and I doubt she would appreciate it, even though I know you are the soul of discretion."

"Of course." Rivers shrugged, and if his gaze filled with a fraction more interest at the subterfuge, he didn't press. "How are things? I know there's been some major change in the last six months."

Jonah sighed. "Yes. Major change and I can't say I'm comfortable in my new role. But…" He glanced over his shoulder toward Ilaria, and the next words dropped away.

A man had approached her. He was seated across from her, leaning over to speak a little closer. She lifted her gaze, found Jonah's across the crowd, and the anxiety on her face was enough. He pushed away from the bar top and started across the room, indelicate as a bull shoving through the crowd.

Because he had to get to her. And he had to get to her now.

~

Ilaria watched as Jonah walked toward the bar across the room. She shifted a little in her seat as she let her expression become less cool. God, she could almost still feel his tongue on her, his fingers pressing into her flesh. She tingled at the thought and hated herself for the lack of control when he seemed to have so much.

She sighed. She'd wanted to be relaxed by that powerful moment between them, moved and changed. Instead she only felt more frustrated. What he'd given her was only a reminder of all she would lose if her mother and her brother prevailed in their vision of her future. Certainly she would never find herself pleasured against a wall in a sex club again if she married a proper man like Lord Bramwell or another of his ilk.

"Good evening."

She glanced up to find a tall, broad-shouldered man in a plain gray mask standing over her. He had approached so quietly she hadn't noticed him until he was right there.

"G-Good evening," she stammered, and glanced past him toward where Jonah had gone. She couldn't see him in the milling crowd.

"May I sit?"

Her heart rate increased immediately. The man was not doing anything wrong, he was polite beyond his incredibly intense stare, but she still felt a jolt of nervousness. Uncertainty.

"Er, my companion will be back momentarily."

There was a flutter of a smile that tilted the man's lips beneath his mask, and he sat even though she had given him no leave. "Then I will keep you company until his return," he said.

She swallowed hard. "Very well."

He leaned back in his chair and examined her closely. "You were here before."

Her lips parted in surprise at that observation. She hadn't been aware her brief appearance here before had been so closely monitored by anyone.

She forced herself to shut her mouth and shrug nonchalantly. "A great many people come here, sir, as indicated by the enormous crowd tonight. Whether I have ever been one of them in the past is my prerogative to share or conceal."

A flash of annoyance passed across his face and she tensed further. There was something uncomfortable about his presence. Something…dangerous…and not in the sensual way that Jonah was. *Truly* dangerous.

But perhaps she was just being foolish. Perhaps she should push aside the discomfort in her belly and try to be polite to appease him.

"Indeed, you are correct," he said, and then leaned a little closer. She scented cigar smoke on his clothes, sweet and smoky. "But you are so lovely, it would be hard to miss you."

"While I appreciate the compliments…" she said, looking again for Jonah. The crowd had parted slightly and she saw him at the bar talking to another man. He turned his head as if he sensed her eyes on him and she flitted her gaze to the person who had joined her. Jonah stopped talking and started across the crowd toward her, unheeding of anyone he shoved aside as he went. "Here comes my companion."

The gentleman, though she hesitated to call him such even though he had done nothing untoward, stood and pivoted to face Jonah. She noted how his stance changed, how his gaze got harder.

"No need to make a scene," he said before Jonah could say anything. He started to walk away but bent slightly and whispered, "Good night, princess."

She stiffened at the word. It could be construed as a cheeky endearment, but what if it wasn't? Could he know her identity? How?

"What did he say to you?" Jonah growled, shaking as he sat down beside her and took one of her hands in his. There was something instantly comforting about that touch. She wanted to lean into him, let his arms come around her so that she could feel even more protected.

But she couldn't. He would never allow that. She was honestly shocked he was letting her touch him at all when he pulled away any time things got too intimate between them.

"Nothing," she lied. "He only said good night."

He didn't look certain, and she knew she ought to tell him the truth. But what if she did? Jonah would panic, he would drag her out of here, he would never return with her. He might even tell her brother. And all for what? A throwaway endearment from a stranger who probably meant no harm?

"Then why do you look like you've seen a ghost?" he asked softly.

She shook her head. "I've been so sheltered my whole life, I am not accustomed to a stranger just coming up to me like that."

Which was true enough. And probably why she was overreacting.

"Are you certain that's all?" he pressed.

She nodded. "I think I'm just…tired. Tonight has been eventful."

"That's one way to put it," he muttered. "Shall I take you home?"

Again, she nodded, even though she wanted to push her luck. She wanted to beg him to take her to his home, not hers. To his bed, not leave her cold in her own. What would he say if she were so direct?

He would deny her. That was what he would do. She knew that like she knew the back of her hand. He'd done so already once. Was she ready to face that again?

"Yes, I think that would be best," she said, and rose. He offered her an arm and she stared at it. Stared at him, this man who aroused such complicated and heated feelings in her. This man who so obviously wanted her and yet had the strength to turn away.

This man who had awakened things in her she had never fully felt before. It was as if she had been sleeping, put up in a tower her whole life, but now she knew what the world looked like and she could never fully go back to what she was before.

"Miss…Crawford," he said, his voice getting rougher as he said his own name. The name she'd stolen for her own, if only for a few nights of pleasure.

"Yes," she said, pressing her fingers into the crook of his elbow. "I'm sorry. I'm ready."

He cast her a quick side glance, but said nothing else as he guided her through the room. She hardly saw any of the writhing bodies anymore. Didn't hear the moans. She was too focused on her own tangled thoughts, her own worries, her own memories of what she'd done here with the man who was guiding her home.

And her fears that she might never get to experience any of it again.

Ilaria had been quiet on the drive back to the gated house where she and her family were staying. She stared straight ahead, her hands clenched in her lap. A thousand questions raced through Jonah's head. Questions about the man who had been sitting with her at the club, because he knew she was withholding *something* on that topic.

But also about their encounter. Was she sorry it had happened? Was she as haunted by thoughts of it as he was? And if he dared to beg her, would she come to his bed and give herself to him?

Only he couldn't ask those things. Not if he wanted to maintain his sanity.

She looked at him at last when he turned the phaeton down the narrow alleyway behind the house. "What...what will we do now?" she asked, her voice trembling just a fraction. But enough that it answered a great many of his questions.

He brought the horses to a stop before she twisted in his seat to face her. He held her stare evenly and he knew he wouldn't be able to keep himself from digging this hole even deeper, not when she was staring at him like he was some sweet treat.

"You mean now that I've eaten your pussy in a public hall until you clawed scratch marks in the wallpaper?"

Her breath shuddered out but she lifted her chin almost defiantly. "Yes."

"I'm not certain," he admitted. "It changes the tenor of our relationship, there is no denying that. Are you still intent on testing your boundaries, even after tonight?"

She drew back and stared at him. "Wait...did you...did you do that tonight in order to frighten me? To make me change my mind about wanting this taste of freedom?"

He hesitated. That was an easy answer to give, a lie to tell that would maybe create the distance he so desperately needed from this remarkable and entirely out of reach woman.

"No, Ilaria. I can say with complete honesty that I wasn't thinking about frightening you in any way. But if you were frightened, either by the power of what we did or anything else you saw or did tonight, perhaps you should put this foolish notion away."

Her breath caught and her eyes narrowed on him. "If you are trying to play some game, I don't like it."

She moved as if to climb down, but he caught her wrist, holding her in place gently. He leaned closer, until he could feel her breath on his lips. Sweet torture.

"Nothing about tonight was a game. We both know that." He brushed his lips to hers, gentle at first, then with increasing pressure. She wound her arms around his neck instantly, practically clawing her way into his lap as she moaned his name into his mouth. God, but he wanted her. He had never felt anything like it in his life.

He pulled away before he lost all control. "Best go inside, Your Highness."

Her mouth twitched and she shook her head slowly before she climbed down from the high rig and walked away. He watched her as she unlatched the gate. She gave him one last, long look and then she was gone.

He scrubbed a hand over his face and stared up at the starry sky. "What the hell are you doing, Crawford?" he muttered before he urged the horses into motion.

He already knew the answer to that question. And the hell he would be led to if he couldn't rein himself in.

CHAPTER 12

Ilaria sat in the parlor, staring out at the garden behind the estate. Well, not the garden, exactly. The alley she could barely see behind it. That was where she had last seen Jonah a few days ago. She had been unable to think of anything else since.

When she went to some stuffy reception, her mind turned to the pressure of his lips on hers. At state suppers? Jonah's hand on her back. And at night, as she slid beneath her sheets? Her hand always stole between her legs as she tried to recapture the pleasure his tongue had given.

"Ilaria."

She jolted as her mother entered the room. Queen Giabella's dark hair was pulled back in a simple style and she wore a plain gown. In that moment, she was more Ilaria's mother than queen. And yet she held herself regally and with a confidence Ilaria had always envied.

"Mama. You look very pretty," Ilaria said, pushing thoughts of Jonah from her mind.

"Thank you." Her mother sighed. "I admit it is nice to have an afternoon away from all the pomp and circumstance. These state visits can be exhausting."

Ilaria stood and motioned her mother to the settee she had abandoned. "Allow me to fetch you tea, then, and you can relax."

Her mother gave her a strange look, but took the seat she had been offered and settled in with a sigh. "I'm surprised you would be so solicitous, Ilaria, considering how at odds we've been these past few weeks."

Ilaria sweetened her mother's tea and then brought the cup over. She sat and shook her head. "I can be...frustrated by what you desire and still care for you."

Her mother sipped her tea and then set the cup aside. "But you don't understand me."

"Nor you me," Ilaria said, and tried not to sound as defensive as she felt.

Her mother bent her head. "No, I *completely* understand."

There was a moment of silence as Ilaria took that statement in. "Because you were also forced to wed."

Giabella nodded. "I was offered no option when the arrangement was made between Alastair's father and my own. Athawick was a treasured trade partner to Everlay and my country wished to make a stronger alliance."

"And look at how it turned out," Ilaria said softly.

Her mother flinched and set her jaw. "We made a family—it was a success."

Ilaria tilted her head. "Mama."

The pain that flowed over her mother's expression was instant and powerful. "What do you want me to say, Ilaria? Will going over the facts help you in some way?"

"Perhaps," Ilaria said. "I saw how it was, Mama. I saw how unhappy he made you, how...cruelly he could treat you and us by extension. I know you did your best, I know you had no choice once it was done. But didn't you ever wish for...for more?"

Her mother's gaze flitted to the door, and Ilaria followed it. Nothing was there, but it was like her mother was seeing something or someone.

"I was not taught to wish for more," she said softly. "The marriage with your father was arranged from the time I was very young. I accepted it because I never knew anything different. It wasn't until later—much later—that I began to long for something else. But what good did it do me? What good does it do anyone to fantasize about a past that cannot be changed?"

"The good it does to help you understand why I'm resistant. When you told me you and Grantham expected a marriage to be made for me here so that you could solidify an alliance, it was as if someone tore a piece of me away."

"Ilaria, you don't need to be dramatic. You knew at some point you would need to marry. And you must have guessed there might be a political element to it. You're the only daughter of a king."

Ilaria closed her eyes. "Yes. That had come up. Father brought it up regularly. Told me again and again how it was my only value as a woman."

"I am sorry about that," Giabella said softly. "That is not how I feel."

"But when Grantham took over, all the talk died. And I thought...I thought I might be allowed to make my own choices. For..." Ilaria shook her head as she trailed off. She could not say the next word, not when images of Jonah were sliding into her mind. Taunting her.

"For love," Giabella said for her, and there was such a longing on her face that Ilaria drew back.

She nodded. Her mother slid over on the settee and covered Ilaria's hands with her own. "I realize what we're asking might seem cruel. But I have purposefully chosen gentlemen for your consideration who are *not* cruel. Who have interests in common with you. Who I think you could be happy with if you would just stop—"

"Stop what?" Ilaria whispered.

"Stop mooning over a man you cannot have," Giabella said. When Ilaria sucked in a breath, her mother raised a hand to stop her from speaking. "I like Captain Crawford. I do. And there is no denying he is very attractive. But his history…his connections…they will not be enough. And your brother needs this. Our country needs it. It isn't fair, Ilaria, and I wish I could make it be so. But…" She shook her head and tears filled her eyes. "Sometimes things just aren't fair."

Ilaria winced. "Are things so very bad for Grantham?" she asked.

Giabella nodded. "Worse than I think he wishes us to know. I'm not certain of the particulars, but Dash—Mr. Talbot has given me some information that leads me to believe it is a harder transition than he has allowed."

Ilaria worried her lip. She loved her brother. She loved her country. And for the first time this request…this *order* that she sacrifice herself made more sense.

"I will try, Mama," she said softly.

The relief that crossed her mother's face was so powerful that Ilaria gaped at it. She hadn't fully grasped the queen's fear until that moment.

"Thank you, love." Her mother released her hands and stood, pacing the room. "There is an opera tomorrow night. I'd like you to go with the Earl of Bramwell, along with his mother and me. Do you understand?"

"To be seen on such a public outing will make the intentions very clear, I think."

"Yes."

She thought of the earl. He was handsome, there was no denying that. He seemed kind enough. She liked his sister and her husband very much, from the short time she had spent with them. And his mother was also friendly and inviting. If she put aside the fact she felt absolutely no attraction to the man at all, it wasn't the worst idea.

She cleared her throat. "Then I will do my best to get to know him better during this outing. I won't fight you anymore, Mama. You may tell Grantham the same."

Her mother stared at her. Ilaria had expected even more relief, perpetrated even the tiniest of celebrations. Instead, there was a sadness to the queen.

"Thank you," her mother said softly. She glanced at the clock on the mantel. "Look at the time. I have yet another engagement tonight, so I must ready myself. You and Remi are staying in, aren't you?"

"Yes," Ilaria said, wishing her voice wasn't so broken. "A quiet night."

"Enjoy it. I think it is the last one for a good while." Her mother squeezed her hand as she passed by, and then she was gone.

And Ilaria placed her head in her hands, and fought the urge to sob.

❧

Two Years Before
The Island of Athawick

Jonah stood at the edge of the dock, watching as the last trunks were loaded onto the ship. It was a funny thing. He had been anxious about this trip, uncertain if he wished to be part of an honor guard for something so frivolous. And yet now he felt melancholy that within hours he would be leaving this place forever. He had tried to tell himself that his regrets were only about how beautiful the island was, or the friendly acquaintance he had developed with Prince Grantham, who was a serious man of intelligence.

But it wasn't either of those things that made him cast a glance back up the hill toward the palace glimmering in the sunshine.

"Captain Crawford?"

He jolted at the very familiar voice that did not belong here at the dock. He looked around and noted a slim figure in a long, pale blue cloak standing beside a pile of pallets off to the side of the dock.

He wrinkled his brow. "Is that—?"

The figure pushed the cloak back a fraction and his heart lurched. It was indeed Ilaria, and she motioned him to follow her with just a jerk of her head. He did so, looking over his shoulder to be certain they were not being followed.

"What are you doing?" he asked when they had walked away from the dock and down the lane that led to the sandy beach along the shore. With every step, they got a little farther away from town and watching eyes.

She didn't answer until she glanced around and seemed satisfied that they weren't being observed. "You've been avoiding me these last few days."

He drew back. He'd been trying to be subtle about that fact, but it seemed he had failed. Still, one didn't just have a conversation like this. With a princess. Especially one who looked like a wood sprite who could easily draw him away to some kind of fantasy land.

"Are you going to deny it?" she asked, and he realized he'd just been staring at her, not speaking.

"No," he said softly. "I respect your intelligence too much to do such a thing. I have been avoiding you, I thought it was best after...after..."

"The ball," she finished.

He nodded. She stared at him a long while and then pivoted and paced up the beach a few steps. She pushed the cloak away from her head and gazed out at the sea, toward his destination, away from her home.

When she looked at him again, her frustration was clear. "Did my father say something to you?"

He drew back. "No."

"Oh. He did to me." She folded her arms but he saw the pain and disappointment behind the shield she created, sharp and undeniable in the fraction of a moment before she covered it. "He has plans for me, I know. So I assumed he made it clear I was not someone you could ever trifle with."

Jonah tilted his head. "He didn't say that, but if he did I would...I would have to agree with him, Your Highness." When her lips parted as if she would argue, he held up a hand. "You are a beautiful woman, a person would be a fool to deny that. But you have a life that most men could never touch. To pretend otherwise would be folly for all parties involved."

Her nostrils flared slightly, as if that statement stung her. It certainly stung him, even if he knew it was true. He sighed. "And I'm leaving at any rate."

"I suppose you are," she said. "And you'll forget me soon enough, as you believe I will you."

He nodded, though he doubted what she said would ever be true. "It would be best, I think, to do just that."

Her expression went a little harder. "I'm glad my father didn't cause you any grief. That was all I wanted to say to you. I have already said my farewells to the rest of the party, so I doubt I will see you again, Captain."

She held out a hand, arching a brow as she waited for him to take it. He did, gently and leaned over it, pressing his lips to the silk of her glove for all-too-brief a moment. When he glanced up at her, her pupils had dilated and her breath was short.

"Goodbye, Captain," she whispered as she tugged her hand from his and hurried away back toward the palace, yanking her hood up as she went.

"Goodbye, Ilaria," he whispered. Then he turned back to the sea that had been his home for so many years. She would welcome him back. She would help him forget any other desires.

She had to.

~

1817
London

Jonah eased his way through Fitzhugh's Club and took a seat by the fire. A precisely liveried servant approached with cigars, but Jonah waved them away and picked up the paper that had been left on the table beside his seat. Splashed across the front was a story about the Athawick royal family. Something about King Grantham's latest meeting with the courtiers for the prince regent. There was an accompanying cartoon that depicted Grantham as larger than life and beautiful as a Greek god while the courtiers were small and feeble at his feet.

"*That* should play extremely poorly in the palace," Jonah muttered. He glanced up and caught his breath. Coming across the room was Jonah's old friend Nicholas Gillingham and Gillingham's brother-in-law, the Earl of Bramwell. He lifted a hand to wave and stood to greet the men as they joined him.

Gillingham switched his cane to the opposite hand before he shook Jonah's. "Good to see you, Captain."

"Gillingham," Jonah said with a genuine smile. One that dimmed as he extended a hand to Bramwell, as well. "My lord. Won't you two join me?"

He didn't really want to sit with the man who was being groomed to be Ilaria's future husband, but there was no way to avoid the societal expectation of politeness without making a scene.

The men took the seats beside him and for a while the talk was general and uneventful. He was somehow able to control his countenance as he chatted amiably with the man he knew was in contention to marry Ilaria. The fact that he was a good man was at least helpful.

But the idea of him having Ilaria, falling in love with her, making a life with her...it was physically painful.

"It seems like it's been an eventful Season thus far," Gillingham said. "My brother, the Duke of Roseford, tells me he hasn't seen anything like it. But you know, Thomas—you are at the heart of this royal family situation."

Bramwell smiled but the expression was tight. It didn't reach his eyes. "Yes. Every party is truly a crush and half the people in attendance have snuck in just to get a look at the Athawick party's gowns and hair. And the rumors run rampant. I think I've been featured five or six times in barely blind items in the *Scandal Sheet.*"

"Are the items true?" Jonah asked quietly, gripping his chair arm just a little harder.

"Some of them, yes, but you know that rag. It's nonsense more than half the time." Bramwell rolled his eyes. "I shudder to think what they'll say after tomorrow."

Jonah straightened up. "What is tomorrow?"

"The opera. It's the performance of the year, people say. The regent will be there—there are rumors Princess Caroline will make some other move against him. And my mother and I will be sharing our box with Princess Ilaria and Queen Giabella."

Jonah's heart sank even as Bramwell continued talking casually about the arrow he had just flung directly into Jonah's heart. Such a public outing would, as Bramwell implied, set the gossips off. Because it meant something. The circling of the two families was entirely clear. And the end result was predictable.

"You're really going to do this, are you, Bramwell?" Jonah asked, interrupting the earl in the middle of his sentence.

Bramwell appeared taken aback and shook his head. "Do...what?"

"Marry her," Jonah said, as quietly as he could.

Gillingham's eyes went wide and he slid to the front of his chair as if he sensed he might have to intervene between the two men. Which made Jonah wonder how wild he looked, since Bramwell appeared entirely calm.

"I..." the earl said, and then bent his head. "I suppose the intention is not a secret, especially since you are so close to the family, I've heard. There are overtures being made in that arena, yes."

Jonah couldn't believe how unmoved this man seemed to be about this subject. He was talking about marrying Ilaria, who was beautiful and sharp-witted and frustrating and wonderful. A woman one couldn't help falling in love with.

Jonah blinked. *He* had fallen in love with her. Not just in the past few weeks when they'd been reunited, but back on Athawick two years before. He had loved her then. It seemed painfully obvious in this moment.

And this man would marry her. This man who didn't seem to give a damn.

"Is that what you want, Thomas?" Gillingham asked gently, his attention fully shifted to Bramwell now.

Bramwell hesitated for far too long, and then he shrugged. "I… sometimes what we want cannot be taken into account in these situations. We must do what is right. What is beneficial to both her family and my own."

Jonah shook his head and growled past gritted teeth, "Ilaria is a person. You understand that, don't you? A woman with desires and dreams, not just a political pawn. Would you crush that for the benefit of your title?"

Now Bramwell's expression hardened and he looked at Jonah as if he truly understood him for the first time. "Why do you want to know so much about it, Captain Crawford?"

Jonah leaned forward in his chair, but before he could respond, Gillingham pressed a gentle hand against his chest. "Steady now, both of you," he said softly. "We are not in some private hall where you two could spar over…over what we both know this is over. We're at Fitzhugh's and half the men of the ton are watching you."

Jonah blinked and shook his focus off of the man across from him. It was true that eyes had slid to them as they talked. He supposed it made sense, given their individual proximity to the family of the day. If he swung on Bramwell, it would do no good. He would attack a man who didn't deserve it, it would change nothing about Ilaria's future, and it would cause nothing but trouble for all parties involved. He didn't want that.

He pushed to his feet. "My lord, Gillingham, please accept my apologies. I am out of sorts and I clearly need to take some air. Good afternoon."

The men both said their goodbyes, but he hardly heard them as he walked out of the club. He felt the eyes on him—he didn't care. All he could care about was the one constant refrain in his mind. One drumbeat.

He needed to see Ilaria.

Because if it was true that tomorrow she and Bramwell would make a first public outing where their arranged attachment would be obvious, everything would change. So he had to see her now, tonight. Because he loved her. That was a fact. He would lose her, another fact.

So he had to cling to whatever moments he could have now before they came crashing down around him.

CHAPTER 13

Ilaria tucked her legs beneath her as she sat on the settee next to Sasha. Remi was across from them, and they were all laughing at his tale of gaming the night before and nearly losing an entire royal carriage.

"If I hadn't drawn that four of hearts," he said. "Grantham would have had *me* drawn and quartered."

"You must be more careful," Ilaria said. "Honestly, he might not have you murdered, but imprisoned in a tower is a good possibility."

"God, he'd love that, wouldn't he? To tuck us all away while he goes about being kingly." Remi sighed and shook his head. "I suppose that is unfair."

Ilaria nodded. "It is. As I was reminded not that long ago, he has a great deal to carry. Perhaps more than we even know."

Remi frowned. "If that is true, then he should tell us. We're his siblings, after all, and I include Sasha in that assessment."

Sasha smiled gently at that. "I think he feels it is his burden, he doesn't want to place it on any of us."

For a short while the three of them were quiet, each contemplating what their brother might or might not be enduring. Then Remi shook his head, like he was clearing those less pleasant thoughts away. "Well, I hear Ilaria has a wonderful time ahead of her at the *opera* with the Viscount Bitteroot," he said.

"It's the Earl of Bramwell," Sasha said, and there was tension in her voice. Ilaria had to wonder if that was because she could tell what this subject did to her.

If Remi had meant to lighten the mood with his teasing, it didn't work. Ilaria felt herself deflating with the reminder. Her conversation with her mother came rushing back, as well, and she bent her head. "Yes," she said softly. "It seems there is no escaping it."

Remi winked at Sasha. "Sasha will go in your place if you don't want to. She seems to like Bramwell well enough."

Sasha pushed to her feet suddenly. "What do you mean by that?"

Remi leaned back in his chair. "I saw you two on the terrace at that little gathering…what, three nights ago? Four? I lose track with all the nonsense we are expected to perform."

Sasha walked away. "You want to talk about nonsense, there it is. I was just talking to the earl outside, nothing more."

Her tone was sharp, and it was clear she didn't think Remi's teasing was funny. It made both Ilaria and her brother stare at her in surprise, because Sasha was never so sharp.

"Very well, as you say," Remi said, holding up his hands as if in surrender. "My apologies."

Ilaria shook her head. "Well, I *wish* I liked him," she said. "I *wish* I could feel something for the man when he is being thrown in my path so obviously, and now it will be so publicly."

Remi's brow wrinkled and he moved from the chair to sit beside Ilaria on the settee in the place Sasha had abandoned. He took her hand, and suddenly his blue eyes, the ones he and only he had inherited from their father, softened.

"I'm sorry, Lari," he said, reverting back to a childhood nickname that hadn't been used in years but made her smile despite the pain that had settled in her chest. "Life is wickedly unfair, I know."

"I realize it was silly to think I could marry for love," she whispered. "That any of us could, given our positions."

Remi nodded, but she could see he didn't understand. Her brother was the consummate rake—he had no interest in such things. He hadn't met anyone that could tempt him to give up his wicked ways and perhaps he never would.

"Sasha can," Remi said with a conciliatory smile for her.

Sasha turned from the fireplace and she was still frowning. "No. I will never marry for love," she said softly. "You may call me sister, but I am not and we both know that. I will spend my life as Ilaria's companion and occasional body double. And I will...I will do my best to help her be happy if I can."

Ilaria's lips parted at the sadness of her friend's description of her future and was about to address it when there was a light knock on the open parlor door. The butler for the home they were keeping for the Season stepped into the room slightly. "I'm sorry to intrude, Your Highnesses, Miss Killick, but there is a message that just arrived for Princess Ilaria and it was given with some urgency."

"A message at this hour for me, Greenly?" Ilaria said, giving her brother and Sasha a confused look before she crossed to take the folded message from the silver tray Greenly carried.

"Will there be anything else?" Greenly asked.

She stared at the message, which only had her name across it. Her heart was racing at the sight of it. She'd never seen Jonah's handwriting before, she realized that now. But she had no doubt this was it. She felt it in her bones. She felt it in the deeply disciplined edges and boundaries of it.

"No, thank you," Remi said when she didn't respond. "That will be all, I think."

The servant left the room and Ilaria rushed to the fireplace, her hands shaking as she broke the hastily melted wax seal and read the message inside.

Ilaria,

This is folly and yet I can't stop myself. I need to see you. Tonight. I will wait for you in the usual spot behind the garden. If you won't meet me, I will understand, but I hope I'll see you soon. I'm waiting there now and will stay for at least an hour.

Yours,

Jonah

She read and reread those words, felt the desperation of them and the connection.

"Who is it from that you go so pale?" Sasha asked.

Ilaria flattened the note to her chest and looked at Remi and Sasha, who were waiting expectantly. There were no two people she trusted more in the world, and in that moment, she had no choice but to give them some information.

"I...I have been spending a little time with Captain Crawford," Ilaria said. "Sasha knows that."

"It's from him?" Sasha burst out, and snatched the letter. She read it and her eyes went wide. "Ilaria!"

"Well, it's not fair that I don't get to see it," Remi grunted, and took the paper next.

Ilaria huffed out a breath. "*That* was a private correspondence."

"Not anymore," Remi said with a chuckle. When he'd read it, his gaze lifted and the playfulness was gone from his look and his tone. "Ilaria..."

"Oh, please don't take a serious tone. I get that enough from Grantham and Mama." She snatched the note back. "I know I'm being a fool, but this is my last chance to be so. Tomorrow everything will change, won't it? Within a few days, perhaps a week or two, my life will be set in stone and I'll never have the opportunity to do this again." She held up the note and shook it. "I'll never have the ability to see...to see him again."

"This is far more serious than I thought," Sasha whispered.

"It *can't* be serious," Ilaria corrected. "But it can be mine, just for one more night. Will you help me? Or at least not thwart me."

Remi sighed. "I won't stop you. But I'm going to go down with you."

She drew back. "You're playing protective older brother then?"

He shrugged. "I have the costume, I might as well since there's no one else to do the duty." He looked her up and down. "Are you wearing that?"

She glanced at herself. She was wearing a rather plain gown because she and the others had been staying in. "I…"

"No, she's not," Sasha said, grabbing for her hand. "If this is your last hurrah, you're going to have it in all your glory. I'll help you."

Ilaria might have argued, but the fact was she did want to look as pretty as she could for Jonah. So she let Sasha drag her from the room to prepare for what might be the last night they would share together, at least privately.

And she tried not to contemplate too closely how much pain that idea brought her.

When the gate opened and Ilaria stepped into the moonlight, Jonah pushed from the wall with a gasp. She was stunning in a dark green gown that clung to her curves with mouthwatering beauty. Her dark hair had been done to perfection, framing her face. When she smiled at him? Oh, the love he could now admit, if only to himself, that he felt for her was almost overwhelming. He wanted to shout it from the rooftops, to claim it with word and deed until no one could deny it.

He moved toward her, but came to a halt when Prince Remington stepped out behind her. Normally the man was a court jester, but tonight he looked serious as the grave as he followed Ilaria to Jonah's side.

She met Jonah's eyes and shrugged. "He was with me when your note arrived and wanted to escort me to you," she explained quietly.

Remi held his stare. "I assume you can be trusted with her."

Jonah almost didn't know what to say. He truly couldn't be trusted. He would protect her from harm from others, of course. He would never hurt her or make her do something she didn't want to do. But he couldn't be trusted, because he loved her. And that made him blind to oh-so very much.

"He has always protected me," Ilaria said when Jonah didn't answer the question.

Remi shrugged, and then he squeezed Ilaria's hand. "Have fun, be careful."

Jonah guided her to the passenger-side of the phaeton and helped her up, but as he came around the back of the vehicle, Remi blocked his path. The prince leaned in closer. "I may seem like a fool to you, Captain. Perhaps I am. But if you hurt my sister, I want you to understand that I will *end you.*"

Jonah cleared his throat. In truth, he was happy to see Ilaria so protected by her family. He nodded. "Understood."

"Good night," Remi said, a little brighter and louder so that Ilaria would hear. Then he turned on his heel and went back into the garden, shutting the gate behind himself.

Jonah climbed up next to Ilaria and urged the horses into a trot back out onto the street.

"Jonah," Ilaria began.

He shook his head. "Please don't speak."

She wrinkled her brow. "Why?"

He glanced at her from the corner of his eye. "Because I'll talk myself out of this. Mask on the seat beneath you."

She smiled slightly and tugged the mask from beneath herself. "Back to Donville?"

"It's ours, isn't it?" he said softly.

She nodded. "Yes. More than any other place in this city, it belongs to you and me."

For the rest of the ride, they sat in silence, but it wasn't uncomfortable. She rested her head on his shoulder and he could almost pretend they were allowed to be together, allowed to be so close. That this wasn't a last, desperate night to steal rather than earn.

At Donville, they both put on their masks and he maneuvered

them through main hall. Neither of them looked at the games around them. Tonight wasn't about games.

A private room was provided, and after he had locked the door and closed the peeping window, he turned toward her and tugged off his mask. She did the same, and for a heartbeat they only stared at each other.

She mouthed his name, not said it, just mouthed it, and it broke him. He crossed to her in a few long steps, caught her cheeks and dropped his mouth to hers. She lifted into him, clinging to him like he was a life raft on the stormy seas.

They staggered back, falling against the soft bed in a tangle of arms and legs and mouths and tongues. He partially covered her, arching against her as he slowed the kiss, deepened the kiss, tried to put aside desperation so he could savor this. Worship her.

How long they kissed, he couldn't have said. It might have been a moment, it might have been a lifetime. He lost himself in her and he didn't want to be found. But at last he lifted his head and looked down into those warm brown eyes that were so soft with emotion and bright with desire.

He traced the line of her jaw with a fingertip. "I want to say something and I know it isn't fair. It isn't right."

She blinked up at him. "What is it?"

"I...want you, Ilaria. I have wanted you probably from the first moment I saw you. You were standing with the royal party to greet the regent and his honor guard at the dock in Athawick and my heart...I wanted you then and I pushed it down, crushed it down. I should do the same now, but I need you to know that I want you so very desperately."

She blinked. "You've told me more than once that we can't...we can't make love. What changed?"

He shook his head. "Because tomorrow you will go out in public with...with *him.*"

There was no need to clarify who *him* was. She turned her face. "How do you know that?"

"I saw him earlier this afternoon. He mentioned the opera and I knew, I *know*, what will happen after that."

"Yes," she said, and didn't look back at him.

He cupped her jaw and turned her face so that their eyes could meet. "After that happens, we won't be able to do this anymore."

Her dark eyes went glossy with unshed tears. "I know that, as well."

"So if all we have is tonight, then I have to tell you what I need." She nodded, but he didn't allow himself to kiss her again even though he wanted so desperately to just lose himself in her all over again. "If you don't want to do anything more than lie in each other's arms and kiss or have me pleasure you, I'll understand that. I don't want you to think you can't say no. But I will regret it the rest of my life if I don't ask. And I fear I'll already regret a great deal when it comes to you."

She shivered at the confession and then cupped the back of his head. "Just like you, I've wanted this for a long time. Perhaps we should deny it, perhaps we should walk away and try to forget this connection we both feel. But I can't. I won't. I want you, too, Jonah. And I want this tonight, here in this bed, in this place. So please—" She drew his mouth closer. "Make me yours, even if it's only for this stolen moment."

He brought his lips back to hers, this time with more purpose and drive. With her permission given, he sank into the love and desire he felt, knowing it would only be this one time, so he had to make it remarkable. For her.

For him.

CHAPTER 14

Even though nothing had changed between them—the future was still coming and it would end this soon enough—when Jonah kissed her again, Ilaria no longer felt his desperation. She wrapped her arms tighter around him, sinking into the taste and feel of this man and tried to forget that this was all they could ever share.

"I want to see you," he whispered against her mouth.

She nodded, cupping his face as they sat up together, following him to his feet. She only broke away to turn her back so he could unfasten her gown. He did so slowly, letting his fingertips graze her skin as he parted the buttons. She shivered as he pushed the dress forward. She pulled it from her arms, then turned to face him as she slowly lowered it and gave her hips a shake to allow the silk to pool at her feet.

She only wore a chemise beneath and he shut his eyes with a quiet curse before he reached out a hand and touched her bare shoulder. He looped a finger beneath her chemise strap and she gasped. Together they watched as he lowered it, draping the thin scrap of fabric at her elbow and letting it fall away from one breast.

He stared. "You are so beautiful."

She shrugged from the other strap and pushed the chemise away so she was naked but for her stockings and slippers. "I hope I'll not be the only one naked tonight."

He was still staring, and he blinked as if coming back to reality. "Whatever you wish."

She sat down on the edge of the bed and watched him as he undressed. He did so slowly, almost as if he wanted to drag out this night as long as possible. She didn't blame him. If this was their fantasy realm, their dream world, she didn't want to wake up.

He threw his jacket behind him, unwound his cravat, removed his shirt, and she caught her breath.

"Wait," she whispered, rising to move toward him. He was beautifully made, with a defined chest and shoulders and a flat stomach. A line of red, curly chest hair trailed into his trouser waist, and she had the strongest desire to follow it with her tongue.

One she refused to resist. She placed her hands on his chest, reveling in the increased thud of his heartbeat when she touched him. In the way his eyes fluttered shut as he let out a long sigh. She pressed her lips to the side of his neck, tasting the hint of salt to his skin, like the sea he loved and had lost. Her mouth trailed lower, and she sucked and licked a path to one pectoral. She swirled her tongue over his flat nipple and he dragged a hand into her hair, cupping her scalp with a rumbling groan from deep in his chest.

She smiled against his skin and trailed lower, sinking back to the edge of the bed and tugged him forward so she could nuzzle his stomach with her cheek and then drag her mouth against the placard of his trousers, where his cock was clearly outlined.

"God's teeth," he muttered.

She glanced up at him. "I don't use teeth, Captain. Never fear."

His eyes went almost impossibly wide and she laughed as she unbuttoned his fall front, dropping the placard away to free his cock. And a fine cock it was. She shivered as she gripped his considerable length and stroked him once, twice, smoothing the droplet of his essence across the head with her thumb.

"Enough of that," he grunted, his voice harsh as he backed away, sat down on the settee before the fire and removed his boots with what had to be record speed.

He pushed out of the remainder of his clothing, but she had no time to admire the muscular lines of his thighs because he came across the room toward her, chest forward, shoulders back, like a hunter stalking prey. She yelped in surprise as he pressed her back to the bed, his mouth finding hers with increasing hunger and purpose.

She raked her nails across his back gently and he moaned into her mouth, his tongue driving all the harder. "You are making it very difficult to go slowly," he murmured, his voice muffled by their continuing kiss.

"Then don't go slowly," she whispered back, letting her hands drift lower to cup his hips, pulling him tighter against her so that his hard cock nudged her stomach.

He lifted his head and glared at her playfully. "My entire plan involves a lack of speed."

She arched a brow, giving him the best powerful princess face she had learned over the years. "And mine involves having you inside of me. So who wins?"

He laughed and she reveled in the sound. He was often such a serious person that she loved softening him.

He leaned his forehead against her shoulder and sighed. "I suggest a compromise," he said, and then gave her a wicked wink before he pressed one last kiss to her mouth.

Then he dragged lower, just as she had a moment before. He tasted every inch of her flesh, pausing at her breasts for a moment. He pressed them together, flicking his thumbs over her sensitive nipples to harden them, and licking them to soothe the sharp thrill of pleasure that followed. She arched beneath him, surrendering a shuddering sigh.

He switched to the opposite breast and repeated the action, scraping gently with his teeth, sucking and licking until her whole body felt like it was tingling and her hands were gripping the coverlet until she feared she might rend it in two.

He glanced up at her, as if he was checking her response as he moved lower down her body. She circled her hips as he neared them, knowing what he would do, already well aware of the pleasure he could bring with that wonderful mouth.

"Seems a bit unfair to get this twice from you when you have yet to take any pleasure yourself," she gasped as he parted her thighs and settled between them.

"Oh, trust me, Your Highness, I get a great deal of pleasure from making you come undone," he growled, his voice rough and breath hot on her flesh before he parted her folds and licked her. "Just as pretty as I pictured in that dark hall," he murmured.

She lifted into him, and he didn't speak again as he dove into his work. He gave with gusto, watching her so he would know when he'd sucked and licked her to the edge and backing off to allow for further torture. She was sweating and panting after he'd done that a few times, and she sat up on her elbows and glared down at him.

"Please!" she gasped.

He smiled. "There's the magic word."

He began to focus his tongue on her clitoris without stopping, increasing the pressure as she flopped back on the pillows with a harsh moan. And just as she reached the climax and began to fall, he pressed a finger, then another, inside of her.

She gripped him as she came, her body twitching and writhing against her will as wave after wave of deep and powerful pleasure overtook her. As she gasped for relief, he withdrew his fingers and crawled up the length of her body, pressing his mouth to his. Once again, she tasted herself on him and it made her even hungrier for more.

She caught his hand, still sticky with her pleasure, and lifted it to her mouth. He drew back a fraction, their eyes locking. Together they licked his fingers clean, their tongues brushing and tangling around them.

"Fuck," he muttered.

She opened her legs wider, offering a place there for him. "Please," she whispered a second time, knowing now what it meant to him when she said that little word.

He shook his head. "You are a wonder. I'm going to be ruined for anyone but you."

She knew he meant it as a teasing compliment, and yet it stung. If this was to be their only time together, she *did* want it to be memorable. It already was, it always would be.

But she didn't want to ruin him. She didn't want to be ruined, either. She didn't want to think of Jonah any time her future husband—probably the poor Earl of Bramwell—touched her. That seemed so unfair to them both.

And yet she feared that was exactly what would happen. But she couldn't stop this. She needed it more than she needed to be wise.

She caught Jonah's toned hips and pulled. He followed that physical order and eased closer, rubbing the head of his cock through the wet evidence of her pleasure before he slowly began to ease into her waiting body.

It had been a while since she did this. Years since she'd wanted someone enough to surrender her body to them. This was different than any of those meaningless times when the attraction had been purely physical, a pleasant way for a bored woman to pass some time.

With Jonah it was something else when he filled her inch by wonderful inch. When he fully seated himself inside of her, it was like she truly became one with him. She stared up into his face, which was as bright with amazement as she knew her own to be, and one truth became desperately clear.

She loved this man. It wasn't a surprise to recognize it. It was just…true.

So when he thrust gently, then harder and faster, she lifted into him, pouring that feeling she could never say out loud into him. Hoping he would feel it, that they would somehow make some tiny part of this permanent, even if the world would intrude and far too soon.

She wrapped her legs around his hips, she met him stroke for stroke. She drew his mouth to hers and tangled their tongues just as they tangled their bodies and her body, still on edge from release a moment before, quickly found its way back there again.

When she came, she keened, jolting her hips hard against his, trying to bring him with her. He didn't resist. His neck flexed, veins suddenly outlined against the muscle. He drew her out as far as he could and then pulled away, splashing his seed across her belly as he murmured her name against her mouth.

He collapsed across her, his arms tightening, like he could cradle her here forever and not let this night end. And for a brief moment, she wondered if that were true.

She pressed a kiss against his neck, her fingers flexing against his back. "Does it have to only be tonight?"

He had been relaxed against her, his face buried in her shoulder while his breathing slowed, but now he tensed and lifted his head. "Ilaria…"

She pursed her lips at that tone to his voice. "I'm not saying there aren't barriers."

He pushed away from her, leaving her arms. From his expression, it was clear he didn't believe there was another way. Or perhaps he simply didn't want to pursue it. She wasn't certain of which, and that cut her to the bone.

"You say *barriers* like it's simple. This isn't simple."

"Couldn't it be?"

"Your family has plans," he snapped, and ran a hand through his hair. "You know this, it's been drilled into you since the moment you arrived in London. This isn't a normal circumstance and we can't pretend it is."

She followed him from the bed and caught up her clothing. She dressed as she spoke, shoving the chemise over her head. "Why not? How many families in this country look to make advantageous matches? And why couldn't we find an advantage to ours? You are a landowner, a gentleman—"

He threw his head back, his frustration plain. "No, I'm not, Ilaria. I'm not a gentleman. I'm a bastard. Do you understand? I'm a bastard son of a third son. The only reason I'm a *landowner*, as you put it, is because he…he couldn't ever see me for what I was."

She stared at him in surprise as he walked away from her, padding naked to the fireplace where he stared into the flames. She saw the tension in every part of him. The pain she had never fully understood existed at the core of him.

"Jonah," she whispered.

He shook his head and faced her, then sighed and came back. "Put the dress on," he said softly. He held her hand as she stepped in and then put her back to him as he buttoned it. "There's no reason to go into particulars that will only make this more difficult," he said, his tone gentler, but firm. "Your family is already well-aware of my background, I'm sure. They might accept me as an acquaintance…even a friend. But as a husband for the only sister of the King of Athawick? No."

Her shoulders rolled forward. He wasn't wrong. "But if we talked to them…"

He turned her to look at him and sighed. "Or we can accept what we already knew coming into this room tonight. All we have is what we just shared. And it was wonderful, Ilaria. I regret nothing. But this is all it could ever be and it has to be over now."

She flinched. "Do you say that because you believe it…or do you say it because you don't want to fight for me?"

His eyes came briefly shut and his mouth twisted like that question was a knife to his heart. But when he looked at her again, there was a hardness to his expression. "If it will help you to believe I don't care, then I have no choice but to allow it."

She backed away, staring at him in disbelief that he would surrender. This man who had fought in actual wars, this man who had stood up for a worthless lay about of a prince...but he would not fight for her. Not even try.

"I…" She shook her head. "I understand. I need a moment."

With that she grasped her mask, slid it back over her head and hurried from the room. She heard him calling, knew he couldn't follow right away because of his state of undress. And that was good because she couldn't take any empty platitudes in that moment.

She re-entered the great hall with all its erotically charged energy and passionate revelers, and for the first time, being there was like a cruel taunt. She stumbled through the room, trying to find a place where she could breathe for a moment, but she kept being jostled by laughing revelers.

She staggered and stumbled against a person. He turned, and she gazed up and immediately recognized his bright, piercing eyes. It was the same man who had come to talk to her during her last trip to Donville.

He gripped her arms with a wicked smile. "Good evening…*Ilaria*," he said quietly.

For a moment the rest of the room faded away and only this man's harsh voice saying her name remained. He knew who she was. He knew what she was. This encounter, the one before…it had all been part of some plan. It had to be.

She yanked back, struggling to escape the hard grip of his fingers against her bare arms, but he didn't release her. Without thinking, she slammed the heel of her slipper against his boot as hard as she could. He released her and she tumbled to the floor, her head bouncing off the wood.

The world began to go darker and the last thing she was aware of was her attacker rising up over her, a knife in his fist. And then…nothing.

CHAPTER 15

Jonah was barely back in his clothes as he raced into the main hall at the masquerade. He searched for Ilaria and found her instantly, halfway across the ballroom floor...and she was being held by some stranger. She was pulling away and Jonah began to run toward her, shouting, though he couldn't be heard above the crowd.

She fell. He wasn't sure if she'd been hit or just stumbled, and when the crowd parted in shock, he saw she was lying still on the floor. The man who had attacked her rose up, a knife in hand, and Jonah realized he wouldn't reach her in time. He wouldn't stop this man from killing her.

"No!" he screamed, but before the killing blow could be stuck, Marcus Rivers appeared out of what seemed to be nowhere, hitting the attacker with his considerable frame and sending the two of them falling away from Ilaria. The knife clattered away, bouncing back toward Jonah, and he picked it up in a daze, pocketing it and the piece of cloth that was wrapped around the handle.

With his heart pounding, Jonah dropped to his knees as he reached Ilaria, skidding the last few inches as he took her in his arms.

"Please," he whispered, and looked up in time to see the man who had tried to kill her thrust Rivers away and run at full speed away into the crowd.

"Fucking follow him!" Rivers bellowed, and half a dozen men complied, running after the man though he had a head start. He pivoted back to Jonah and Ilaria. "I think we'd best move—the crowd is getting restless."

Jonah looked around at the people who were beginning to gather around them, whispering and pointing. He nodded and swept Ilaria up. She made a soft sound and turned her face into his chest.

"Follow me," Rivers said to Jonah, and then spoke to the crowd, "The young lady will be fine and the culprit will be apprehended by my men, I assure you. Please, go back to your pleasures."

The music lifted from somewhere in the room, and Rivers guided Jonah through the throng, past the guard at the bottom of the stairs that led to his office. As he pushed into the big room that overlooked the club below, his wife, Annabelle, leapt to her feet from behind the desk.

"What in the world?" she began as she raced around the desk and followed Marcus and Jonah into the bedchamber attached to the office. Jonah set Ilaria down on the bed and smoothed her hair back from her head, careful not to disturb the mask she had put back on before she fled the room a short while before. A small bruise was forming on her temple.

"It's Princess Ilaria," Rivers said softly.

Jonah jerked his head up. "You knew?"

"I deduced her identity after the last time we spoke," Rivers admitted.

Jonah blinked. "How?"

"Your relationship to the family, the fact that you were so desperate to keep her a secret, to protect her." Rivers shrugged. "And the sketch made of her in the paper was quite good. The lips."

Annabelle leaned closer. "Oh yes, I see it."

"I think we must send for her brother," Jonah said.

Rivers nodded, and he and Annabelle departed the room. When Jonah was alone with Ilaria, he kissed her forehead. "Wake up. Please, wake up. I love you."

She groaned a little, her fist gripping on his lapel as she opened her eyes. "Jonah?" she murmured.

He nodded, relief flooding him as tears leapt to his eyes. "Yes."

"That man," she said, lifting from the pillows and then collapsing back. "Oh, that makes me dizzy."

"You hit your head," he said, and examined her eyes. Her pupils looked fine, which was a relief. He'd seen men felled by head injury, but hers didn't seem to be as dangerous. "Did he strike you?"

"No," she groaned. "He grabbed me. When I pulled away, I fell. Jonah, he was the same man who approached me a few nights ago. The one you frightened away."

He wrinkled his brow. "You're certain?"

"Yes," she whispered. "And he…he knew who I was. He said my name."

Jonah gritted his teeth. That was certainly not good. And all the more reason to report this situation to the king as soon as possible. He grabbed for her hand and squeezed gently. "I'm going to step out. I must talk to Rivers. Just rest now. You're safe."

She released his hand with a shaky sigh and he got up and left her, as much as he didn't want to do so. He wasn't lying. She was safe in the room in this fortress. But he wasn't sure if that would apply once she left here. Because if this man who had approached her tonight had known her identity, that could mean nothing good.

Ilaria had lain in the bed for a while, she didn't know how long because the room would not cooperate and stop spinning. Too long. Now she struggled to sit up. Her head throbbed. It was getting better, but the bruise on her temple pounded beneath the strap of her mask. She reached up and touched it as a pretty woman with chestnut-brown hair and friendly eyes entered the room.

"Would you like to remove that?" she asked, stepping up to the bed.

Ilaria leaned away. "I-I shouldn't."

"There now," the lady said as she sat down beside Ilaria on the edge of the mattress. "I know who you are and your identity is safe with me, Your Highness."

Ilaria shut her eyes. "Does everyone know?"

"No. My husband did, and he told me after you were brought up here." The lady carefully unfastened Ilaria's mask and pulled it away, tilting her head to look at the bruise. "I'm Annabelle Rivers. This is my husband's club."

"I would normally say I'm pleased to make your acquaintance."

"These aren't the best of circumstances, I know," Annabelle said with a friendly smile. "But I hope I can assure you that your identity will remain private. Even if it weren't in our own best interest to keep the anonymity this place requires, my husband and I are not of a cruel bent."

"Thank you," Ilaria said, and felt she could trust this woman's words were true. There was just something about her. "Is Jonah…"

"He and my husband went to talk to his right-hand man. Paul will fetch the king."

"No!" Ilaria said. "He can't…"

"You were just attacked and thanks to that knock on your head, it would be better if you stay here a while longer," Annabelle said. "Someone in your family must know about this."

Ilaria rested back on the pillows with a groan. "Grantham will be so angry with me. And my mother—oh, I shudder to think of the look on her face."

"You won't be in…in danger, will you?" Annabelle asked gently. "From them?"

Ilaria's mouth dropped open. "Oh no, nothing like that. They'll just be disappointed in me."

"Ah. Well, that can cut just as deeply."

Ilaria worried her lip. "You see a great deal of women in danger?"

"From time to time," Annabelle said. "The nature of our club makes it a safe place for courtesans and lightskirts to make a little coin. Marcus does not require a percentage and the guards protect them. Other women are here simply for pleasure without any other kind of transaction and are more open with themselves then they are allowed to be in the greater world. There is vulnerability to pleasure. Especially that of an anonymous nature between strangers."

Ilaria bent her head. In her case, she had experienced the vulnerability, but with a man who was anything but a stranger. She sighed. "Your rules for the club must help keep things safe."

Annabelle nodded. "They are meant to do so. But men are…*men*. And many are not to be trusted. From time to time, keeping this club a safe haven entails more than merely keeping watch on them. Like tonight."

"My world is so far removed," Ilaria breathed.

Annabelle looked over her shoulder. "It sounds like it won't be now. Prepare yourself."

Ilaria held her breath because she heard her brother's voice echoing from the other room and the door slammed. "Where the hell is she?"

Jonah had not expected the entire royal family of Athawick to arrive at the secret back entrance to the Donville Masquerade, but that had been what happened. The moment Grantham exited the carriage, his anger was plain. As was his concern for Ilaria as the family followed Rivers up the back stair to his office.

Now Jonah stood before the door where Ilaria was resting, braced for the censure about to come when Grantham realized exactly what was going on here.

"Where the hell is she?"

"Your sister is in the other room, Your Majesty," Rivers said, his voice calm but firm, as if he managed royalty every day. And he might. His club was a popular place.

"Rivers saved her life," Jonah said softly.

For a moment, Grantham stared at Rivers, all his gratitude clear in his eyes. But then he spun back toward Jonah. "I thought that's what *you* were supposed to be doing. Instead you let her come to this place, this...this sex club." He glanced at Rivers. "No offense, Mr. Rivers."

"None taken," Rivers said mildly.

"Grantham," Queen Giabella said. "Why don't we let these gentlemen explain? And I want to see my daughter."

"I'm here."

The entire room pivoted as the door to the back chamber opened and Ilaria stepped out, Annabelle Rivers at her side. Jonah flinched at how tired she looked, how worn down and still afraid. His foolish actions had put her in this position and he hated himself for it.

"Ilaria," Grantham breathed, crossing to her and tugging her in for a gentle hug. Jonah watched her collapse against her brother a little, leaning on him for support.

When Grantham pulled away, Ilaria stared around the room. "Why in the world would all of you risk coming here?" she asked. "You could be seen and the stir that would create is—"

The queen silenced her by stepping up to embrace her. "As if I could hear that my daughter had been injured and not come to her," she said, her voice shaking, tears sparkling in her dark eyes.

Prince Remington embraced her after her mother had released her and Ilaria's companion, Sasha, did the same. They each said something to her that no one else in the room could hear, but Jonah didn't have to guess what it was. Both of them had helped in her escape her earlier in the evening and their guilt was plain on both their faces.

Once the family had stepped away from her, Granthan's face hardened. "You have some explaining to do."

"I know," Ilaria said softly. "But please don't shout. None of this is anyone's fault but my own."

"Why don't we all sit?" Annabelle Rivers said. "I have tea or something stronger. Please." She motioned to the settee and the chairs scattered about the office.

There was a moment's hesitation before Queen Giabella led Ilaria to the settee. Her lead was one the rest else followed, and soon the entire party was seated, save for Jonah and Rivers, who exchanged a brief, knowing glance with him before he handed him over a whisky.

He downed it in one gulp and said, "I don't even know where to begin."

Ilaria met his gaze. "From the beginning. None of this is Captain Crawford's fault. I came here of my own volition, and he simply intercepted me and tried to help."

She was lying. Trying to protect him despite the fact that Sasha and Prince Remington knew the truth of how this night had started.

"Yes," Grantham said. "I asked him to do so. To watch you because I feared you might make a desperate choice in your anger toward me. Though not quite this desperate."

Ilaria stared at Jonah. "Wh-what? You were…were you spying on me for my brother?"

He winced. That wasn't the way he'd wanted her to learn that fact. But perhaps it was best that the truth was out in the open. "Yes," he said softly.

She stared at him wide eyed for a moment, and then she lifted her chin and a calm went over her face. The same mask she wore for others but had begun to discard around him. How it hurt to see it back.

She cleared her throat. "This was my third time coming here," she admitted.

"Ilaria," he mother murmured, a hand coming up to cover her mouth.

Ilaria shrugged. "You may express your disappointment at length later, all of you. But perhaps I should first tell you what brought us to tonight."

Grantham folded his arms. "I think that's a good idea. Because it isn't every day that a princess of Athawick is attacked. I want to know who did this, I want to know why and I want this person brought to justice. I will do everything in my power to make sure that happens. So tell me."

CHAPTER 16

Ilaria saw the steel in her brother's eyes, and it reminded her of their father. The cold, distant king, the man with ice in his veins. Only Grantham wasn't quite that. The way he'd clung to her when he hugged her told her how deeply he loved her. And she loved him. Even if she hated that his direction had been why Jonah lied to her.

She cleared her throat. "The first time I came here, I was jostled in the crowd. When I got into the carriage, I realized my gown had been…well, I told myself it was torn. But it was sliced. With a knife."

She watched as Jonah's lips parted. "You…you didn't say anything when I saw you next."

Grantham tossed a glare at Jonah. "And you said nothing to me about my sister coming here. So I suppose we were all kept in the dark."

Ilaria caught her brother's hand. "I asked Jonah—Captain Crawford—not to tell you about my being here. He kept watch over me, just as you apparently asked and he protected my secret as I asked."

Grantham gave Jonah another look but said nothing. "Continue."

"The second time I came here…" She looked again at Jonah as she thought of that night in the hallway when he'd dropped to his knees in the hallway and made her come until she could hardly breathe, hardly speak. "The second time I was approached by a man, the same one from tonight. I thought he was just being forceful in his interest, but when he walked away he called me princess."

Now Jonah took a long step toward her. "Ilaria! I asked you what he said."

"And I lied," she admitted. "I suppose we're even on that score. I tried to convince myself it was just some silly endearment said by a man who was too familiar. It's obvious now that he knew who I was all along. And he must have been planning his attack."

"How did he attack you?" Remi asked.

Ilaria looked to Jonah. She couldn't say it, she hoped he could see that. And he did, for he stepped forward and told them all about her fall and the knife and the struggle afterward that she had not been conscious to see. With a shudder, he withdrew the knife in question from his pocket.

"He dropped this," he said, holding it out.

Grantham got up and stared at the knife, taking it and yanking the fabric that was wound around the handle, rending it from the weapon and unfurling it. The flag was similar to the flag of Athawick, with its swan centerpiece and dancing whales to each side. Only instead of being blue and white, the background was black, the swan and whales a disturbing blood red.

"This is the flag of the rebellion," he whispered, holding it out toward Jonah once again.

"Rebellion?" Queen Giabella said. "What are you talking about?"

Grantham's jaw set and the rage in his face was nothing like Ilaria had ever seen. "Grantham," she whispered.

He paced to Rivers' desk and slammed the knife down on the tabletop, tossing the cloth next to it. He faced Rivers and Annabelle, "I realized this is your establishment, Mr. Rivers, and that you saved my sister's life tonight, for which I am eternally grateful. But what I am about to say is highly sensitive."

Rivers straightened his spine and Ilaria caught her breath. There were few people who had ever stared down her brother when he was in full king mode. But there was no hesitation to the club owner as he did just that. "I assure you, Your Majesty, that highly sensitive is my business. I recognize your hesitation to speak of private things, but those private things have entered my club now and threatened more than just your sister. So I won't leave." He inclined his head slightly. "There may even be a chance that I can help."

Grantham held Rivers' stare for a long moment, sizing him up, Ilaria thought. And then his expression grew less hard. "How?"

"I have connections," Rivers said softly. "And I can find things that perhaps even your courtiers would find difficult to uncover. I will offer my assistance in any way I can. But I must understand what happened in my club tonight and why."

Grantham ran a hand through his hair and looked at his family, then back to Rivers. "Very well. If I have your word that nothing I say here leaves this club, I don't suppose I have much choice."

"I swear to you that nothing you say will ever leave these walls," Rivers said, his gaze intense on Grantham's.

"I think I believe you." Her brother sighed heavily. "I suppose we're all being revealed as liars tonight. There has been trouble since I took the throne, a trouble I…I kept from all of you. There is a faction of our people who do not wish to have a monarchy anymore. Apparently they would go so far as to murder my sister to make that point abundantly clear."

As Sasha and Giabella gasped, Remi got up and crossed to the desk. He squeezed their brother's arm and picked up the flag. "They want you to, what…abdicate?"

Grantham nodded. "I'm receiving regular reports of their behavior from home. My advisors keep telling me to squash them, do it swiftly and harshly enough that it will never happen again during my reign. I've resisted—I do not wish to turn might against my people. But I never thought it would go this far."

"It seems odd it would." Remi fingered the cloth. "Odd to leave a calling card like this when they must know you are being pressured to retaliate. It feels too obvious."

Jonah cleared his throat. "I don't disagree with Prince Remington," he said softly. "But I think the matter at hand is that Princess Ilaria's life has been threatened, not once but three times in a short period. She is the target, no matter what the purpose of the attacks is in truth. And she must be our focus. Your Majesty, you asked me to do a duty. To protect your sister. And I have a suggestion as to how that needs to be carried out."

Grantham glared at him, and Ilaria had to force herself not to stand up, to insert herself between the men, defend Jonah in a way that would make their bond all the more obvious. "You have a suggestion after you have failed three times? After you allowed her to come here *three damned times*? For what purpose, I can only imagine."

Jonah flinched, but did not defend himself. He cleared his throat. "She needs to be removed from London," he said. "Secreted away, even if only for a short time while you investigate."

The queen got to her feet. "I don't disagree with Captain Crawford," she said softly. "My daughter must be protected at any cost."

"Then we should return home," Grantham snapped. "We could be on the boat by tomorrow."

"And destroy all your hopes for this visit?" Ilaria gasped in horror. "Undo all you've built?"

Jonah shook his head. "With all due respect, Your Majesty, I'm not sure that solves your problem. You are dealing with a person or persons who are driven to make some kind of point. They might be with this rebel group you describe, or your brother might be correct that they are not. Going home may not alleviate the pressure and if you cannot trust someone within your own household——"

Ilaria's stomach turned. "You think the culprit could be someone in the household?"

"No," Grantham said. "I cannot believe it."

"Then you'll leave yourself open to danger," Rivers said softly.

Grantham cast him a dark look, but Rivers seemed unmoved. "We don't like to think that those we trust haven't earned it. But it is sometimes terribly true. If Crawford could take the princess to safety, I could have my own people, people you can trust completely, look into this attack and its true origins."

"And how do we explain a missing princess?"

"You don't." Sasha's hands shook as she grasped Ilaria's. "I will stand in her place."

Grantham jerked his face toward her. "Sasha!"

"Please don't pretend that this isn't exactly what my presence was always meant for. Ilaria's schedule includes many events where most will not get too close to her. Even those who do, most of them only have seen sketches of her in the papers. I look close enough to pass if need be."

"And what of the Earl of Bramwell?" the queen interjected. "He would know you weren't Ilaria, so he would have to be told the truth."

"Yes. But I think he and his mother could be trusted." Sasha straightened her back. "We carry on just as you intended, only with me in the place of threat rather than Ilaria."

Ilaria clenched and unclenched her hands before her. "No. That is too dangerous."

"That is what a double does," Sasha said, touching her face gently.

"You are more than my double," Ilaria declared. "For God's sake, you are my friend. My sister. Grantham, Mama, tell her this is outrageous. Unacceptable!"

Sasha didn't allow the king or queen to do that. "It is *because* I am your friend and your…your sister that I am willing to take the risk. Now that the danger is known, I will be well-protected, I'm sure."

Grantham ran a hand through his hair as he paced the room. "I don't like this. I don't like that we would endanger Sasha, nor that the rest of my family may be at risk. I don't like that Ilaria would go away with Crawford. God's teeth, this is a mess." He rested both hands on the desk top and leaned heavily there.

Jonah stared at Ilaria for a moment. Too long. She felt how desperate he was, how afraid for her. How he would do anything to protect her, even at great cost to himself. "I can protect her, Your Majesty. I vow that to you now. I will die if need be to see her through this."

"Jonah," Ilaria whispered, and that elicited several looks from those in the room, including her brother.

Grantham let his breath out in a long sigh. "Fine. I see no other choice at present. Sasha, you and Remi go back to the house. Gather some of Ilaria's things...quietly. She won't return until we all feel this danger has subsided. No one else in the household must know what is happening. If anyone asks about her, she is taken ill and only Sasha and her mother are seeing her. We close off her room, we close off everything. Come back in the unmarked carriage."

"Understood," Remi said, taking Sasha's arm. "Come."

They left together quickly, and Ilaria stood to take her mother's arm. She felt how tightly her mother clung to her. How her fear seemed to ooze from her like an unstoppable flow. Her mother who had lost so much.

She hugged her tightly as Grantham, Rivers and Jonah all put their heads together to talk about their plan further. It didn't really matter what it was now. She would be sent away, with a man who she loved but still could never have. And she had no idea what would come of it all.

"Is he trustworthy?" her mother whispered against her shoulder.

Ilaria pulled away and looked into her mother's eyes. "Yes," she said. "I trust him. Whatever happened here, it was my fault, my willfulness that caused it, not his failure."

Her mother held her stare. "Including whatever is between you?"

Ilaria caught her breath. "Mama—"

"I must be very old in your eyes," her mother whispered. "But I assure you, I am not incapable of understanding what is right in front of me." She glanced over her shoulder at Jonah. "He is hand-some. I can see the attraction. But be careful, Ilaria. Whatever happens, the future remains unchanged. I cannot stop you from pursuing whatever you will pursue when I'm not there to act as a shield. But I don't want to see you hurt. Not by these blackguards who pursue you. Not by your own heartbreak."

"I know," Ilaria said, and glanced at Jonah again. "I won't."

She said those words, but they were lies. Deep in her heart she knew she might not, in fact probably could not promise that. Not to her mother. Not to herself. Not when she was finally alone with a man who held the key to all her happiness…and all her heartbreak.

To avoid the eyes of the public and to allow Ilaria more time to clear her head, they did not depart the Donville Masquerade until dawn, long after the club had cleared and the staff had gone home for the night. Jonah trailed behind the royal family, watching as they flanked Ilaria, bearing her up, speaking to her softly as they moved toward the carriages parked behind the club. When they had reached the one she and Jonah would escape in, she hugged each of these people who she loved and then the king, himself, helped her into the rig.

Rivers clapped a hand on his back, jolting Jonah from his obser-vations. He turned to face his friend. "I am sorry, Rivers, Annabelle, for all the trouble," he said softly.

Annabelle smiled gently, but Rivers tilted his head back and laughed. Normally he was such a serious person, Jonah almost didn't recognize him.

"Friend," Rivers said. "This isn't *trouble* in the slightest, I promise you. Just as I promise that I will do anything in my power to bring this to a swift and good end."

"Thank you." It was Grantham who replied as he stepped up to their small circle. Jonah looked back over his shoulder and saw the rest of the royal family had stepped away to their own rig and were climbing in, ready to go home after this unfortunate adventure.

"My pleasure, Your Majesty. My people will be in contact with you shortly," Rivers said, then took Annabelle's hand and the two stepped back into the club.

Which left Jonah alone with the man he had failed. They stared at each other for a beat, and then Grantham shook his head. "If I hadn't been so distracted, I would have noticed that you are in love with her."

Jonah set his jaw, but didn't deny the charge. This man was too intelligent to sport with on this topic. "I am dedicated to her protection," was all he said in reply.

Grantham looked at him closely. "I suppose you are. And she is an adult, despite the occasional fit of pique."

"But nothing changes," Jonah said softly. "I know that. She knows that. When this is over, there remain expectations that she will do her duty. And she won't fail you. At least not because of me."

"We know where you are staying with her," Grantham said. "And I will send word the moment we feel things are safe."

He turned as if to go, but Jonah caught his arm. The touch seemed to surprise the king, for he jolted and stared down at the hand clenched on his forearm.

"I know you know this, but I must repeat it," Jonah said. "Be careful with that information. You want to trust those in your employ, but until we are certain, only the family must know about Ilaria."

Grantham pulled his arm from Jonah's grip. "Yes, so you and Rivers say. I will be careful," he promised with a shake of his head. "And I'll ensure the rest are careful too."

"Good," Jonah said. "I hope we're both wrong about the threat."

Grantham drew in a long breath. "If you love her, then you must understand I love her too. She is my only blood sister, and if anything happened to her it would..." He bent his head. "It would destroy me. And my mother. It would break all of us. So please, whatever else you do or don't do, keep her safe."

Jonah was surprised by the emotion that wavered in the Grantham's voice, that was bright in his eyes in that moment. But it vanished as the king turned on his heel and walked away without a backward glance for Jonah or for Ilaria, staring out the carriage toward her family. Grantham thrust himself into the vehicle, and off it went. Ilaria sagged in defeat at the door to their rig.

Jonah moved to her, trying to look calm and in control when he felt anything but after the last twelve hours. She slid back to allow him entry and he climbed up. The driver—who Marcus had provided and vouched for, rather than a family driver—already knew the destination, and once Jonah was settled, the rig began to move.

He stared across the carriage at Ilaria. She had always seemed a big presence to him with her jewels and her crowns and her effortless confidence. Her entire life, she had been trained to come into a room and draw every eye to her, make every person feel as if she was the center of the world.

But right now she looked so small as she sat in the corner of the carriage seat, her head bent and her hands clenched in her lap. Her pain, her fear...they were palpable, like a drumbeat between them in the quiet.

"Ilaria," he said softly.

She lifted her gaze. "Why didn't you tell me the truth?" she whispered.

He hesitated. "Are you referring to the fact that Grantham asked me to watch you?"

She nodded.

"I thought," he began, and then he shook his head. "I thought you would try to escape me if you knew I was another person sent to thwart your desires. And, to be honest, I wanted to be near you."

She worried her lip at that admission. Foolishly made, considering their conversation earlier in the night when he had told her that they could have no future. When he had asked her to believe he didn't care about her. But so much had changed in the hours after that, including the fact that he'd almost lost her.

"So where are we going?" she asked, her voice suddenly rough.

He cleared his throat. "It's a small estate, not so far outside of London. We'll be there in a few hours. You should sleep if you can after all the evening's excitement."

She snorted out a breath. "As if I could get comfortable with everything that happened."

He hesitated a moment and then moved to her side of the carriage. She watched him but didn't recoil when he slid an arm around her. He pulled her to his side, and she shivered before she rested her cheek to his chest and wrapped an arm around his waist.

It was quiet for a while, almost to the point where he thought she might have fallen asleep already, but then she lifted her head to look at him. "Jonah?" she murmured.

"Yes."

"I'm...I'm glad you were there. I'm glad it was you. If I'd ever had to choose anyone, it would have been you."

She didn't clarify what she meant by that as she settled herself back against his chest and shut her eyes. She didn't need to really. He knew she meant to protect her. But also more. All the more that they couldn't have no matter how much they both wanted it.

He held her tighter as she slipped into sleep. He loved her. That was what mattered. So he would do anything in this world to protect her.

CHAPTER 17

"Ilaria."

Ilaria heard the voice through darkness and cuddled into the warmth around her even closer. "No, not yet."

"Ilaria."

Her name came again, and this time she recognized that it was Jonah saying it. She'd had this dream before, back in Athawick after his visit there, definitely since her arrival in London. If she opened her eyes, he wouldn't be there and she'd be empty again. But if she stayed in her dreams, she could pretend he was real.

"Ilaria."

She opened her eyes and jolted as she found herself looking up into Jonah's face. Everything came back in a rush and she sat up straight. The carriage was slowing now, and through the window she could see a little cottage outside with whitewashed walls and a pretty blue door.

"What is this?" she breathed.

"It is the place I had during my time in the Royal Navy," he said, and she heard the strain to his voice.

She glanced toward him. "And you didn't let go of it after you inherited?"

His jaw tightened and she saw the same pain she had witnessed when he talked to her about being a bastard the previous night. The still waters of his heart ran very deep, it seemed, and she wanted to explore them all. Only he refused to let her.

"No," he said softly. "This was the last vestige of the life I had before."

The driver opened the door before Ilaria could push further, and Jonah looked relieved as he stepped out onto the drive and extended a hand back to assist her in her departure. He said something to the driver, who nodded and moved back to pull the carriage to the back where the small stable was located.

"I warn you there are no servants here," he said. "I was here so rarely, I could not justify the expense. There's a woman in the village just up the lane who will bring food and do a little tidying for us. But there won't be fanfare."

"I don't think I want fanfare," Ilaria said.

"You have always had it—I hope that will be true."

She pursed her lips. "Do you think me an entirely silly person, Captain Crawford? I realize I've always been...*spoiled* might be the word some would use, but I hope that I have enough character to accept new circumstances with as much grace as I can muster. And the idea of not having to be *on* all the time is actually an intriguing one. I will make the best of this and prove you wrong if need be."

He shook his head, but he was smiling. "I have no doubt you will prove me wrong a hundred times in during our hopefully short stay here. But on your ability to make the best of things, I actually have faith in you. Go inside while I help our driver unload the rig."

She blinked in confusion at that idea and then realization dawned. "Oh...yes, because no servants."

He arched a brow at her and then guided her to the door. He unlocked it and opened it, motioning her inside before him.

She caught her breath. If the outside of the home was charming, the inside matched. The foyer had a tall ceiling and sunlight streamed in through the windows beside the door. There were double doors open to a parlor off the entryway and from what she could see through them, it had pretty white wainscoting and bright corners to sit and read. The house was cold at present, and everything was covered with cloths to keep the dust away, but she was already enchanted. No wonder he hadn't been able to sell this place when he inherited. Though she couldn't help but think about his expression when he told her that.

She stepped from the foyer into the parlor she'd been admiring. The brightness of the room came from the sunlight streaming from the bay window which faced out onto the lane. She moved toward it, running her hand over the sheet-covered chair near the fireplace across the room. She tugged and pulled the sheet away. A sparkle of dust filled the air and she waved her hand to clear it. Then she smiled and went around the rest of the room, pulling the sheets away and piling them in the middle of the room until everything was uncovered and ready to be used.

Then she stared at the fireplace. Wood was already laid there, and there was a flint set on the mantel to start it. She'd never done this, but she'd seen it many times. It couldn't be that hard, could it?

She grabbed the flint and knelt before the fireplace, worrying her lip as she pondered what to do next. She scraped the steel across the flint and a spark lit. She smiled as the mechanism became clear and went about scraping and scraping, letting the sparks fall onto the wood, and yet it never caught. She was beginning to get frustrated when she heard the clearing of a throat behind her.

She peeked back to find Jonah standing there, looking around the room. "You've been busy, princess."

"I thought I could help," she explained. "Since you said you had no servants. But I can't seem to figure out the fire." She scraped the flint again and the sparks fell on the logs. "See?"

His mouth twitched as if he found all this entirely amusing, then he stepped up and dropped down beside her on the floor. "You're trying to light the logs, but they're too large. See the smaller kindling and dry matter beneath?"

She tilted her head a little closer to his and peeked beneath the wood. "Oh, yes, I see."

"That will catch much easier." He took the flint from her and scratched it, letting the sparks fall. Unlike when she had done it, the lighter elements beneath the logs caught. He blew on them gently and her body clenched as she recalled him doing exactly the same thing between her legs the night before. It seemed like a lifetime ago now.

She cleared her throat and tried to refocus on the fire. "That is helpful. I suppose I'll have a great deal of practice while we're here."

He blinked at her. "Why?"

"Well, I'm not leaving you to wait on me hand and foot. I must try to be useful, mustn't I?"

Something shifted in his gaze. "What if I want to wait on you hand and foot?"

Their gazes held, and for the first time since she was attacked she no longer saw the concerned protector, but the lover she'd come to long for. She swallowed hard and leaned up toward him.

"Well, I wouldn't refuse you," she whispered, and then brushed her lips to his.

He was perfectly still for a moment, and then he made a soft groan in the back of his throat and cupped her neck, tilting her for better access as the kiss deepened. She wrapped her arms around him, holding him closer, letting the desire she felt for him build deep within her chest, her core, her everything.

He wouldn't allow it, though. He pulled away after far too short a time and scooted back, his pupils dilated and his breath short.

"I…I should show you the rest of the house," he said as he got to his feet. "Such that it is."

She nodded and her head no longer ached. Very good, considering how much she wanted to forget the events of the night before and focus on far more pleasurable pursuits. She allowed him to help her up. He released her immediately and didn't touch her again as he took her through the first floor of the place, which included a small dining room, a study and a kitchen.

"I've sent the driver along to the village to take a message to Mrs. Williams there. She's a widow who occasionally helped me here when I was in residence. She'll bring supplies and come around here and there to help."

Ilaria wondered if Mrs. Williams was a young widow or an older one, but had not the heart to ask. She simply nodded to acknowledge what he'd said.

Then he took her up the backstairs and into a hall. "There's a drawing room there," he said, pointing to a closed door. "And then the one…the one bedchamber."

"Oh," she said softly. "Just the one?"

He nodded. "It has always been my bachelor residence. I thought maybe in the future the drawing room down the hall could be transformed into a nursery if I ever married. But it isn't that yet."

She blinked. So he had thought about marriage and children, even in some distant way, in the past. She was rather jealous of that nonexistent woman and her children.

He dropped his gaze from hers. "You will have the bedchamber, of course," he said. "And I will take the settee in the drawing room."

Ilaria stared up at him, still seeing need in his gaze. Still seeing emotions that reflected her own. Ones she didn't want to ignore.

She caught his hand and drew him to the door, through it. "I would rather share the chamber."

He shut his eyes, and a ripple of emotion worked over his handsome face. Desire and duty, give and take, control and surrender. A war that she forced him to fight and hoped she would win, even though he had far more experience in battle.

"Ilaria," he whispered.

She reached around him and pulled the door shut. "Please," she said. "This is a gift, Jonah, this time together. I'm not letting it go, not after coming so close to losing my life last night."

At that he opened his eyes, and desperation flashed within the gray depths. He nodded. "Very well. This place is like a fantasy anyway, and I can't deny that I want you. Still. Always. Forever."

She shivered at that vow and watched as he moved into the room. He pulled the sheets that covered the big bed, and she worried her lip at the way he folded the edges so the dust wouldn't go everywhere.

"Did I…did I make a huge mess of your parlor downstairs?" she asked.

The corner of his mouth quirked into a smile. "I like your mess, Ilaria. It's…exciting."

Heat flooded her cheeks and she laughed. "You're kind to say so, but I'll try to learn. I don't want to be a burden to you, nor to anyone who comes here to help us."

He set the sheet aside and reached for her. His fingers threaded through hers and he tugged her against his chest. For a moment he simply stared down at her, his gaze darting over her face like he was trying to memorize the lines. Then he smiled again.

"You could never be a burden to me. Never." He bent his head and kissed her, and she forgot everything else. All the danger, all the uncertainty, everything but the pressure of his mouth on hers and the promise of passion in the way he held her close.

Jonah's hands shook as he cupped Ilaria's cheeks gently and kissed her slowly and deeply. He didn't want to rush this, even though his body declared a different intention. This whole experience was a dream now, one he would wake up from and far too quickly, so he wanted to savor every moment of it.

She lifted her hands to cup his wrists, a little sound of pleasure escaping her lips as she backed up toward the bed. His bed. Their bed for a little while. In a place where he could pretend they belonged together, that this wasn't a stolen moment.

She pulled from his kiss and looked up at him, dark brown eyes soft and pupils dilated with desire. "Don't think about the future, don't think about the past. Just be here with me."

He hadn't realized he'd been thinking so loudly, but she'd caught him. He nodded and then wrapped his arms around her. His fingers found the back of her gown, flipping each button free. He pushed her dress forward, then down around her hips between them so that it fell away. She kicked it aside as her fingers tugged at the buttons of his jacket. When it was open, her hands found their way inside, pressed to his waistcoat. Her fingers flexed there, pressure against his stomach, and it was an electric current through him, sending pleasure to every nerve ending.

This was wrong. Nothing about this had ever been right, not from the first moment he arrived in Athawick and saw Princess Ilaria holding out a hand to greet him and his heart had stuttered. Not since he saw her again and all the longing had come rushing back. Not since he foolishly let himself believe that one touch, one kiss, one night of pleasure would somehow ease this ache she caused in him. He knew now it would never end. It would stay with him forever, long after she was gone.

But none of that mattered when she looked up at him in the filtered sunlight coming through the gauzy curtains, her expression soft and welcoming. The previous evening she had asked why this couldn't last for more than one night. And now it could.

"You're thinking again," she whispered.

He smiled. "I'm always thinking, I'm afraid."

She sighed. "Then tell me what you're thinking about and maybe we can take care of it."

"I'm thinking that if we're going to do this, if we're going to let this time together be…this…then we'll need some rules."

"You want rules to go with how you—I'll use the crudest terms possible, Remi would approve—how you fuck me?"

His eyes went wide at that word coming from those pretty lips. Rarely had he heard a lady use it, but it was intoxicating watching her mouth form such a vulgar word. "Yes. That."

"Of course you do, you military men and your discipline."

"I think you've benefitted from my discipline," he murmured.

"And I'd like to again, so move along, Captain. We are wasting valuable time," she teased.

He playfully saluted her and then stepped away. As he spoke, he shed his jacket and carefully folded it across the back of a chair before he started unbuttoning his waistcoat. "We will only be here a few days, I would imagine," he said, and laid his waistcoat on top of the jacket.

She swallowed. "Er, yes. I assume so. This is a desperate measure taken by my brother because he isn't sure what to do next. But he's too clever and strategic not to work out a plan within short order and demand my return, both so he can control how I am protected and to move forward his plans for me."

Jonah heard the bitterness in her tone and hated how helpless she felt. How helpless he felt.

"So we must assume," he continued, untying his cravat and slowly winding it around and around his neck to loosen the long swatch of fabric. "That we will have limited time together. We must carefully plan what we will do with it."

She tilted her head. "What I want to do, Jonah, is stay in this bed and just...pretend like things won't change. Pretend that we could be like this forever."

His fingers fumbled as he moved to drape the cravat with the other items he'd already removed, and it fluttered to the floor instead. He made no move to pick it up.

"That is fine with me," he said softly. "More than fine. I can easily protect you if I've got you pinned to my bed, screaming out my name."

She swallowed. "Exactly. I'll be very obedient in that situation. And since we won't be inviting anyone else in...correct?"

He snorted out a laugh. "While that sounds intriguing, I think it best just to have it be the two of us."

"Very good. Then we won't have any problems with outsiders

threatening us. Unless that widow you mentioned, the one who cleans and cooks for you a bit, is the jealous type."

He cocked his head. "The lady, Mrs. Williams, is old enough to be my mother. Were *you* jealous?"

She folded her arms. "Had the widow in question been a beautiful young woman who was offering solace to a handsome former captain of the Royal Navy? Yes, I suppose I can admit that I would have been jealous."

The sense of pleasure that admission granted him was enough to make him focus on what he'd been doing once more. He unbuttoned his shirt slowly, taking his time because Ilaria had begun to squirm and he liked watching that, especially when she was only clothed in a short chemise.

"So we are agreed then," he said. "You and I will spend this small amount of time we have been granted exploring all the pleasure we can manage." He tugged the shirt over his head and she caught her breath, clutching her hands together in front of her. As he draped the shirt with the rest of his clothes, he let out a long sigh. "But Ilaria..."

She shook her head. "Don't say 'but Ilaria'...not like that. Not like you're about to tell me something horrible while you stand here looking like a statue in a garden."

He shut his eyes. "If we're going to do this, we must be honest with each other."

Her shoulders rolled forward a fraction and she sighed. "Very well. Burst this beautiful bubble. I'm ready."

"When your brother sends for you, when we return to London—"

"Then it's over," she said softly. She lifted her chin with defiance and strength. "You made that very clear last night, Jonah. I understood it then, even if I wished to escape it. I understand it now, and I think I have no choice but to accept it."

He should have been pleased about that. Her fighting the

inevitable was useless, and it had led her to danger. And yet there was no relief that she had agreed to his terms. Just a sense of loss.

One he couldn't take time to evaluate, because she stepped toward him, looping her fingers beneath her chemise straps as she did so and pushing the thin fabric to pool at her feet. She was naked and he stared at those lush curves that he wanted to worship for a while.

"Are you satisfied, Captain, that I understand the terms of the arrangement?" she asked softly.

He forced his gaze to lift to hers and he nodded. "I believe you understand, Your Highness. But I'm far from satisfied."

She smiled, that little wicked, knowing expression and moved the rest of the distance to him. She pressed her hands to his chest and slid them down slowly. When she reached the fall front of his trousers, she looked up at him.

"I think I can fix that," she whispered, pressing a kiss to his chest as she unfastened his fall front and let his now-fully hard cock bounce free.

CHAPTER 18

Together Jonah and Ilaria looked down at his cock. The little smile that quirked up the corners of her lips as she took him in hand did nothing to relieve his tension. She stroked him once, twice, and he dropped his head back with a long groan as pleasure streaked up his cock.

She pushed at his trousers, and managed to ease them down. They caught on his boots, but he didn't give a damn as she dropped to her knees on the floor and stared up at him. She stroked her cheek against his length and smiled.

"You've pleasured me twice with your mouth, Jonah," she whispered. "I think it's time I returned the favor."

His eyes went wide, and he opened his mouth to speak, though he had no idea what to say at that offer. She didn't give him the change to argue or agree, though. She darted her tongue out and swirled it around the head of him.

All words, all thoughts, emptied from his mind, and Jonah grunted as he dug his fingers into her hair. Pins scattered on the floor around them as her locks curled around his hands and her shoulders and his cock.

She smiled around him, then took him deeper into her mouth.

Deeper still. He pressed gently on the back of her skull, and she grunted as she took a little more. She sucked and he let out a breath of pleasure.

It had been a long time since a woman took him into her mouth. And none had ever been so good at it as this woman. Ilaria stroked and sucked, she swirled her tongue around his length, she withdrew until he almost popped from her mouth and she took until he felt her throat quiver against the head of him.

What was better was that she seemed to like doing this to him, for him. She moaned as she took, she stroked a hand over her naked flesh while she gripped him firmly with the other.

It was all building to an explosive release of that pleasure. He wanted to come this way, to have her drink every drop of him, but right now he wanted to be inside of her even more. To take her and feel her flex around him in orgasm.

So he tugged himself from her mouth and grasped her elbows, dragging her to her feet. His legs were still tangled in his trousers, and he didn't want to take the time to free them, not when his cock was actually throbbing in time to his rapid heartbeat.

He kissed her, hard and hot and fast, then spun her around so that her back was to him, bent her over the bed and cupped her sex from behind. She jolted back, her hips hitting his as she cried out his name in the quiet. She was wet, proof that she had enjoyed sucking him. He aligned himself to her, feeling her sex give way to him, flex as she welcomed him into her tight heat. Slowly, he took her, reveling in the quiver of her, the sound of her, the way she gripped his coverlet when he seated himself fully.

And then he fucked her. Not made love to her, not gently took her—no, this was animal. This was desperate. This was every pleasure he'd ever desired and every moment he had pushed away to be proper or right. He gripped her hips hard enough that she would likely have marks on them tomorrow, he drove into her body like a man possessed, and when she buried a hand between her legs to stimulate her clitoris and began to grip harder and harder against him, he was almost unmanned.

When she came it was glorious. She quaked around him in long, heavy waves, her back arched, and she cried out his name until it felt like it was music. Pleasure crashed through him, pulling him toward his own release, driving him harder and faster and wilder until he felt control snap. He withdrew, his seed splashing across her skin.

He grabbed her hips and rolled her on her back. Her skin was flushed pink with pleasure and she had a languid expression that grew shocked when he pushed her legs wide and dropped his mouth to her. He tasted the sharp tanginess of her release on her wet sex—he lapped it up, sucking her sensitive clitoris as she dug her fingers into his hair and ground up against him. She was writhing within moments, her breath short and sharp, her legs trembling around his shoulders, and then she let out a cry and twisted in his bed. His tongue was flooded with her flavor, she fluttered against him wildly and then she collapsed back, her eyes wide as she stared up at him.

He crawled onto the bed beside her, their legs dangling over the edge because they were cockeyed. She slung an arm over his chest and pressed a kiss to his neck.

"That was what I needed," she murmured. "You."

He didn't respond in words, but gathered her closer, memorizing the feel of her warm body against his. The way her breath slowed as she fell asleep in his arms. The way it felt as he did the same, sliding into a dream world that would never be better than the reality he had just experienced.

A reality that would end just like a dream soon enough.

~

Ilaria woke up slowly, cuddling into the warmth of the bed around her. She had been having the most wonderful dream about Jonah and his hands and his tongue and...

She opened her eyes and looked around at the unfamiliar chamber. She was naked, tangled in the sheets, her body beautifully tender from his touch.

Memories crashed back. Their time together in this bed had not been a dream after all. She sat up slowly. The light outside was far dimmer than it had been earlier in the day. How long had she been sleeping?

More to the point, when was the last time she'd slept so soundly? Not since her arrival in London, certainly. Probably not since the death of her father.

"Jonah?" she called out in the quiet, but he didn't respond. She got up. Her gown had been laid out carefully on the back of a chair. She stared at it. It buttoned along the back and she didn't think she could manage it. Had she ever dressed herself? That seemed like a skill one should have, though she'd never considered it.

She opened the wardrobe. Jonah's things hung here. Not many—she supposed most were at his home in London or the estate he had inherited. But a few shirts and some trousers were folded on the shelves of the wardrobe. She reached out to touch one of the shirts. Soft linen, beautifully made. She preferred him out of such things, but he did cut a fine figure when he was dressed.

She tugged the shirt from the stack and shook it out. It was big, far too big for her, but she pulled it over her head nonetheless and buttoned it. The long tails brushed her thighs and she could smell the lingering hint of Jonah on the fabric. She shivered and closed the wardrobe to take a longer look around the room.

It was a plain chamber. Whether it was that way because he no longer lived here as often or because he intended it to be austere, she didn't know. The fact was, she didn't know much about this man...the man she loved.

He was decent, he was kind, he was dependable. He was outrageously handsome, he was a wonderful lover. But she only had hints of his past. Of his dreams now that his life had changed.

She wanted more.

She left the room and gasped as the chill in the hall hit her bare legs. She wasn't accustomed to being so exposed, but there was little else to be done about it. She wandered down the hall, peeking into the drawing room he had mentioned when they first arrived. Jonah wasn't there, though, and the furniture was still covered in cloths, so it didn't look like he'd been there at all.

She came down the stairs, carefully and quietly so that if any other person were in the house, she would hear them before they heard her and then saw her in such a state. But the cottage seemed still as she came down. The parlor was empty, so she went to the next door.

When she opened it, she smiled. Jonah was seated at an oak desk. His jacket was off and his sleeves were rolled to his elbows as he leaned over the desk, writing. He glanced up when she entered and his quill froze, hovering over the sheet of vellum until a blot of ink dripped onto the surface.

"Ilaria," he breathed as he set the quill down and leaned back in his chair. "I must say I approve your choice of outfit. You in that shirt is…"

"Ridiculous?" she asked, turning around so he could see the full effect.

"My cock says otherwise," he muttered.

Heat filled her cheeks and she turned away slightly. "How long did I sleep?"

"Half the day," he said. "You needed it after being up all night and then the hasty escape. How are you feeling?"

"Better," she admitted. "Though I admit I was a little lonely when I woke up by myself. You must have needed the sleep as much as I did."

He shrugged. "Perhaps. But I also had things to do. Mrs.

Williams has come and gone. There is a larder full of food for us now—we will feast like kings."

"Oh, excellent," she said with a laugh. "I've always wondered how kings feasted...I've only ever feasted like a princess."

He smiled. "Then I'm happy to oblige that little...fantasy." His smile faltered a fraction and he cleared his throat. "I was just writing a letter to your family, telling them of our safe arrival. I'll have Mrs. Williams take it to be posted when she calls to check on us tomorrow afternoon."

"You think of everything," Ilaria said. She smoothed her hands over the shirt restlessly. "I would have dressed in my own clothing," she explained. "But I am useless, apparently. I might have a gown that fastens in the front, but I don't know where my trunk is."

He nodded. "There's a small adjoining dressing room to the chamber. The door isn't obvious. We put the trunk in there earlier. I'll show you when we go back up." He stood and came around the desk at last. "Are you hungry?"

She was about to nod when her stomach growled. They both laughed again. "Apparently," she said. "Lead the way to my kingly feast."

He motioned her toward the door and they walked up the hallway together. She was very aware of his presence at her side with every step, even as she tried to remain nonchalant and unbothered by it. He took her into the kitchen, and she sat at the small table there as he gathered food together for them.

When he placed a plate before her, she almost clapped her hands together in pure glee. He had piled cheese and meat and bread, along with olives and preserves. She dove into the food without much ladylike or princess-like grace. Her mother would have been horrified, she was certain, but she was too famished to care.

Jonah laughed as he poured them each some wine and then started in on his own plate. "When you came into my study, you said something that has been bothering me."

She tilted her head. "What is that?"

"You said you were useless."

She nodded as she took a sip of wine. "I *am* useless. I couldn't even dress myself."

He glanced down and let out a long breath. She followed the stare and found that his shirt had hiked up even more when she was seated, revealing almost the entire length of her thighs. She blushed at his regard but didn't adjust the shirt. Let him look. She wanted him to touch later.

He blinked, as if he were trying to clear his mind. "You are anything but useless, Ilaria."

"Am I?" she asked, chewing more thoughtfully. "I'm not so sure. Normally I'm surrounded by people who have been as privileged as I have been. With more money than they know what to do with and servants who take care of the real business of life. People with titles whose entire job is like mine."

"What do you think your job is?" he asked.

"Wave prettily from a carriage? Make an appearance on a terrace during island celebrations? And, I suppose, marry some titled man to keep English encroachment at bay a little longer."

She sighed as the reality of those facts sank in. They were things she had considered before, of course. She felt the emptiness of that existence from time to time, wondered if there was more for her in the world. But never so keenly as now, staring across a plain wooden table at a man who was so different from herself.

"And just why are you looking at me that way?" he asked.

She shook her head. "I think I just feel it all the more when I'm… when I'm with you?"

He drew back a fraction. "That you are useless? I would never wish to make you feel that way, Ilaria."

She heard the upset in his voice and reached across to catch his hand. "No, I know that. I think it's just that I…I look at you. You have lived a life of duty, you had a profession, you have such dedication. And it makes me realize I have never been useful." She pursed her lips. "I'm sure my father would have agreed."

He stroked a thumb over her hand. "When I visited Athawick, your family seemed close."

She held back a humorless laugh. "Oh, then we did as he expected. Demanded. Good."

"What do you mean?"

She pulled her hand from his, unsure she could say these things out loud when he was touching her. She cleared her throat and took another, much larger, gulp of her wine. "Family unity was his mantra. He thought if the public ever saw us as anything less than perfect, they would begin not to want us. He was terrified of the monarchy being overthrown, especially after the horrors of the revolution in France. Of his legacy being destroyed because of the failure of his children. He demanded we put on the public face of closeness."

"But the reality?"

She shrugged. "He was very cold. Distant. The only one of us he had any real interest in was Grantham, and that was just to rail about his future duties." She shook her head. "Poor Grantham. When he told us that there was a threat to the throne last night…his face. It was my father's every nightmare come true."

Jonah nodded. "Yes. He seems to feel the pain of it keenly."

"Because my father linked uprising to failure. He screeched it at him for decades. It was horrible." She shivered. "To choose to inspire such terror in your own children, even for what you believe is a good cause, is…" She caught her breath. "At any rate, the closeness you saw was more of an act then the truth."

"The rest of you are truly attached, though," Jonah insisted. "I've seen how you interact when no one else is around, when you believe no one is watching. You do love each other."

She nodded. "We do. There may not be the warmth to it that other families are allowed to show, but I adore them. I want to help and keep them safe." She bent her head as the reality of that hit her too. "Even if that means not being entirely happy myself."

They were quiet together for a moment, and then he leaned

across the table and cupped her cheek. He kissed her and she tasted wine on his lips as she sighed against him. When he pulled away, she felt empty without him. That was the future, she knew. Never being able to touch this man again. Because he wouldn't fight for her. She couldn't fight for him.

And yet she continued to hand over her heart, piece by piece. Eventually he would take all of it with him when they were parted. And she was trying so hard not to let that fact destroy her before the time came.

CHAPTER 19

I laria and Jonah were quiet together for a while. It wasn't an uncomfortable silence, not something she felt like she had to fill. Which was odd because that was her entire existence: filling silences, working to keep things from being awkward with dignitaries and subjects alike.

But with Jonah she could just...be. He held her hand, not pressuring her, not expecting anything from her.

She had no idea how much time had passed before he said, "I know what it's like to long for the father you don't have. To mourn what you wish had been, as much as what was. And I'm sorry that you didn't get what you deserved from him, which was love and support."

There was the hint at the edges again about his past, linked to her own story. "Thank you," she whispered. "He has been gone for a year and I still have such complicated emotions about him. Some days I miss him. He was not a warm father, but he was a very certain king. I didn't worry about the future—I assumed he would know what to do."

"You don't feel that way with Grantham?" Jonah asked.

She bent her head. "My brother is just finding his way. I can see the weight of it on his shoulders. It isn't that I don't think he'll determine his own path, it's that I fear he will be broken by it in the end. That crown is very heavy on his head."

"I don't disagree," Jonah said.

"You knew about the uprising before last night, didn't you?" she asked softly.

As she waited for the answer, she realized she wasn't angry about it either way. She didn't like that he'd hidden his true motives for following her, but she didn't believe what he'd concealed had been done out of malice or cruelty.

He sighed. "He told me before, yes."

She drew her hands from his and worried them before her. "I am glad he has a friend in you. I'm glad *I* have a friend in you."

That seemed to move him in some way because a muscle in his jaw twitched. "You shall always have a friend in me, Ilaria."

"But not the rest," she said. "I won't always have the rest. So I don't want to waste this time we have together." She stood up and moved around the table to him. He pushed his chair back as she reached him and didn't resist when she settled herself into his lap. She wiggled her bare backside against his cock and felt half-hard go to full attention, even through the heavy layers of his trousers.

She pushed aside everything but this. The sensations, the closeness, the love she felt for him. That was all that mattered in this moment. That was the gift.

She lowered her lips to his and he opened to her, letting her in with a soft grumble from deep within his chest. His arms came around her, his fingers pressing into her back as he pulled her even closer. The kiss deepened, his tongue tracing patterns against hers. She found herself lifting into him, as if she could somehow get even closer, even deeper.

She shifted in his lap, straddling him so they were face to face. He cupped her backside, sliding his fingers beneath the edge of his shirt so that the heat of his hands held against her bare skin. She hissed out a sound of pleasure as her head dipped back. He gripped harder when she rotated her hips against his.

Already pleasure spiked, even though they were separated by the fabric of his trousers. It didn't matter. She could grind here to release if she tried. She knew that. It wouldn't be enough. But then again, nothing would be enough. Not with this man.

She wanted it all. Selfishly and recklessly and blindly, she wanted it all.

But instead of saying that, she found the buttons of his shirt and fumbled to open them. When he laughed at her bumbling, she pulled away, loving how close their faces were in this position.

"See?" she whispered as she stroked her nose along the side of his. "Useless."

"Never, never, never," he murmured. "Just overly eager."

He covered her hand with his, and together they unbuttoned him as he stared up into her eyes, never parting his gaze from hers. In that moment she felt more molded to him, more one, than she had any time they made love. This was something else, something special and rare and beautiful.

She sought his lips again as he worked his shirt free of his trousers, quite the feat with her perched on his lap, and then tugged it away so he was naked from the waist up. She pressed her hands to his chest, raking her nails against his skin gently and memorizing every line of his body with her fingertips.

He muttered something, low and lost against her lips, and then he shocked her by grasping the fluttering edges of the shirt she wore and tugging. Buttons flew across the kitchen floor and the fabric rended as she drew back with a laugh.

"You ruined my shirt!" she gasped.

He shook his head as he pulled the torn fabric away and left her utterly naked in his arms. "*My* shirt," he clarified. "And since I intend to keep you in nothing at all for the next few days, that is a sacrifice I'm happy to make."

"Anything for the cause," she murmured, arching against his

chest so her breasts rubbed against the line of curly red hair there.

He grunted with pleasure as he cupped the back of her head and pulled her down to find her lips with his. Everything felt more urgent now, a shift that had happened instantly. She needed what he would give, he needed to give it.

So when he cupped her backside with both hands and then stood, lifting her along with him, she wasn't even surprised by the move. It made sense that they should shift as one, never even break the kiss as he pushed the plates on the table aside and set her on the edge.

She wrapped her legs around him out of instinct and it aligned their bodies. He dug his fingers into her hair, tilted her head for better access as his kiss grew more wild and unfettered and deep. She clung to him, her island on this ocean of desire as her body pulsed with a heartbeat of need only he could fulfill.

"Please," she whispered against his lips. "Please, please."

He drew away from her mouth and rested his forehead against hers instead. "Do you know what you do to me?" he muttered, she thought almost to himself more than to her.

So she didn't answer in words, but wedged her hand into the tight space between them and let it slide down over his chest, his stomach, until she found the fall front of his trousers. She opened the fastenings and angled herself back just far enough to pull the fabric away.

He cupped her hips, drawing her to the very edge of the table as he took her in one, easy stroke. She gasped against the quick invasion and locked her legs harder around his hips. They circled together, slow and steady, grinding for her pleasure. She gripped him hard with every stroke, their mouths tearing at each other, seeking more and more until there would be nothing left.

Except pleasure. This wicked pleasure that mounted inside of her, pulsing between her legs. He seemed to sense her building toward it, seeking the release from the pressure. He kissed her one last time and then lowered her on the tabletop, flat on her back. She gripped the edge, watching him as he pressed his fingers against her clitoris.

He slowed his thrusts and smoothed her own wetness against the sensitive nub, peeling the head back to reveal the pulsing pearl beneath. She gasped, turning her head, squeezing her eyes shut as he tortured and soothed her all at once. She lifted against his hand, losing control of her body as he took her to the edge and then pushed her over.

She was flying, soaring through the rippling waves of pleasure he built higher and higher in her body with just his touch. She gripped his cock harder, unable to control the squeezing of her body anymore. He grunted as his thrusts increased, grew harder, and just as her crisis ended, he withdrew with a curse.

He came in thick spurts that splashed across her stomach and breasts. She gazed into his face in this moment of pure vulnerability, lost in the expression of pleasure that softened his hard edges. When he opened his eyes and saw the mess he had made, he shook his head and reached for the ripped shirt he had discarded.

"My apologies," he began.

She ignored him and instead rubbed the wet evidence of his release against her skin. He stared as she did so, his pupils dilating all over again.

"I want it," she whispered. "I want you, all of you, for as long as I can have you."

He grabbed her hand to pull her to a seated position on the table. He kissed her, not gently, but firmly and with promise, then said, "Then come back up to my bed, Ilaria. Because I have a thousand ways I want to debauch you and we don't have that much time."

"Yes, yes, yes," she said.

He handed over the torn shirt. Instead of putting it on, she slung it over her shoulder and padded out of the kitchen. He was hard on her heels, his arms coming around her from behind as they staggered up the stairs, toward his bed, toward the slender opportunity they had and neither wished to squander.

CHAPTER 20

Jonah rolled over on his side and found Ilaria flat on her back, gorgeous breasts uncovered. He slung his arm over her stomach and tugged her a little closer. She murmured, some empty sound of pleasure and connection as she curled farther into his chest.

It had been three days of this. The only time he left this bed was to get them food or deal with matters when Mrs. Williams came to bring him mail and supplies. Or when he went to fetch water to fill the tub.

Otherwise, he was in this bed, with this woman, and it was heaven. One he'd soon be forced to leave, but he was trying not to think about that at present.

"What time is it?" Ilaria muttered without opening her eyes.

He glanced on the clock by his bedside table. "Almost ten. Not too early."

"Nor too late," she said, turning on her side and pressing a hand flat against his chest. Her fingers flexed, tracing little patterns there that made his blood run hotter. It was unbelievable how much she set him aflame. It was like he was a green young man when he was with her, always randy and ready to have her.

183

"I know you got up earlier," she said. "Did you receive a letter from my family?"

He shook his head. "No. It was Mrs. Williams with eggs. No letter this morning, but the afternoon post could change that. Are you so eager to escape this prison?"

She glanced up at him. "This is far from a prison and you know it. If I could stay here with you forever, I would, but only if I also knew my family was safe and happy."

He stroked his hand along her back gently. "But that's a fantasy."

"So you keep saying any time the subject comes up," she said with a sigh.

He shifted slightly. "Because it's true. It would be too easy to get wrapped up in the idea that we could stay here, that we could be like this for more than a few days. It's for myself that I say those things, as much as for you."

Her expression softened. "Are you saying you would want to stay here with me if you could?"

He drew in a long breath. He'd said too much, revealed too much, but what else could he do?

"I can't, Ilaria." He tried to say it as gently as he could when it tore a hole in his heart. "So what I want doesn't really matter."

She frowned, and some of the light went out in her dark eyes. She rolled onto her back and stared up at the ceiling above the bed for a few moments, silent. He wanted so much to fill that space between them, to explain his heart and how much it broke with the idea. But that would only make it worse for both of them. And once he told her that he loved her, he was afraid he wouldn't be able to let her go. Not ever. No matter the consequences that would tear them both apart.

"And all of that is because of who our parents are," she said slowly. "My royal ones...and yours. That you're a by-blow."

He tensed. This was a subject she had danced around but never fully addressed. He'd been anticipating it, though. The closer they got here, the more he knew she wanted to hear about his life, his past. He hadn't offered the information because it opened so many more doors to his true feelings.

But perhaps if she heard the truth, she would more fully grasp why a future together was impossible.

"Yes," he said softly.

"Will you tell me?" she asked, turning back on her side and propping herself up on her elbow so she could really look into his eyes. She reached out a hand to trace the line of his jaw and he let his lids shut as he reveled in her soft touch.

"It's not something I generally talk about."

"Not even with friends?" she asked.

He shrugged. "What would be the point? No one can change the past, can they?"

"But they can commiserate, support," she said. He opened his eyes and stared deeply into hers. There was an oasis there, someplace warm and safe. A place he wanted to go to with all his heart. She shifted slight. "I won't push you. But I'd like to know, given that you know so much about my life."

He cleared his throat. "Did you do any digging into my life over the years?"

She tilted her head. "No. I'm certain my brother did, but I don't really care about your past, except for how it has affected you. Changed you. But your bloodlines don't mean anything to me. I have seen many a man with an impeccable pedigree turn out to be a rotter and those with little respectability to recommend them turn out to be the best of men."

"It remains to be seen where I fall on that spectrum."

She sat up fully and stared at him. "No, it doesn't. You are the best of men, Jonah Crawford, and no story about your past or your lineage will change my opinion on that matter."

She meant it, he could see that. Her acceptance was pure and deep, without conditions placed on it or him. And he loved her even more desperately in that moment than he had in the hundreds of moments before.

So they would do this. He scrubbed a hand over his face and drew a shaky breath. "My father was a solicitor in London. He and my mother had married the same year I was born, and they ultimately had three more children together in the years that followed." He tried so desperately not to go back in time, but it was difficult. "We were middle-class people, with enough to be comfortable, and I should have no complaints about my growing up."

Her brow wrinkled. "Except?"

He didn't speak for a moment as images of his father leapt into his mind. That coldness to his eyes, the cruel tilt his mouth had sometimes taken.

"He hated me." He said the words out loud and felt them all the way to his soul.

Ilaria blinked. "Who?"

"My father. He despised me. There was never warmth between us, never gentleness. And that distance didn't exist between him and my siblings, Alec, John and Olive. He was a proud and joyful father to those three. So I knew he hated me, but I didn't understand why."

She shook her head. "I'm so sorry, Jonah. That seems an impossibly cruel thing to do to a child."

"It was," he said softly. "He would bring them all gifts when he came home from work. Not me. He would take them to the market, but leave me behind."

She flinched. "Jonah," she said softly, only just a whisper of his name, but it was filled with such empathy, such pain for him.

"When I was eight," he continued while he still could, "my mother took me to a fine house in London and introduced me to a man named Harlen Grisham."

"Harlen," she repeated. "Like the name you give at the Donville Masquerade."

Jonah winced. "Yes. He was the youngest son of Viscount Grisham. It was important to him that I know that. He gave me sweets and looked me over and was generally jolly and friendly. As we were going home, my mother kept telling me not to tell my father, never tell my father."

Ilaria shook her head. "Oh no."

He sighed. The path was so clear, she could already see it. They could walk down it together to the moment that had changed his life. "He already knew. When we got home, he already knew where we'd been," he said softly. "And he exploded. I'd seen him be cold, even cruel, but never violent. But he grabbed my mother and he was shouting and shaking her. I tried to intervene, to step between them."

Ilaria lifted a hand to her mouth. "At eight?"

"He hit me so hard my ears rang," he whispered, his father's red, enraged face rising up before his eyes like it was yesterday. "And that was when he told me Mr. Grisham was my…my real father."

"Jonah," she breathed, and reached out to catch his hand. Her touch centered him, brought him back to his safe room with this woman he loved.

He cleared his throat. "After that, everything changed. Norland Crawford let me keep his name, but he made no effort to pretend to be a father to me. Nor was he careful about who he let know the truth. My parentage became common knowledge and the judgments about it followed. The only good thing was that I was suddenly allowed to visit Grisham. Twice yearly, just the two of us."

Ilaria tilted her head. "He was welcoming?"

"Yes, very." He pursed his lips. "He had not been allowed to marry my mother, you see. She wasn't elevated enough for his family."

"So they were separated by circumstance. That is very sad," Ilaria said.

He snorted out a laugh. "Don't create too romantic a story for them. By the time I was visiting him, Grisham had long since fallen out of lust or love or infatuation. Sometimes he would call her Franny—not her real name, Fanny, because he couldn't remember it."

"Oh." Ilaria wrinkled her nose. "Yes, far less romantic than I had pictured."

"Life went along, but I longed for acceptance. For a real father. And after a particularly unpleasant exchange with Crawford when I was thirteen, I ran away. I went to Grisham and begged him to let me stay there. But all that jovial warmth and fun he showed disappeared in an instant. He reminded me I was nothing but a bastard and there was no place for me in his hallowed halls."

"No," Ilaria said.

He nodded. "Our relationship wasn't the same after that. Though Crawford did become a little less cruel, so I have to assume my real father paid some coin or made some threats to mitigate the pain I experienced at home." He shrugged. "When I was sixteen, Harlen Grisham bought me a commission in the Royal Navy. And I went. I suppose it was a way to dispose of his duty to me, but I could never repay him because it changed my life."

She smiled slightly, watching him as he became more animated with the subject. "It was evident when you came to Athawick that you loved your role in the military."

"I did. I fought in many battles, I made bonds with the men around me that can never be broken. I moved up in the ranks. I found my purpose and I intended to serve for the remainder of my life. And then…"

He broke off because now they were coming to a pain that was so near, so close that it still stung as if the wound were fresh.

"Grisham died," he whispered. "My father, my real father, died."

She covered his hand and clung there. He felt her pouring her strength into him, and it was like a light that glowed inside of him. The feeling was unlike anything he'd ever experienced, and he stared at her in wonder at what she was capable of creating with just a look or a brush of her hand.

"That was why you inherited," she breathed.

He nodded. "He never had any legitimate heirs, and he was hell-bent on enraging his own father, the viscount who has never acknowledged me. Grisham's small estate and his London town-house were not entailed. They were free and clear inheritance, and he left them to me. Along with all his numerous debts."

She swallowed. "You had to resign your commission."

"Yes." His voice was thick now, heavy with the regret this story inspired. "To settle with his creditors and get the estate back into some kind of manageable state. There were dozens of people who depended on it. Depended on me now. What could I do but take care of it? Even if it meant…"

He trailed off, and a tear slid down Ilaria's cheek. "Even if it meant losing your own dreams."

He was quiet for a moment, trying to gather himself so his voice wouldn't break. "Yes."

She scooted closer to him on the bed and wrapped her arms around him. She threaded her fingers through his hair and gently guided it to rest on her shoulder. They sat like that for a while, and then she sighed. "Jonah, I'm so sorry."

He lifted his head and shook it. "You needn't be. This is my life now. I must accept it." He met her gaze and held it there. "*We* must accept all these things we cannot change."

Her lips trembled for a moment. "I suppose we must."

She pushed from the bed and walked away to the fireplace. Her naked curves would have normally been the sweetest distraction, but right now all he could see was how sad she was.

For days, he had been feeling something when they were together. Something he tried to suppress and deny and ignore, pretend away. But now there was no way to do it, it was just too obvious. She loved him. He felt that as keenly as he felt the same emotion toward her. She loved him, and the reason she was hurting was because his story further proved that she couldn't have him. That whatever future she longed for, he longed for, it could never be theirs because of his class, because of the expectations around her marriage…because he was a bastard.

"You know," she said without looking back at him. "I think I'm getting a little tired of being trapped within these walls."

"You wound my masculine pride," he said, hoping that teasing would draw her back to him, even just a fraction.

She smiled at him over her shoulder, but the expression didn't reach her eyes. "Oh, come now, Captain, you know you have been a fine lover these past few days."

He arched a brow. "*Fine?*" he repeated.

She blinked at him innocently. "Very nice."

"Nice!" He pushed out of the bed and folded his arms, trying to suppress a laugh at her needling. "I think I've been better than nice. Your squealing and writhing makes me believe I've been spectacular."

"God's teeth, the ego on this one," she said with a shake of her head. "Fine, if it makes you feel better, you were…amazing. Spectacular. Far above average."

He puffed out his chest. "I'm glad we're in agreement."

"But I'm tired of you now," she said, and giggled when he grabbed for a pillow and pitched it at her. "And I want to go for a walk."

He glared at her playfully for a moment and stroked his chin, pretending to be deep in thought. "So you *do* wish to be released from this prison."

"Oh yes, please, sir. Only for a while." She clutched the pillow he'd thrown in front of herself and gave him the most adorable innocent look.

Which made him think not particularly innocent thoughts.

"Why don't we make a bargain?" he suggested, coming toward her and tugging the pillow from her arms to toss it behind him. "You come back to that bed with me for just a while longer so I can prove to you once more that I am spectacular in bed."

She swatted his chest as she giggled. "And then?"

"And then I will take you out of this house for a while."

She eased closer and wrapped her arms around his neck. She lifted on her tiptoes and kissed him. "That, Captain, is a bargain."

He stood there for a moment, reveling in the warmth of her, the joy of her, the absolute connection between them. And then he leaned forward to kiss just the tip of her nose. "Carefully, Your Highness."

She blinked up and him and some of her teasing faded. "Very carefully," she promised, and then tugged him in for a kiss once more.

And for just a little while longer, he allowed himself to forget everything but her.

CHAPTER 21

Ilaria squeezed the inside of Jonah's elbow gently as they walked along the lane. It had taken three tries to get out of the bed, three very pleasurable tries, but eventually they had made their way down to the village and seen the shops. Now they were strolling arm in arm in the sunshine like they were a couple. Like this was just a day in their life together.

"You just let out the most contented little sigh," Jonah said.

She laughed. "I was pondering the pleasure of this experience of normalcy outside the castle walls."

"I've been to that beautiful castle in Athawick and your equally lovely townhouse in London—do you consider them prisons?"

"A prison can be pretty," she said softly. "But I don't think I can say that exactly. I never felt…held captive, but I've certainly been limited. Even before we came to London, I was not allowed to just roam the streets or go into a shop like I just did. I feel almost like an average person."

"I do not think you could ever be that." He covered the hand on his elbow with a gentle squeeze.

"Do you think anyone recognized me?" she asked. "That gentleman on the street was watching me quite closely."

He glanced down at her. "Oh yes, I marked that interest, I promise you. But I don't think he stared because you are Princess Ilaria. He stared because you are impossibly lovely."

She felt her cheeks heat with a blush and ducked her head. "It's so strange. When people look at me while I have a tiara on my head or am standing beside the king or queen, I know they are looking at an institution. To have them see me as just a person is truly a revelation."

"Well, I'm glad you had a good time," he said. "Come, let's go off the path a moment."

He guided her from the road and down a small hill. She caught her breath as she gazed down at the valley beyond them. It was all green rolling hills and a small lake in the distance. They walked in comfortable silence until they reached it.

"Beautiful," she said on a sigh. "No wonder you haven't sold the house here."

He released her arm and walked away, the quiet suddenly turning from comfortable to something else. She watched him pace to the lakeshore and pick up a stone. He worried it in his hand a moment before he threw it in.

"I know I *should* sell the cottage," he set. "Or let it at the very least. But it is…it's the last vestige of the life I had before. The life with actual meaning."

"The loss is keen, I know," she said softly. "And I do understand it, I think. But Jonah, I think it's a fallacy that your new life couldn't have meaning."

He pivoted back. "How? Strutting around Shrewsbury, being a bloody landowner?"

She wrinkled her brow. "First off, being a bloody landowner is no small future. You said yourself that the reason you resigned your commission was so you could focus on those who depend upon you there. I may be a sheltered little fool in a great many ways, but even I know that a good landlord can be a lifeline and a bad one can destroy everything."

He shook his head. "Wonderful, so I'll fill in little boxes in a ledger and approve improvements to retaining walls. What a life that is."

She put her hands on her hips. "Then stop moaning, Jonah, and make it a better one."

He blinked. "I beg your pardon?"

"I realize that the shock of having your entire world changed has thrown you into a…a funk." She moved toward him and caught his hands. "But you *aren't* trapped, Jonah. No one is going to force you to do anything you don't wish to do."

She realized she was referring to herself, but pushed those thoughts aside to focus on the man standing before her. The one who was looking at her like she had sprouted a second head.

"If you don't like your path, change it," she continued. "Why not go into politics? What do you call it here…stand for a seat in the House of Lords—"

"I'm not eligible for that. I would have to stand for the House of Commons," he said. "And half those constituencies are owned by aristocrats. The entire system is corrupt to its bones."

"A Whig to your very core," she said gently.

He lifted his chin and fire snapped in his eyes. "Proudly so."

"Then do what will change what you don't like: work to reform that system. It seems the world is ripe for it. You could make your corner of it a better place, Jonah, not just for yourself, but for those without a voice, without a vote, without a hope. Is there any more meaning than that?"

He stared at her for a beat and he almost looked impressed. "The princess is an idealist."

She nodded. "I am. I may have to accept that my world is set in stone, but I must hold on to hope that the wider world isn't. That people who care about what is right and good and just will change the course of the future for the better." She reached up and patted his cheek gently. "Rather than mourning what they've lost."

He pursed his lips. "Yes, so you've said."

"I just think that your father, difficult as he was, gave you an opportunity as much as a curse. You can see it as one or the other, but you will choose your own path in the end. And *that* is a lucky thing, Jonah. Not everyone gets to do that."

"You mean you."

She sighed and stepped away from him. She couldn't touch him when this topic was in play—it seemed too cruel. "You and I have been over this subject again and again. No matter what I want, my future, like yours, could and I suppose *should* be for bigger things. Knowing my brother's position is being threatened from within makes the consolidation of power via my marriage even more important. It is not my choice, but my choice can be to accept it. To stop fighting it as I have been."

"So you will marry Bramwell," he said, his tone hollow.

She swallowed past the lump in her throat. "I must, it seems. To believe otherwise was a fallacy from the start, I think."

He threw another rock into the water, this time much harder, and the splash created waves that eventually faded to ripples and then disappeared. Like they had never happened. She couldn't help but see the metaphor to this time with Jonah. Right now it mattered more than anything, like those waves that had disturbed the water. But eventually she would have to forget, or at least not dwell on the past, on the moments with him.

"May I make one more suggestion about your future?" she asked.

He snorted out a laugh and glanced at her over his shoulder. "As if anyone could ever stop you from doing anything."

She would have smiled at the quip, but she couldn't manage it, considering what she was about to say. "You should..." She trailed off, unable to say the next word.

"I should what, Ilaria?" he asked, facing her. "I may be a bit of a prick about it, but I do value your counsel."

"You do?"

"Yes." He moved toward her a step. "You are cleverer than anyone I've ever met by half. I see you watch those around you, making a study of them and then formulating little plans of how to use what you see. You even did so with me when we first met."

She smiled. "I was there to meet the ship and the dignitaries and I saw you and…it was like everything else fell away. All I could see was this dashing man in his uniform, with gray eyes that seemed to see far more than the surface. And then you talked and you were intelligent and amusing and it was very much not fair."

"Not fair?" he repeated with a light chuckle.

"Yes. I was rather hoping you would be uninteresting so that the attraction would fade. Instead, you made me spend the next month tracking your every move, trying to find ways to be seated next to you or be part of any party you were a member of."

"And here I was, just trying to catch a glimpse of you," he murmured.

"It seems we wasted a great deal of time," she said.

He shrugged. "Not that I could have done anything about it, even if I'd known you felt an attraction. Can you imagine? I would have been court-martialed. Thrown out of your country if not beheaded or taken to a dueling field by your brother."

"Grantham has obviously guessed about you and me now, and he seems to have no desire to duel you," she said.

He pursed his lips. "You were about to tell me more about what you think I should do with my life. What is your suggestion?"

Her distraction had kept her from thinking the dark and dangerous thoughts she had prior but they returned now. Her breath became shaky and she knew her voice was the same when she said, "I think you should marry, Jonah."

His lips parted and he backed a long step away, as if he could escape the inevitable. "Ilaria, this is not a topic you and I should discuss."

"Of course it is," she said. "It may be painful, but you and I are exactly the people who should discuss it. Because I…"

She stared up into his eyes and wished she could just pause this moment forever, never have to say the next words, never have to walk away from this man. But that was not possible.

"I love you, Jonah."

His expression twisted in enormous pain, as if she had stabbed him through the heart. And perhaps she had done so at that.

She continued, "And I know you love me too."

Jonah had always remembered his dreams. Sometimes he wrote them down when they were particularly interesting or he thought they contained some important message he needed to explore. In so many of them in the last two years, Ilaria had played a starring role. And her one line, the only thing he could ever remember her saying in them, was exactly what she had just said.

I love you, Jonah.

Only the difference was that in a dream he could wake and push those words aside. Dismiss them as some silly game of his mind. But now Ilaria stood before him, sunlight glinting off her dark hair, tears glistening in her brown eyes, and there was nothing but truth and certainty on her face as she said those words in reality.

As she called him out for his feelings without a thought for what it would do to him. To them.

He pivoted away, trying to calm his racing heart and shaking hands. Loving her for saying out loud what they had been avoiding. Hating her for peeling away the binding on a wound he knew would never heal.

"I've never said that I…that I feel such a way," he whispered.

She caught his arm, her fingers burning him even through all the layers of clothing. He was marked by her, branded—he could never erase that from his mind or his body or his soul.

"Then tell me you don't love me," she said.

He ground his jaw. "I can't," he admitted at last on a huffed out breath of frustration. "Does that please you, Ilaria? To make me admit it?"

"Does it please me that the man I love with all my heart, the man I will always love, feels the same way about me?" she asked. "Yes. There are only a handful of people in this world who would be so lucky."

"Lucky?" He lifted his eyebrows and anger sparked in his chest. "You are trying to tell me that this feeling that is burning me alive, that will haunt me until the last day I draw breath, is *lucky*? When one moment ago, you were demanding that I find someone to marry? Someone who isn't *you*, princess."

She squeezed her eyes shut and wavered a moment. Then she swallowed hard and said, "Yes. It is unfair that we can't be together. Neither of us asked for the circumstances of our birth or our lives, but who does? So if I cannot have you, Jonah, then I would wish you to be happy. To not be alone."

He caught her upper arms gently and drew her closer. "Understand this, Ilaria. If a person cannot be with the person they love... they are *always* alone."

Her face crumpled and she leaned forward to rest her forehead on his chest. His anger dissipated and he wrapped his arms around her, holding her close. How many more times would he be allowed this opportunity? A handful? A dozen? And then it would be over.

"I'm not trying to hurt you," she said, her voice muffled against his coat. "I'm just trying to find a way where we have some control over what is about to happen. I'm trying to move on with my life but to be able to know that you are well and as content as you can be. So that I can be the same."

He cupped her chin and tilted her face toward his. "I know," he whispered. "I know that you are very much accustomed to being able to dictate what happens. But there is no amount of your blessing that will make this right. We're going to have to feel this heartbreak, Ilaria. Sooner rather than later, I think."

A tear slid down her cheek and he caught it with his thumb, wiping it away gently. His own eyes burned with similar tears as the reality of their situation was magnified by the declarations of their hearts.

"Then I don't want to waste another moment that we do have," Ilaria said softly. "Let's go home, Jonah. Back to this dream we're able to live in for a while. Let's go home and pretend that we're living our future together."

He nodded and leaned down to kiss her. Her arms came around his neck and she clung to him, her desperation plain in the way she trembled in his arms. He felt the same and he hated it. He didn't want this to be desperate or painful. He wanted these moments they had left to be wonderful.

So he broke their kiss and caught her hand. "Come on," he murmured, his voice rough with desire and emotion.

She walked bedside him the rest of the way without speaking. Her fingers merely flexed against his, little tremors that were like a vise grip around his heart. The tension between them seemed to rise with every step, and by the time they reached his door, longing all but vibrated between them.

He struggled to get the door open, and the moment he did, he caught her waist, dragging her against him as they staggered inside. He kissed her while he kicked the door shut and then they stumbled into the parlor off the foyer. She lifted into him, cupping his face just as he cupped her backside, and shifted her against him with a heavy groan.

She sucked his tongue, gently at first, then harder, and starbursts of pleasure erupted all over his body. He pressed his fingers into her skin, grinding her against him as he sank onto the settee in the middle of the room. She straddled him, her skirts tangled around her legs, her kiss growing more and more desperate when he unfastened the first button along her spine.

He was vaguely aware of a rapping sound, constant and piercing through the haze of desire and heartbreak that swirled around them. She pulled away.

"Someone is knocking," she murmured, shifting onto the settee beside him.

He glared toward the door. "So they are. Stay here?"

She nodded and reached up to refasten the top button of her gown as he got to his feet, trying to think of anything that would ease the raging erection pressing to his trouser front and exited the room. When he pulled the front door open, he found a young man waiting there.

"What is it?" he all but snapped. Ilaria was in the next damned room, after all, and their time was limited.

"Sorry to disturb, sir," the intruder said, and it was then that Jonah noted he was dressed in Athawick livery. "But I have a message from London." He handed over a folded sheet. "Marked urgent by the king himself."

Jonah felt the blood leave his face as he snatched the message and turned it over. The crest on the wax seal was, of course, not of his own king, but Ilaria's. He broke it open and read over the few lines within, his heart sinking with every word.

"Do you have a reply, sir?" the messenger said when Jonah had lowered the missive with a shaking hand.

"I...not yet," he said. "The driver who brought us here, Baker, he is at the Cresthold Inn up the lane in the village. Join him there and wait for the reply. I will bring it myself shortly."

"Yes, sir," the messenger said, and then executed a sharp turn that any military man would have been proud of and hustled to his waiting horse.

Jonah shut the door and pivoted back toward the parlor, but before he could move toward it, the door opened and Ilaria appeared, face pale. "A message from my family?" she whispered.

He nodded.

"What does it say?"

He moved toward her, hand outstretched as if he could make this better for her. Fix it when he knew he couldn't. All he could do was be here.

"Sasha was attacked in London last night," he said softly. "They think by the same man who tried to harm you."

CHAPTER 22

Ilaria's ears were ringing as she backed away from Jonah into the parlor. As if she could escape what he was saying.

"Sasha," she repeated, unable to say anything else.

Her friend, her sister since Ilaria was eight and Sasha merely six, had been harmed, perhaps even worse than harmed. God, could she be dead? Sasha, with her sweet laugh and her smart mouth and her warm embraces? The very thought tore Ilaria's world to shreds in a horrible instant.

Jonah was still reaching to comfort her in this moment that tore her apart. "She is alive," he said.

Relief nearly buckled her, and Ilaria leaned into his embrace for a moment. Then she straightened up. This wasn't the end of this situation. She needed to know it all, so she retook her place on the settee.

"What else?" she whispered. "Please tell me everything."

"There is little to the note, but that her injuries were not life threatening. She will recover fully. The family is shaken, of course. And they fear for your continued safety, since you were…" His voice broke. "You were obviously the true target of the attack."

"Let me see it," Ilaria demanded, holding her hand out for the letter.

He gave it without hesitation and sat down next to her as she read the short message. "It is from the king, himself," she breathed.

"I think he wrote it more in capacity of brother than king," Jonah said gently. "Look at how his hand shakes here and here."

He motioned to two places in the letter and she, too, saw the tremble of Grantham's writing. It made her heart ache for him and for all of her family, most especially Sasha.

"She was hurt because she was pretending to be me," she whispered. "Because I ran away from my responsibilities to be your lover in the country."

Jonah drew back slightly. "This is *not* your fault, Ilaria. There were good reasons to remove you from London, this very incident being one of them. It might have ended far differently for you. And Sasha has played your double for years. She knew the risks of taking your place and hoped to do her part in saving you."

Ilaria shook her head. "But she's still hurt because of me." Waves of guilt washed over her one by one, and she lowered her face as tears rushed to her eyes. "These people...whoever they are...they aren't going to stop pursuing my family, pursuing *me* as some kind of a message to Grantham."

"Perhaps not, but that's all the more reason to—"

"Return to London," she finished.

He stared at her. "No, I was going to say stay here."

She stood and pressed the message back into his hand. "How can you say that when almost everyone I love is in the midst of danger?"

"And I can't take you back into the middle of that, especially if you're the focus of the men who are doing this," he said, grasping her hands.

She held tighter to them and stared down into his eyes. "If I'm the focus, then I could also be part of the solution."

"That's ridiculous," he snapped, rising to his feet. The emotion that laced his voice was that of the man who loved her, not someone detached.

She touched his face. "I know you're afraid for me, but *please*, Jonah. I need to be with my family. I need to be part of solving this problem, before anyone else gets hurt trying to protect me."

He pressed his lips together hard, but she could see he knew she was correct, as much as he wished to deny it. Deny her. Keep her safe in this little bubble they had created where it was only him, only her, only them. The bubble she had to burst at last.

"If we left for London now, we wouldn't be there until dark," he said with a sigh. "And I'm not comfortable with the idea of bringing you in without the ability to see potential threats. We'll return tomorrow morning. And I can send the man who delivered this," he held up the folded pages briefly, "back to your family to let them know of our plans. They can increase security further overnight."

She nearly sagged with relief, though it was tempered with fear. Jonah didn't want her to go to London because she would be in danger, and the idea that someone wanted her dead was a terrifying one.

He lifted her hand to his lips, and it was only when his warm breath brushed her skin that she realized how cold she was. "I need to hurry to the village to send a message back," he said, "and tell the driver to prepare everything for tomorrow morning. You should pack your things."

She blinked. Oh yes, she would have to do that herself. An interesting exercise in independence, for certain. "I will," she said, and then she stepped closer. "And then tonight is...it's..."

He caught her hand. "Our last night here. Our last night together."

"Then we had best make it memorable," she whispered. She leaned up to kiss him and he buried his fingers in her hair, gripping her scalp with possessive heat before he drew back, panting. "Write your message and deliver it," she said softly. "I'll be ready for you when you return."

He nodded and stepped away to go to his study to write the note, leaving her alone in the hallway for a moment. She drew in a ragged breath. Once she returned to London, everything would change. And she doubted Jonah would like the thoughts that were beginning to form in her mind.

But they had tonight, and she intended to make it memorable.

Ilaria stood in her chemise, standing over her open trunk in the hidden dressing room, staring at the mess she had made of her gowns. Her maid, June, would be upset when she saw how wrinkled everything was, but she'd done her best and that was all one could do. She closed the trunk but didn't fasten it. She had a handful of things to add to it later...after...

After she and Jonah shared their last night together.

She blinked and pushed aside the pain of that statement, then walked from the dressing room and into the bedroom.

After struggling out of her dress, a feat that had taken a good quarter of an hour thanks to the buttons along the back, she had spent a long time preparing this room. She'd lit candles, she'd made the bed...well...almost. The coverlet was still cockeyed, but it was good enough. She'd taken a bottle of wine from the kitchen and set it on the bedside table with two glasses.

Everything was in place. All she was missing was...

She heard something from downstairs and peeked from the window to find Jonah dismounting from his horse below. It would take him a moment to put the animal away, so she made her final preparations. She splashed a bit of lilac water behind her ears, took her hair down and combed through it with her fingers to make messy waves around her shoulders. And finally she slipped from her chemise so she was naked.

She climbed into his bed, settled herself on the pillows and opened her legs just a fraction to give him the best view when he entered.

He came into the room, head partially bent. "We are ready for tomorrow. Baker will come to help me load the carriage at…"

He looked up and saw her on his bed.

"…seven," he finished, his voice rough.

She leaned up on her elbows and arched a brow in his direction. "Then we have only half a day left."

"Just enough time," he murmured, and shed his jacket as he came across the room, purpose in each step.

He caught her thighs and used them to pull her forward to the edge of the bed. He bent and brushed his cheek against her exposed sex. She shivered at the roughness of the shadow of a beard there, abrading her tender flesh. She lifted into him, seeking the pleasure she knew he would give.

"So greedy," he said with a rough laugh that blew warm air against her inner thigh and made her quiver again.

"With you? Always. I want it all. I want everything you have to give," she whispered.

He lifted his head and their eyes met. "You have it."

There was a moment of silence where the small room seemed to shrink even further, down to just them. Just this moment. Just what they could share, had shared, would always share, even when this was over.

But before the moment could overwhelm or destroy, he bent his head and languidly licked her sex. She dropped back against the bed, pushing all thought away and widening her legs to open herself to him. He peeled her outer lips back, massaging her gently with one hand as he licked her again, this time slower and more thoroughly.

Immediately, she found herself on the edge, because being near him put her there, being touched by him was almost too much to take. She rose to meet his mouth. He cupped her backside to steady her and feasted on her fast and hard, slow and sweet until her legs shook. Until she was soaked by both his tongue and her own trembling reaction to the pleasure he gave so easily and generously.

He nipped at her, scraping his teeth gently against her clitoris, and she jolted, clutching the coverlet and arching her back against the sharp blast of pleasure that he soothed by sucking the sensitive nub. Waves crested over her, building higher and higher, and at last she could hold it back no longer. She came, keening out his name in the quiet, rolling her hips against him, her vision blurring and her mind emptying of everything but this sensation.

She had not yet come down from the high of that when he stood to his full height, unfastening his fall front, and freed his cock. She wrapped her legs around his waist, tugging him, gasping as his cock nudged her entrance, and then he was sliding home.

He took her hard and fast, his expression lined with passion and desire, but also with the impending loss, the fear, the regret of all that was to come. She cupped the back of his neck, drawing his wet mouth to hers so she would see, wouldn't feel. She just wanted this now, wanted him.

She ground up against him, holding fast to his shoulders. Her body, already sensitive from release, found the rhythm to bring her back up to the height of pleasure. This time when she came, gripping his cock as she arched her back, he let out a low, heavy groan. He pulled from her, his essence splashing across her stomach, into his hand.

She tugged him forward and he collapsed on the bed beside her, flopping an arm over her. They were quiet a moment there in the silent room. Then she turned on her side and traced his still-clothed arm with her fingertip.

"That was an excellent way to start, Captain."

He lifted his head from the bed and stared at her. "Start, eh? Not finished with me yet?"

She didn't wince at that statement, but it took everything in her not to do so. Instead she dragged her fingertip along his jawline, let it cross his lips. He kissed her skin and she shivered.

"Not by a very long way," she whispered. "Now take off your clothes, Jonah. Time is wasting as we speak."

He smiled at her, that warm and wonderful expression that he so rarely showed the world but had become hers to enjoy since her arrival in London. But as he stepped back to make a grand show of undressing for her, her heart hurt.

The fact that they had little time remaining was a fact, not part of the game they were playing here in their bed. And soon enough she wouldn't have the delight of these moments with him ever again.

So she pushed all else aside, and decided to savor this wonderful man for all the hours they had left. Even if these last hours left her exhausted for whatever dangers she would surely face back in London.

CHAPTER 23

If the carriage ride out of London had felt like it lasted a lifetime, the one back to the city felt like it took but a snap of the fingers. Ilaria leaned against Jonah's arm, watching out the window as the buildings multiplied all around them, the traffic slowed the rig, the sounds of merchants and residents shouting and laughing and living their lives pierced the barrier and reminded him that he couldn't hide anymore.

As the scenery changed, so did everything else. The sense of duty this remarkable woman had abandoned during their time in the country rose in her. He saw her transform from his lover back to a princess. It was something in the way she held herself, something in her expression that shifted. That placed her back out of his reach, just as she always should have been.

He felt her pulling away. Their conversations had dwindled, become less personal, especially in the last hour of the ride into the city.

He knew he had to separate himself just as much. Perhaps even more. With difficulty, he shifted, patting her knee before he moved to the opposite side of the rig. She stared at him as he did so, pain flashing in her eyes at the withdrawal.

"I'm sorry," he said softly. "But I need—"

"I know," she whispered. Then she leaned across the carriage and caught his hands. He couldn't pull away as she lifted them to her lips and kissed his knuckles, then his palms. Her touch was so gentle, but it was like fire. "Whatever else, I will never be sorry."

Relief washed through him at that. He prayed it would remain true for the rest of her life. He knew it would for him. "Neither will I," he whispered, and scooted forward on the carriage seat so that he could kiss her.

Her breath hiccupped into his mouth on a strangled sob, his fingers flexing against hers as he tasted her deeply and slowly. Only when the carriage stopped did he do the same, leaning away from her just in time for the door to open. She blinked at the tears that filled her eyes and glanced toward the footman who had come to escort her out.

"Your—Your Highness," he stammered, the color leaving his cheeks. "I didn't realize you were returning today."

Jonah wrinkled his brow at the statement. So odd considering the chaos this return should have created in the household, but perhaps Grantham had thought it best to keep things quiet. Jonah couldn't fault him for that.

Ilaria took the young man's hand and allowed herself to be helped out of the carriage. She didn't glance at Jonah over her shoulder as she made her way toward the steps up to the door. It opened and the household butler, Greenly, executed a quick bow. "Your Highness, I am happy to see you."

He sounded as confused as the footman had outside, and it made no sense. Perhaps some lower house servant wouldn't have heard of her impending return, but one as elevated and on top of things as Greenly? There was no way he wouldn't be aware.

The hairs on the back of Jonah's neck began to rise in warning and he glanced around to ensure there were no hidden villains lying in wait.

"I will...I will ascertain where the family is," Greenly said as Ilaria moved into the house before him.

"They are not expecting me?" Ilaria asked, and now she did look at Jonah. He shook his head ever so slightly, indicating he didn't understand either.

"Not that I am aware of, Your Highness. Please..."

He motioned to the parlor off the foyer, and she stepped in with Jonah on her heels. When the servant had bustled off and they were alone, she turned toward him. "Why wouldn't they know of our arrival?" she asked softly.

He shook his head. "The messenger left late yesterday afternoon, heading back to London. On a fast horse, it shouldn't have taken him very long. He should have been here before supper was served. Something could have waylaid him."

She lifted a hand to her lips. "Or...or perhaps he was injured. Even killed to keep him from delivering his message."

Jonah's heart began to pound as he caught her arm and drew her away from the window, back into the foyer. He needed to get her away from the front of the house, he needed to find her family and figure out what the hell was going on. They had begun down the hall when Grantham, Remi, their mother and her mother's secretary, Dashiell Talbot, stepped out of another room.

The queen saw Ilaria first and made a sound of surprise and joy. She rushed toward Ilaria and snatched her into an embrace. The queen smoothed her hands over Ilaria's back, her fingers shaking as she did so, revealing her fear.

"You are here," Giabella whispered. "It isn't a dream or a lie."

"I'm here, Mama, and I'm fine," Ilaria reassured her as she pulled away gently and once again glanced at Jonah from the corner of her eye. "You were afraid?"

"Of course we were, especially after the attack on Sasha." Giabella wiped a tear from her cheek with the back of her hand, and Mr. Talbot stepped up to produce a handkerchief from seemingly nowhere. Queen Giabella glanced at him quickly and then back to Ilaria.

"Is she well?" Ilaria asked, gripping her mother's hands.

"She is," Grantham answered instead of the queen, and then took Ilaria's hand to draw her into a brief embrace. "I'm so glad to see you."

"As am I," Remi said, and also hugged her. Ilaria kissed his cheek and squeezed his hand.

It warmed Jonah to see her reconnect to them this way. They were not allowed much public affection as a family, but behind their doors, he could see they adored her.

"I need to see Sasha," Ilaria whispered. "Please, I must."

Giabella nodded and took her arm. "We'll come back shortly, gentlemen," she said, and Ilaria allowed herself to be hustled away. Jonah tracked them as they went, and only when she was gone from his sight did he turn toward the king.

"You didn't know we were coming," Jonah said as he followed Grantham, Remi and the queen's man, Mr. Talbot, into the study they had exited from a few moments before.

"No," Grantham said, pacing the room restlessly.

Talbot said nothing, but went to the sideboard and began preparing drinks. Jonah stepped toward the king. "The messenger never returned to you?"

Grantham gave him a strange look. "What messenger?"

"The one who came to us to deliver your message about the attack on Sasha," Jonah said. "I sent him back here last night to tell you we were returning. If he didn't arrive, I must think he was waylaid…or worse."

Grantham was just staring at him, unspeaking, and then he shook his head. "Captain Crawford, I didn't send a message to you and my sister about the attack on Sasha. I don't know what messenger you're talking about."

~

I laria felt her mother trembling as they entered Sasha's chamber just up the hallway from her own. There was a figure on the bed along the back wall, the firelight dancing across her.

"Sasha?" Ilaria breathed.

The lump on the bed moved and Sasha's head lifted. Ilaria's stomach turned. The left side of her friend's face was a mass of bruises. She had clearly been struck multiple times.

"Sasha," Ilaria sobbed, and raced to her. Sasha opened her arms and drew her in.

"Hush, I'm safe," Sasha whispered. "I'm fine."

Giabella snorted her derision and reached out to trace a gentle finger across the damage. "We are very lucky, my love," she said softly.

Sasha touched the queen's hand, and for a moment Ilaria felt their connection. Giabella had, after all, been as much a mother to Sasha as to Ilaria. And though she could be cool and distant, the perfect queen, none of her children had ever doubted her love for them. It was written all over her face right now.

"I'll leave my two girls alone," she said gently. "And see what Captain Crawford is talking about with the king, Remi and Dash."

"I'll be down shortly," Ilaria said.

Her mother nodded and then slipped from the chamber, leaving her and Sasha alone. Ilaria perched on the edge of the bed next to her friend and shook her head. "Tell me."

Sasha closed her eyes with a weak, shuddering sigh. "Very well," she whispered.

There was a moment of silence, and Ilaria realized Sasha was trying to find the words, trying to fight the tears that now sparkled in her eyes. And her chest hurt with how terrified she had been.

"Unless you don't want to," Ilaria whispered, pushing her slippers off and coming around to get into the bed with her, as they had done hundreds of times as little girls. She put her arm around Sasha and rested her adopted sister's head on her shoulder.

"I need to," Sasha said. "The danger is to you, after all. Not me."

"I knew it was my fault," Ilaria breathed. "I'm so sorry, Sasha."

"It's not your fault." Sasha shook her head. "I was…I was out. Don't ask me more about it. I was out and I stepped onto a terrace, and suddenly there was a man there, coming toward me, his arms raised and his gaze wild. He stopped short when he got close enough to see I wasn't you."

"Did he have a piercing stare?" Ilaria whispered, thinking of the man who had approached her, attacked her, at the Donville Masquerade.

"Like he could see down to my every fear." Sasha let out a soft moan. "I tried to back away, but he was too fast. He was enraged that he'd been tricked. That he thought I was you and I wasn't. He hit me so hard I fell and…and then everything gets dark and quiet and painful. I don't know what happened next until I woke up in Thomas's arms. He saved me."

"Thomas?" Ilaria repeated, trying to think of who they knew with that name. A servant, perhaps?

Sasha looked at her. "The Earl of Bramwell."

Both Ilaria's eyebrows lifted. "I…oh!"

"Yes." Sasha's gaze darted away. "He knew you were in hiding, he knew I was pretending in your place at things like the opera and a few other events. He and I were much thrown together, you see."

Ilaria wasn't certain of what to say. There was something in Sasha's tone. Something she understood, because the tremor was much the same as the one in her own voice whenever she spoke of Jonah. But that couldn't be true. Sasha couldn't care for Bramwell.

Not when the inevitable would still happen. Had to happen.

"I'm glad he was there," Ilaria said at last. "We owe him everything for saving you."

Sasha dropped her gaze. "How were things with Captain Crawford?"

Ilaria wanted to press Sasha more, but she could see her friend didn't want to speak on what had happened. Not at the moment.

She shifted. "Wonderful," she whispered. "Brief. Over."

Sasha reached out a hand, bruised on her palm, as if she had lifted it to protect herself in the attack, and covered Ilaria's. "I'm sorry, love."

"I am too," Ilaria said. "I'm so sorry you were hurt because of me. But I'm glad Grantham sent word to bring me back. I need to be with you now, be with everyone. I need to stop this."

"Grantham sent for you?" Sasha asked. "I didn't realize he was doing that, though they certainly haven't spoken to me about everything in the last two days since the attack. And what do you mean that you need to stop this?"

Ilaria stood up and leaned over to kiss Sasha on her uninjured side. "Don't you worry about it, my dearest. Try to rest now and I'll come back up later. Would you like me to sleep with you tonight? Like we used to do when we were little."

"You snore," Sasha teased.

Ilaria laughed. "I do not! I've never snored in my life—it isn't what princesses do."

Sasha smiled. "I would like your company."

"Then I'll see you later," Ilaria said before she slipped from the room. But her smile fell as she headed back downstairs. No one was going to like what she was about to propose.

And she didn't give a damn.

"What do you mean you didn't send the message?" Jonah asked, his chest constricting with those words, those terrible words and all that they were beginning to mean.

Grantham shook his head. "I wanted to wait to write to Ilaria about Sasha until we knew she would be safe to return."

"You should have seen the fight *that* inspired," Remi drawled, taking a drink from Talbot and downing it in one slug. "This one actually got passionate for once."

Grantham's jaw tightened, as if he were ready to get passionate again. "We've gone over this a dozen times—if I told her, she would have rushed back, just as she apparently did. Sasha is not badly injured, thank God, and I didn't want to further endanger yet another member of this family." The two brothers glared at each other a moment, and then the king turned toward Talbot. "You didn't send something, did you?"

"Don't blame Dashiell," the queen said as she came into the room and crossed to stand beside her secretary in an almost protective stance.

Grantham's lips pursed. "It isn't that outrageous a thought. You and Remi made yourselves very clear about your opinion on the matter. You might have asked Dashiell to go behind my back."

"But I didn't," Giabella said. "I would never put Dash in that situation."

The secretary cast a quick glance at her and then nodded. "Her Majesty is correct. I didn't write anything."

"The message was in *your* hand, King Grantham," Jonah said, drawing the note from his pocket and handing it over to Grantham.

Grantham read it and shook his head. "I...I didn't write this."

"Which means it was a ploy to get Ilaria back to London," Remi said softly.

Before anyone could say anything else, Ilaria stepped into the room, herself. She opened her mouth to speak but then looked at those around her, all pale and digesting the new information.

"What is it?" she whispered.

Jonah crossed to her, not caring how it looked, and guided her closer to her family. Softly, he explained what they had determined and watched as horror came over her features, fear. How he hated that, hated that she was drawn into such madness at all.

She held his stare for a long moment when he was finished and then let out a shuddering sigh. "There is only one thing to do," she said.

The king nodded. "I agree. We must go home to Athawick."

"No," Ilaria said. "I must put myself out there in order to draw this villain in. I must make myself bait to end this once and for all."

~

I laria expected the eruption that followed her statement and waited, not so very patiently, as it happened. Jonah staggered back, Grantham and Remi both began to shout, the queen shook her head and Ilaria could hear her speaking even though she couldn't make out the words over the cacophony. Everyone seemed to have an opinion and all of them were of the same vein: a resounding no to her suggestion.

She let them go for a moment and then cleared her throat. "All of you yelling at once isn't going to change my mind," she announced over the fray.

Grantham strode forward and raised a hand, silencing the others. "Put aside this foolish notion, Ilaria. We're going back to Athawick."

He said it in his best kingly tone, the one people didn't defy. But she put her hands on her hips and did just that. "You are the fool if you think that will do any good. These people, they are the rebels against you and your reign, yes?"

"Thanks to Mr. Rivers help, we have increasing evidence that is true, yes," Grantham said.

"I still say it's bollocks," Remi muttered. "But no one cares about my opinion, I'm just the spare."

Grantham glared at him as he stalked off, but then returned his attention to Ilaria. "They want you dead."

"If that was all there was to it, I would *be* dead."

"What do you mean?" Jonah asked, tone choked.

She allowed herself to look at him, and she wavered slightly. He looked so broken, so desperate to protect her, just as he had been protecting her almost since she set foot in London. And now she was asking to take that duty from his hands, to offer herself as sacrifice.

"Jonah, they knew where I was," she said, now speaking only to him even if the rest of the room could hear. "They brought a message to us. If they wanted me dead, just dead, they could have easily done that. They want to do something public, something loud."

He held her gaze for a moment, then turned toward Grantham. "She is correct. Every attack on Ilaria has been in a public sphere. A message to you."

"But one with no demands," Remi said. "Almost as if they just want to be known. Which doesn't really align itself with the idea of rebels, does it?"

"Oh, you know so much about rebellion now, Remi?" Grantham asked.

"Most definitely, it's my specialty," Remi said, slamming his glass down. "And when I do it, I do it so that you know what I want. What I am. Who I am. Don't I? I don't just rebel so that you look at me, I rebel so that you *see* me."

Grantham's chest lifted and fell—Ilaria could see he was trying to calm himself. Then he inclined his head. "Fine. But rebels or not, whatever the motive, the action is the same. These people keep coming after our sister, so what would you have me do, Remington?"

Ilaria stepped up between them, holding a hand up to Remi even as she faced Grantham. "Don't ask him. Ask me."

Grantham's face crumpled a little and he refocused on her. "Father would have…"

"Father would have asked no one." She touched her brother's hand gently. "But you are not Father. So ask me, Grantham. Ask me."

He shut his eyes briefly and then nodded. "What would you have me do, Ilaria, to protect you? To end this?"

"Going home will change nothing," she said. "If these people are trying to undermine your reign, then they followed us to London and they will follow us home. And if they are trying to do something else, like Remi implies, then they'll do the same. We need to end this, once and for all. And since I am the center of it, though I don't know why, I must have some part in it."

"Do you truly not know why?" Grantham asked. When she shook her head, he leaned forward and cupped her cheek. "Because if I lost you, Ilaria, a part of me would die. You are my baby sister, you are my frustration and my joy. And I cannot lose you."

She blinked up at him as tears filled her eyes. In the last few years especially, she and Grantham had grown more distant. It made sense that as he took on more duties, took the crown, that it would happen. But right now she looked up into his eyes and saw the older brother she had adored all her life. The one who had gotten her into, and out of, scrape after scrape. The one who had kept her secrets so her father didn't explode. The one who smiled and laughed far more freely than he could now.

"You won't lose me," she said softly. "Because this time we'll create a situation *we* control. I'll know there's danger, and Jonah will be there with me. And he'd never let anyone harm me."

Jonah cleared his throat. "I would not, Your Majesty. Ever."

He moved to stand beside her, and his hand touched the small of her back briefly before he let it fall away. The touch electrified her, though. Gave her strength and faith.

Grantham let go of her and stepped back, looking at the two of them together. "It seems there is a great deal to discuss about your time in the country."

"But not now," Ilaria said, arching a brow. "And not ever if you intend to pound your chest about things that are none of your business. I know my duty, Grantham."

"And what is your duty?" her brother asked.

"To do whatever it takes to protect this family, this crown," she said. "No matter what I will lose in the process. Now let me do it."

Grantham seemed to consider it a moment, but before he could speak, their mother moved toward Ilaria. As Jonah stepped aside, she wrapped an arm around Ilaria's waist.

"The princess is correct," Giabella said. "As much as I hate to see my daughter in danger, nothing else is working. These fiends seem to be one step ahead of us—even the intrepid Marcus Rivers and whatever connections he has cannot seem to find them. So let's get ahead of them for once. Let Ilaria do as she suggests."

The color left Grantham's face and Remi jolted forward. Together, they both gasped, "Mama!"

"We all make sacrifices for our country," Giabella said, her gaze going distant. "You cannot require less of your sister out of some sense of chivalry. There will be guards, no matter what we do. And Captain Crawford will not be parted from her, it seems."

"Not until she is safe," Jonah said.

Grantham paced away, his hands gripping in and out of fists at his sides. His expression was unreadable as he faced Ilaria again. "Very well. I can see you will not be turned from this and I am not fool enough to fight a war I cannot win. What is your plan, Ilaria? What do you have in mind of what to do next?"

She turned toward Jonah. "Would Mr. Rivers be amenable to helping us further?" she asked. "Because I think I have a plan that just might work."

CHAPTER 24

Jonah gazed across the carriage at Ilaria. She looked the part of a cool, sophisticated princess, in one of her most beautiful gowns and her hair done to perfection. She wore a mask that matched the fabric of her dress and it was wound carefully into her hair so it rested against and accentuated her high cheekbones.

Yes, she looked the part, but he felt the nervousness coming off of her in waves.

"We've prepared for this night for three days," he said softly, and her attention shifted to him. "Rivers has everything in place. Most of those in attendance tonight will be there for your protection. I will be at your side the entire time. And your brother took our advice and kept this plan a secret from almost everyone in his employ."

She nodded. "And it is my plan, after all. I should not be fearful of it."

He pursed his lips. "You are risking yourself, risking everything. You have every right to be anxious."

She was quiet a moment, and her gaze snagged his. "I haven't been alone with you since we returned to London."

He swallowed hard. As if he hadn't counted every hour, every moment since he'd last touched her, last kissed her. Last taken her and made her his, even for just a moment.

"We've been together," he said.

"*Alone*, Jonah," she whispered. "As we formulated this plan it was always with others. Do you know how many times I wanted to go to you? To put my hand in yours and just…"

He leaned across the carriage and took her hands at last. They were as soft as he remembered, as warm against his fingers as he could hope. He had only meant to do that, to comfort her in this simple way, but now that he'd touched her, he couldn't stop.

He leaned across the space and she met him halfway. She let out a great, shuddering sigh as their mouths met, and then she was moving, coming into his lap, winding her arms around him as the kiss deepened, slowed, became ever more powerful.

She released him only when the carriage slowed, and moved to her side of the vehicle again. "I know I shouldn't have," she whispered. "It only makes me want—"

"Don't say it," he said, turning his face from hers. "Please."

She nodded, and both were silent as the carriage door was opened. He went first and helped her down, keeping a close eye all around them for danger. She really had created a good plan. The Donville Masquerade was public, and if she were attacked here and word got out, it offered a bit more scandal to go along with the message her attackers would send. But it was also a limited space— they could control it thanks to Rivers' generous agreement to what they wished to do.

"You've given us every advantage with this plan of yours," he said softly as they entered the antechamber. "And I'm with you."

The man at the door didn't ask them questions tonight. He merely inclined his head as the doors to the main room were opened. It was the middle of the week, a detail Rivers had suggested because it was a naturally slower time for the club. There were half the number of attendees as had been there the times they came before. And it was early enough that most were still gaming. Only a few were tangled together, kissing or touching playfully, rather than in a purely sexual way.

Still, Jonah's reaction was almost reflexive. He passed into the room and he wanted Ilaria. He had to push those desires aside and carefully watch as all eyes turned to the newcomers. No one stayed particularly curious, though, and went back to their games.

"You're so tense," Ilaria said softly. "Calm yourself and let's get a drink. We can't rush this."

"When did you get so wise?" he asked as he guided her through the crowd toward the bar in the distance.

She glanced up at him. "I spent a great deal of time in the country with a wise man."

"Sounds old and boorish," he teased as he motioned to the barkeep.

She laughed. "Only a little."

He glared at her playfully and ordered them each a drink. As they waited, he looked across the room again and found that Marcus Rivers and his wife, Annabelle, were coming across the room toward them. Although both were heavily involved in this scheme, neither looked in the least troubled or nervous.

"Good evening, friend," Rivers said. He smiled at Ilaria. "And Miss."

She smiled back and then reached out to touch Annabelle's hand. "Thank you again for your help in all this. I know it puts you out."

"Not in the slightest," Annabelle reassured her. "This is traditionally the club's slowest night. It was easy enough to fill the room with friends and employees who we trust entirely."

"Is the back room prepared?" Jonah asked softly.

The drinks arrived and Rivers waved off the barkeep, indicating they weren't to be charged for their libations. Jonah raised a glass to his friend and took the smallest sip. He needed to appear casual, but not lose his head. This night was too important.

"We aren't allowing anyone into the viewing hall," Rivers said.

Beside him, Ilaria shifted. Jonah wondered if she were thinking of the night they'd watched the lovers in the bedroom in that hall and he had pleasured her for the first time. God knew he thought of that night often enough.

"Will that be suspicious to those who might know the normal workings of the hell?" Ilaria asked, her voice rough.

Annabelle shook her head. "We often close the hall when it becomes too busy. If someone asks, they will be told that it is full and to return shortly. In reality, it *is* too full."

"Full of my guards," Marcus murmured.

Annabelle smiled up at her husband. "Some of whom are likely very much enjoying the show until our guests here take their places."

"They earned a bit of fun before the action," Rivers said with a shrug. "They'll be ready when it's truly time."

"Then I suppose all there is left is to take our places," Ilaria said softly.

Annabelle leaned forward and brushed a hand to Ilaria's again. "You are a strong woman, Your Highness," she whispered. "With an equally strong partner. You'll be fine. We'll be watching."

Jonah saw how much those words meant to Ilaria. How her shoulders relaxed a fraction and some of the tension went out of her perfectly formed lips. "Thank you."

"When this is over," Annabelle continued, "we're going to have a stiff drink and a very long talk."

"I look forward to it." Ilaria turned toward Jonah and looked up into his eyes. She nodded slightly, and when she next spoke it was louder, meant for listening ears, not just for their group. "Come, I want a more private party."

She caught Jonah's hand and flitted across the room, drawing him behind her as her hips twitched provocatively beneath her gown. It was for show, of course, just in case some blackguard was watching. But his body didn't care. After so many days without her, her confident display set him back on edge. Wanting her, loving her, needing her.

But right now was about saving her. And that was a sobering thought, indeed.

They reached the entrance to the private rooms and she tilted her head playfully at the guard there. "What's available, sir?"

The man smiled at her and held up two fingers. She patted his cheek as she passed by, all flirtation and bravado until they moved down the sparsely lit hallway. Then Jonah felt her grip on his fingers relax and she sucked in a harsh breath.

"It's hard being here with you, knowing we can't...we can't be together," she whispered, low enough for only him to hear.

"I know," he said. At the door to the second room, he caught her elbow and turned her back. "But at least in the show we get to pretend."

With that he cupped her cheeks and pressed her against the door for a long, deep kiss. When she relaxed against him, he pushed the door open, steadying her as they backed into the room. Once inside, he released her and shut the door, looking toward the place where others could watch. Guards were there, he knew. So there could be no reality to this show.

Ilaria moved to sit on the bed. Jonah was torn back in time once again to that first night when they had come here and he had sat next to her and kissed her. Wanted to do so much more than kiss her, tried to ignore that he already loved her and had for a very long time.

Now he didn't want to deny those things.

"Can they hear us?" she asked as he sat down beside her and took her hand. She rested her chin on his shoulder and looked up at him, those beautiful brown eyes filled with sadness that echoed his own.

"Not unless we're very loud in our passions," he said.

"I love you," she whispered. "And I wish we could just stay in this room forever and make love and talk and never go back to a world where our various duties make a future impossible."

"I know." He smoothed a strand of hair away from her cheek and smiled. "But perhaps one day we can be friends."

She snorted. "One thing I shall never be, Captain, is your friend. There will never be enough time or space to pass that will let *that* happen. I'll pretend it well, though. It was what I was raised for."

They sat together in silence for what felt like a very long time. At last he glanced at his pocket watch and sighed. "A moment or two more and then you can make your grand exit."

She stiffened at his side. "You won't wait long to follow?"

"Not long at all." He smoothed his thumb over her lower lip and she shivered before she stood up and paced across the room. She stood that way for a long moment, her back to him, her shoulders tight and lifted like she was tense. Then she glanced back.

"I never trained to be an actress," she said as she moved to the door. "So you'll forgive this poor performance."

Then she winked at him and headed out into the hallway, hands clutched before her, for all the world looking upset and abandoned, bait for a trap he could only pray would snap shut on the people who threatened her.

I laria could hear her own heartbeat pounding in her ears as she fled down the dim hallway and back into the brighter light of the main hall. She glanced around, trying to look desperate and upset. It wasn't a stretch considering everything going on in her life, considering what would happen if she failed and if she succeeded.

She staggered forward, purposefully tripping over her feet and righting herself, shaking her head, creating as much of a scene as she could without being too melodramatic. She moved toward the exit, praying those in the crowd who were part of this farce were watching, that Jonah would come soon and watch her, as well. Because her plan or not, the danger she felt was real and she was terrified of how it could play out.

She was almost to the door when there was a gentle touch on her elbow. "Miss, are you well?"

She pivoted at the dark richness of a male voice and turned. She caught her breath. She was staring up into the eyes of a tall man. Eyes she'd seen before, though he was dressed far differently, his hair styled differently, his mask different. But he was the same man who had approached her here before, frightened her, called her princess.

"Miss?"

She shook her head and remembered herself. "Oh, it's nothing, thank you. You are too kind. My—my…a gentleman…it was just…"

The stranger's fingers tightened around her elbow. "A cad hurt you, did he?"

She nodded slowly. "He tried."

"Even with the rules, some try things they should not." He motioned her toward the door. "Perhaps I could escort you to your carriage, miss. For your protection?"

She shifted. Here was the moment. "Oh yes, that would be wonderful. I would feel better with a decent man as my escort."

She could barely say those words since this man was clearly not decent. He was a blackguard bent on destroying her to send a message to her brother, to destroy what they had always been told was his birthright. Why? Well, that remained to be seen.

They moved toward the door together and she was proud of the fact that she didn't look over her shoulder to find Jonah. He would follow. She trusted that. He had never let her down, nor would he.

"You don't belong in a place like this," the man at her side was saying, and she focused on him as they exited the building back onto the street.

Here was where the plan was tricky. If she had played her cards right, she hoped he would see an opportunity to make a public statement in front of her carriage, in the busy street where many would be watching.

"My carriage is this way," she said, motioning him toward the rigs lined up in the distance. Just a little farther and she could make the signal and bring a dozen men swarming.

But he didn't take her that way. Instead, he caught her around the waist and lifted her as if she weighed nothing. With no warning, he darted across the street, toward the docks in the distance.

She let out a scream at the sudden and unexpected action. Certainly Jonah and those who were part of this plan must have seen what he did, but it was not something they had planned for.

"You think you can trick me, princess?" he hissed. "You think all this planning is going to culminate with my end and not yours?"

She kicked him in the shin, and he grunted but didn't stop moving. A fog had begun to rise from the water ahead of them, and she glanced back. Men were coming, but they were at a distance. If this person dragged her into the fog, they could be lost.

"Let me go!" she screamed, as much to alert the others to her location as to ask for reprieve. She didn't expect it, after all. "Why are you doing this?"

They were in the fog now. She heard the shouts of those in pursuit, but the bastard who held her crouched behind some barrels, pressing his hand to her lips so she couldn't cry out.

"I suppose I'm to tell you for rebellion. For Athawick," he said. "Does it really matter? You won't be alive to see the consequences of what I'm going to do to you. You won't be alive to see the rewards or the punishments."

She bit him then, sinking her teeth into his finger as best she could. He let out a yelp and tugged his hand away. She was pleased to see she'd drawn blood just before he hauled back and hit her with the back of the same hand.

"Little bitch! He said you were a fighter. Not much longer."

He shoved her down on her back against the rough wooden planks of the dock. She kicked at him, pushing against his hand, but he was stronger than she was by far—he had more leverage. She tried to scream, but this time he pressed his hand down over her nose and her mouth, cutting off her air. She gasped against what little she had left and watched in horror as he reared back, this time with a knife in his hand.

But before he could slam it into her body, end her life, a shadowy figure hit him with full force and he was thrown off of her.

She pushed herself back in horror. It was Jonah, and now he and the man were grappling together on the dock. She screamed, calling out for the others as she staggered to her feet. Jonah had had the upper hand, but her attacker rolled on top. Their masks were both cockeyed, but she didn't recognize the stranger, only his intentions.

He slashed with the knife and Jonah held up his arm. The blade cut into his coat and, from his cry of pain, deeper. With another scream, Ilaria launched herself onto the attacker's back, clawing at his eyes, beating at him with her fists, pulling him back by his nose to get him off of Jonah.

It was a surprising enough attack that it seemed to throw the stranger off. His knife, slick with Jonah's blood, slid from his hand, clattered onto the dock, and he fell backward, half pinning Ilaria behind him.

But it was enough. Jonah grabbed him, and three other men ran in from the fog. In moments the attacker was subdued. He glared at Ilaria.

"It will never be enough, not for those who want you dead," he murmured. Then he twisted his mouth and seemed to bite down on something. His expression changed, as if he were in sudden pain. With a gurgling moan, he slumped in the arms of those who held him.

Jonah pivoted back to Ilaria and offered her his hand. She was pulled up, and they stared. "What is wrong with him?" she asked.

One of the guards tugged the stranger's head back and it was a sickly color, bright red, and foam was coming from his mouth.

"He's…he's dead," the man breathed.

Jonah steadied Ilaria and then released her, moving to check for the attacker's heartbeat himself. "Poison," he said, holding up the other man's hand. There was an empty packet there, clenched in lifeless fingers. "Somehow he managed to get whatever was in this into his mouth and eat it. He killed himself rather than be caught."

"Oh God," Ilaria breathed.

Jonah turned back to her. "Are you injured?"

He touched her face where she had been struck, but she brushed his hand away. "I'm fine, but you were cut. Let me see."

He glanced toward the gathering crowd and reached up instead to adjust her mask and cover her face. "Not yet," he murmured. "You lot take care of this."

"They will." It was Rivers who answered. He was coming out of the fog to join their group. "I'll send word when it's done, and anything else I can determine."

Ilaria moved toward him, this tall, stern man who had come to her aid without ever asking for anything in return. "Thank you, Mr. Rivers. And thank Annabelle, as well. I look forward to that long conversation with her soon."

He smiled at her. "Good evening…Miss Crawford."

She jolted at the use of the pretend name she had given. Jonah's name, and now it stung because with the threat to her at least temporarily assuaged, that meant their time together might be at a permanent end.

If he felt the same, he didn't say it. He simply wrapped an arm around her and guided her away to the carriages. He opened the door for her, and as she stepped in, she gasped.

Grantham was seated there already, his face long and serious. As Jonah stepped in, they nodded to each other.

"What—?" Ilaria began.

"King or not, I am your brother first," Grantham said softly. "And I wasn't about to let you come to this place, to do this thing, without being here to protect you if I could."

"I'm fine," she whispered. "But Jonah's arm…"

Jonah peeled his jacket off gingerly, and Ilaria gasped. His shirt arm was soaked with blood. Grantham let out a curse and swiftly removed his cravat. Together they bound the wound, and Grantham pounded on the wall of the carriage to urge the drive to go faster.

"It's fine," Jonah said. "A flesh wound, nothing more."

"That remains to be seen," Grantham said. "I'll have the doctor sent for as soon as we get home. For both of you." He cleared his throat. "I was prevented from following once that blackguard disappeared into the fog."

"Good, then Rivers did his job," Jonah said.

"If he were my subject, I would have him flayed," Grantham retorted.

"No you wouldn't," Ilaria said with a shake of her head as she continued to apply pressure to Jonah's wound. "You'd give him a medal."

"I still should at that, for all he did for us," Grantham said. "But first I need to deal with the man who attacked you. Will he be brought to us or to the English authorities?"

"He's dead," Ilaria said. She swiftly explained what had happened and what his last words had been.

Grantham wrinkled his brow. "Odd words."

"Yes. But I can tell you he was the only man I ever saw during this nightmare. I would have recognized those eyes anywhere. What if he was acting alone?"

"I'm not entirely willing to accept that," Grantham said. "Nor to dismiss that he is part of the rebellion against me. We'll increase your guard and have to hope that if he was the leader of an uprising, perhaps his death will send a message. I'll make sure word of it spreads back to Athawick. Blairford can make those arrangements. But for now, we go back to the house here in London. The rest can be worked out."

Grantham looked from one of them to the other. "*All* the rest."

CHAPTER 25

Jonah watched as the physician who had been called wrapped the final bandage around his arm. It hurt like the devil, but it had been stitched and the cut, though deep, would certainly heal in time. He was lucky. Luckier still that Ilaria hadn't taken that knife.

The door to the chamber where he was being attended to opened and the king stepped through. Grantham leaned back against the wall next to the door and watched in silence as the doctor packed up his things.

"Will the patient live?" he asked.

The doctor looked puzzled rather than amused at the quip and glanced back at Jonah. "As long as he is careful about infection, I don't see why not. He has his instructions on changing the dressing and I'll check on him in a few days, Your Majesty."

Grantham nodded and motioned the doctor toward the door. "My mother would like you to look in on Miss Killick again, if you don't mind."

The doctor nodded. When he had stepped from the room, Grantham shut the door and faced Jonah once again.

"You realize that this is impossible," Grantham said without preamble. "Loving her."

It was a statement, not a question, but Grantham held his stare as if daring him to deny it.

Jonah didn't. He couldn't. "I do love her, Your Majesty. And I also know that the situation is complicated. I knew that a long time ago."

"Complicated," Grantham snapped with a humorless laugh. "Oh yes, it is that. So how do you feel about that fact?"

Jonah pondered the question and drew a long breath before he answered. "Ilaria once told me she was lucky to know that the man she loved felt the same in return. Whatever happens, I know that was a once-in-a-lifetime opportunity. And I am grateful to have been loved by her and to have had the ability to love her with all my heart."

Grantham tilted his head. "Whatever happens. So you would give her up?"

Pain ripped through Jonah, but he was accustomed to it now. After all, he'd been building toward this since the moment he first met Ilaria. He'd never had any illusion it would end any way but this. "I don't want to do so. The very thought of it is worse than if you shot me where I stand. But if I knew she was happy and safe, I would give up everything."

Grantham pursed his lips and indicated the wrapping on Jonah's arm. "Apparently including your life."

Jonah looked at it, felt the pain of the injury mingle with the pain of this conversation. "I would have, gladly, to see her safe."

"This is an untenable situation." Grantham paced away, running a hand through his hair. "I either give up the possibility of solidifying the connection between our countries and leave my island at risk of colonization while a rebellion puts me at my weakest point, or I lock my sister into a marriage that will break her heart and, eventually, her spirit."

Jonah watched him pace, felt his friend's true torment. And felt a strange frisson of...hope. "Perhaps Remi would be open to a marriage for duty."

Grantham pivoted toward him, and they stared at each other for a moment. Then Grantham laughed, and this time it was filled with more true humor. "Somehow I doubt that."

Jonah managed half a smile. "Then what about you, Your Majesty? You will also have to marry someday, and likely soon. Would none of our English lasses tempt you into a union?"

Something flickered across Grantham's expression, but he erased it instantly. "My future remains to be written, I suppose. My sister is pacing in the hall right now, desperate to see you once your injuries have been tended. Shall I allow her in?"

Jonah winced, and not from the pain of his injury. After this conversation, he knew that this would likely be the last time he would see Ilaria before her future was set in stone.

"Yes," he said. "I would see her."

The king inclined his head and left the room. He did not return, but a few moments later Ilaria burst into the parlor and raced to Jonah's side. She gave no heed to the fact that he was shirtless as her arms came around him, her heart fluttering like a hummingbird against his bare skin.

"Hush now," he said, smoothing her hair. "I'm fine. Just a scratch, little more."

She frowned. "The doctor said there were twenty stitches, Jonah. Hardly a small thing. Does it hurt?"

"Not anymore. Not now that you're here." He pulled her into his lap and rested his head against her arm. He said nothing more, but drew in a whiff of her sweet scent, knowing time was down to seconds, mere moments and nothing more. So he had to savor each one of them.

Ilaria sat in Jonah's lap for a few moments, and they were both quiet at the end of the storm that had been the last few weeks. Her mind raced with thoughts, though, with hopes and dreams that she feared would be soon dashed. She had pictured a hundred scenarios in the last hour while Jonah's wound was tended and her brother spoke to him.

None had the outcome she wished most for.

Finally she sighed. "He'll come soon. Too soon."

"Your brother?" Jonah's voice was muffled against her arm, his breath warm through the thing fabric.

She nodded. "He said he'd give us privacy for a short time."

"Then should you get up off my lap?" he asked.

She smiled down at him, then cupped his cheeks. "Later."

She kissed him gently. He was injured and she feared breaking him. But of course he didn't allow her that. With his good arm, he cupped the back of her head and deepened the kiss. But at last he released her, just as Grantham returned to the room. Ilaria stood without haste or embarrassment and faced her brother.

He looked at the two of them and shook his head. "I was devastated that I almost lost you, Ilaria," he said. "Not as your king—as your brother."

She shut her eyes. He had said something similar in the carriage when she found him there and it had brought a flood of love for him coursing through her. She felt the same now, despite what his appearance would bring.

"I love you," he continued.

She pressed her hand down against Jonah's shoulder, squeezing gently as the warmth of his bare flesh filled her palm. "And I love him."

"I can see that," Grantham said softly. "And he has told me he loves you as well, even though I had already guessed. Enough to give you up if it would save you from grief."

"It will *cause* me grief," Ilaria said. "And I know that isn't fair to say to you, Grantham. I know you ask me to do this duty, to marry someone else, because it is for the good of everyone else. But I selfishly want to do what is good for me."

"I often think about our father and what he would do in situations I face as king," Grantham said. "In this case, I'm sure he would point out that walking away from a marriage with Bramwell will put us in a worse position. He would also mention, I think, that Captain Crawford is not only middle class but there is the matter that he is…that his father was…that he…"

"Is a bastard," Jonah said softly. "I've never tried to hide it."

"No. You haven't. You have always been unfailingly honest." Her brother bent his head. Ilaria couldn't read his thoughts, only his struggle. At last he looked at her. "You know, this man has saved the only princess of Athawick. As king, I have the right…no, the obligation to reward him handsomely."

She blinked. "I suppose that is true."

"In the past, men who have behaved with such bravery have been awarded financially, with medals…and also with title."

Her eyes went wide. "I…have they?"

Grantham nodded slowly. "I'm sure our people, those who still support us at any rate, would agree that naming Captain Crawford to be, say, Count Crawford and award him a ceremonial responsibility over Southern Athawick would be fair trade."

Ilaria could hardly breathe as she stared at her brother. "What are you…what are you saying?"

"I would never desire to be the cause of the kind of grief that separating you from one you love would create. We had a very personal vantage point to watching an arranged marriage that was resented and all the pain it created. I think I would regret forcing you into our mother's shoes more than I would regret losing whatever advantage a marriage to the Earl of Bramwell would create. Creating a title for Crawford and tying it to his incredible act of bravery seems a best way to resolve both our problems. And it opens a door to a further solution. Assuming…" He faced Jonah, who looked as confused as Ilaria felt. "Do you wish to marry my sister, Captain Crawford?"

Jonah rose and his hands were shaking as he took hers. "I would like nothing more if you'd allow it, Your Majesty."

Grantham smiled. "My siblings call me Grantham when we are not in public, Crawford…Jonah. And I hope you will do the same once my sister accepts your hand, which I will allow her to do privately."

Ilaria stared at him and then up at Jonah. Back and forth between them so long that Grantham laughed. "Once you can get her to understand what has just happened. Excuse me."

He stepped from the room, quietly closing the door behind himself, and Ilaria pivoted to face Jonah, grabbing for his good arm with both hands. "Did he—?"

He nodded and looked as confused and joyful as she felt. "Yes."

"He'll let us—"

"So it seems." Jonah shook his head. "I rather thought I'd be wearing a shirt every time I pictured this moment. But one makes due with what one has." He sank down on one knee and stared up at her, his gray eyes dancing with joy and hope and a beautiful future she could see laid out before her.

"Princess Ilaria of Athawick, I have loved you from almost the first moment I saw you. I've fought it and denied and surrendered to it in body, but now I ask you, with all my heart and soul, will you please marry me?"

She felt the tears streaming down her face. Joyful tears that warmed her to her very toes and washed away all the regrets she'd had at the thought of losing this man. Now she never would.

"Jonah, I will gladly marry you."

He stood in a graceful unfolding of long, lean arms and legs and wrapped her into his embrace. She leaned up into him and kissed him. Unlike the earlier kiss, there was no desperation here, only love. No fear, only certainty.

She pulled away and laughed. "Shall we go tell the rest of my family and celebrate with them?"

Jonah held her tighter and shook his head before his mouth descended again. "Perhaps in a moment, love. Just a moment more."

**Coming September 21, 2021!
(Bramwell and Sasha's Story)**

She sighed heavily and backed away from the window, moving toward the shadow again. She leaned against the terrace wall's stone edge and gazed up at the stars. The English had their own constellations, but she saw a few of her favorite Athawickian ones like the butterfly, the sailing ship and the crown. She sighed in pure pleasure and for a moment all was calm and right in her world. She had no duties or fears or anything but the sweet connection to the sky above.

"Your Highness?"

She froze at the words coming from behind her and all good thoughts fled. She'd thought she'd hidden herself well enough from eyes, she'd thought that no one would wish to miss the end of the dance between the Regent and the Queen of Athawick.

She was apparently wrong and now she had created a situation that could go very wrong, very quickly if she didn't use her wits and manage the intruder. She only hoped she was capable of doing just that.

Sasha turned slowly and lifted her chin, trying to put herself in as much shadow as possible.

The stranger, on the other hand, was fully lit by the ballroom window and she caught her breath. He was uncommonly handsome and put her to mind of Paris from the ancient mythology of Troy. The only man beautiful enough to pair with Helen, the one who would start a war to have her.

This man had thick dark hair, full lips, a jawline that could cut through metal and warm, kind brown eyes that widened as he moved closer.

"Oh…I beg your pardon, you are not Princess Ilaria."

Sasha wasn't certain that his observation made this situation better or worse. She cleared her throat. "Er…no. But I thank you for the comparison."

His brow furrowed a little and he came to a stop, tilting his head. "You are wearing the same gown."

Sasha's eyes went wide. Here was the perfect excuse. "Indeed, I am. I was embarrassed by the fact and slipped from the ball to keep from further humiliation."

He arched a brow and she could see his disbelief on his face. "But you are also wearing a copy of Princess Ilaria's crown. And your hair is styled in the same way. You mean to look like her. For what purpose?"

She folded her arms. "If I am to be interrogated, I would expect to know the name of my inquisitor. Who are *you*, sir?"

"The Earl of Bramwell, madam."

Sasha's breath caught. Earlier in the day, before their disembarkation at the port, she had stumbled upon a list on Dash's desk that included this man's name. A list of potential suitors for Ilaria. Her heart sank a little when she ought to have no reaction at all.

"And I think you will find that I cannot be so easily put off, even by one so lovely as you," Bramwell continued, his eyes locking with hers. "Do you dress like the princess for some nefarious purpose?"

She shifted. Only the royal family and staff knew of her role. She had never been so uncareful as she had been tonight to reveal it to someone who was unaffiliated with the Crown.

His jaw tightened and his lips thinned. "I will fetch someone from inside, do not move."

He pivoted as if to march back to the ballroom and she stepped forward. This entire situation could easily escalate in a very bad way if she didn't end his curiosity.

"No, wait. Sir, I *can* explain myself. But first I will need to know that you can be discreet."

He hesitated and turned back, his gaze flitting over her from head to toe in one smooth motion.

"It depends upon your answer. I will not do anything that would put someone in danger."

"Especially the princess?" she asked, searching his face.

His brow wrinkled. "It seems you might be a threat to her in this situation so I think of her, but not just the princess."

He seemed unmoved by Ilaria and that threw Sasha off even further. After all, men were always drawn to her even when she didn't notice them at all.

"Have you met the princess?" she asked.

He tilted his head. "Yes, earlier this evening. We danced."

She blinked. So he had met Ilaria and yet seemed unaffected. Very interesting. "You must see that a lady of her position and her beauty attracts a great deal of attention. Sometimes attention that is unwanted or even dangerous."

He nodded slowly. "I can imagine that is true." He examined her a little closer and then he drew in a sharp breath. "You are a double."

She drew back a fraction. Here she had been trying to find a way to describe her role and he had guessed it without any additional help. "Er…"

"Of course," he mused, almost more to himself than to her. "In her role, she would not always be available or safe in public. To have someone who looks enough like her to wave from a balcony or carriage…to step in under duress…"

Sasha let out her breath gently. "I admit no one has ever guessed. Though I suppose not many see me dressed as her. When I am in my own clothing, when my hair is different, they just see me as…"

"Sasha Killick," he finished for her. "That is who you are, aren't you? The adopted daughter of the family, the princess's companion."

She wrinkled her brow. "You certainly seem to know a great deal about Ilaria and the family, my lord."

He shrugged. "At my mother's behest, it seems I do. God, what have I become?"

There was something about his tone that she couldn't help but laugh and when she did so, he smiled. Her breath was all but sucked from her lungs. Great God, but he was not just handsome, but beautiful. Utterly, perfectly beautiful. She had never met a man his equal and she hated herself for being so drawn to him in this moment.

The Duke of Hearts

The Duke Who Lied

The Duke of Desire

The Last Duke

The Scandal Sheet

The Return of Lady Jane

Stealing the Duke

Lady No Says Yes

My Fair Viscount

Guarding the Countess

The House of Pleasure

Seasons

An Affair in Winter

A Spring Deception

One Summer of Surrender

Adored in Autumn

The Wicked Woodleys

Forbidden

Deceived

Tempted

Ruined

Seduced

Fascinated

To see a complete listing of Jess Michaels' titles, please visit:

http://www.authorjessmichaels.com/books

ABOUT THE AUTHOR

USA Today Bestselling author Jess Michaels likes geeky stuff, Vanilla Coke Zero, anything coconut, cheese and her dog, Elton. She is lucky enough to be married to her favorite person in the world and lives in the heart of Dallas, TX where she's trying to eat all the amazing food in the city.

When she's not obsessively checking her steps on Fitbit or trying out new flavors of Greek yogurt, she writes historical romances with smoking hot characters and emotional stories. She has written for numerous publishers and is now fully indie and loving every moment of it (well, almost every moment).

Jess loves to hear from fans! So please feel free to contact her at Jess@AuthorJessMichaels.com.

Jess Michaels offers a free book to members of her newsletter, so sign up on her website:
http://www.AuthorJessMichaels.com/

facebook.com/JessMichaelsBks
twitter.com/JessMichaelsBks
instagram.com/JessMichaelsBks
bookbub.com/authors/jess-michaels

www.ingramcontent.com/pod-product-compliance
Lightning Source LLC
Chambersburg PA
CBHW021129190726
48288CB00008B/2572